DEADLY MISTAKE

Tony glanced past Charley and stiffened. Suddenly bending at the waist, he whispered, "Let me do the talking. Whatever happens, it is not to involve you."

Before Charley could ask what Tony meant, three men walked up to their table—burly, broad-shouldered men wearing suits and polished shoes, one with a diamond stickpin in his tie.

"Well, well, well." Stickpin's voice was like two rocks grating together. "All evening I've been trying to figure out how in hell I lost my roll. Then who should I see across the room at the most expensive restaurant in Denver? The water boy I always buy water from." He leaned on the edge of the table and glared at Tony. "You made the worst mistake of your life picking my pocket. I've beat people to a pulp for a lot less." His smile was ripe with menace. "So where do you want it? Here or outside?"

Ralph Compton
Do or Die

A Ralph Compton Novel
by David Robbins

A SIGNET BOOK

SIGNET
Published by New American Library, a division of
Penguin Group (USA) Inc., 375 Hudson Street,
New York, New York 10014, U.S.A.
Penguin Books Ltd, 80 Strand,
London WC2R 0RL, England
Penguin Books Australia Ltd, 250 Camberwell Road,
Camberwell, Victoria 3124, Australia
Penguin Books Canada Ltd, 10 Alcorn Avenue,
Toronto, Ontario, Canada M4V 3B2
Penguin Books (N.Z.) Ltd, Cnr Rosedale and Airborne Roads,
Albany, Auckland 1310, New Zealand

Penguin Books Ltd, Registered Offices:
80 Strand, London WC2R 0RL, England

First published by Signet, an imprint of New American Library,
a division of Penguin Group (USA) Inc.

First Printing, August 2003
10 9 8 7 6 5 4 3 2 1

PUBLISHER'S NOTE
This is a work of fiction. Names, characters, places, and incidents either are the product of the author's imagination or are used fictitiously, and any resemblance to actual persons, living or dead, business establishments, events, or locales is entirely coincidental.

BOOKS ARE AVAILABLE AT QUANTITY DISCOUNTS WHEN USED TO PROMOTE PRODUCTS OR SERVICES. FOR INFORMATION PLEASE WRITE TO PREMIUM MARKETING DIVISION, PENGUIN GROUP (USA) INC., 375 HUDSON STREET, NEW YORK, NEW YORK 10014.

THE IMMORTAL COWBOY

This is respectfully dedicated to the "American Cowboy." His was the saga sparked by the turmoil that followed the Civil War, and the passing of more than a century has by no means diminished the flame.

True, the old days and the old ways are but treasured memories, and the old trails have grown dim with the ravages of time, but the spirit of the cowboy lives on.

In my travels—to Texas, Oklahoma, Kansas, Nebraska, Colorado, Wyoming, New Mexico, and Arizona—I always find something that reminds me of the Old West. While I am walking these plains and mountains for the first time, there is this feeling that a part of me is eternal, that I have known these old trails before. I believe it is the undying spirit of the frontier calling, allowing me, through the mind's eye, to step back into time. What is the appeal of the Old West of the American frontier?

It has been epitomized by some as the dark and bloody period in American history. Its heroes—Crockett, Bowie, Hickok, Earp—have been reviled and criticized. Yet the Old West lives on, larger than life.

It has become a symbol of freedom, when there was always another mountain to climb and another river to cross; when a dispute between two men was settled not with expensive lawyers, but with fists, knives or guns. Barbaric? Maybe. But some things never change. When the cowboy rode into the pages of American history, he left behind a legacy that lives within the hearts of us all.

—*Ralph Compton*

Prologue

Wind River Reservation
Wyoming Territory

Five riders came out of the night to the ridge above the old man's lodge and reined in. They wore dark hats and dark slickers and were next to invisible. Their leader rose in the stirrups to study the valley they had traveled so far to reach, and when he gestured, they descended in single file until they emerged from the pines. Then they spread out and moved toward a gurgling stream.

On the far side stood the lodge. It was old, like its owner. Mat-ta-vish had lived more winters than most Shoshones and liked the old ways better than the white ways many of his people had adopted. He refused to wear white clothes. He refused to own white cooking utensils. Under no circumstances would he allow a white blanket to soil his lodge or his person.

Some of the younger Shoshones thought Mat-ta-vish was stubborn and silly. They pointed out that white-made pots and pans were easy to clean and lasted a long time. White-made knives were of fine steel and held a sharp edge even after hard use. And it was a lot easier to buy or trade for a white blanket or white clothes than to make them. But to Mat-ta-vish, the fact they were *white* meant all the difference. He wanted nothing to do with the despoilers of the world he had once known. He wanted nothing to do with those who treated his people like cattle, to be herded up and penned in as the whites saw fit.

This particular night Mat-ta-vish had turned in early, as was his habit. Although grey of hair, his senses were keen, and when his dog growled, Mat-ta-vish threw off his heavy buffalo blanket and sat up. "What did you hear?" he quietly asked. He had not named the dog. He never named an animal he might need to eat.

The mongrel stood and stared at the hide that covered the lodge opening. The hackles on its neck rose, and it bared its teeth.

"Is it a mountain lion? Or another bear?" Mat-ta-vish talked to his dog all the time. The dog was the only companion he had. His devoted wife had died ten winters ago, and his sons and daughters rarely came to visit.

Rising, Mat-ta-vish took down his ash bow and quiver of arrows. His oldest son, Gro-wot, had once tried giving him a rifle even though Gro-wot knew how he felt about whites, but Mat-ta-vish had refused to accept it. "Let us go see."

A brisk wind stirred nearby cottonwoods. Other than the rustle of leaves, Mat-ta-vish heard nothing to account for his dog's unease. He made a circuit of his lodge, an arrow nocked to the sinew string of his bow, but saw nothing out of the ordinary. "Dogs that bark at the wind do not live as long as dogs that do not," he remarked.

As if to prove him wrong, the mongrel suddenly snarled and streaked off into the cottonwoods.

Mat-ta-vish walked halfway to the cottonwoods and stopped. It would not be wise to venture into the trees if a grizzly were on the prowl. While the giant bears were far fewer than they had been in the days of his youth, it was not uncommon for one to pass through his valley. Usually they left him alone, although during the last Blood Moon he had lost a fine mare. Gro-wot said he had brought it on himself by living apart from the rest of the Shoshones, and maybe that was true.

The mongrel began barking. It had spotted whatever was out there.

As Mat-ta-vish raised his bow, he heard the underbrush crackle with the passage of something large. Hooves thudded, and a darkling shape swept toward him. He sighted down the arrow, but before he could let it fly, another rider came at him from the right.

Mat-ta-vish turned. The second rider was closer and posed the more immediate threat. He loosed his shaft. Mat-ta-vish was a skilled bowman, and the arrow should have caught the rider in the chest. But the man swung onto the side of his horse and clung there like a Sioux warrior. It was no Sioux, though. Mat-ta-vish glimpsed a hat and a long coat such as whites wore. He snatched another arrow from his quiver and was nocking it to the string when he realized a third night rider was bearing down on him from behind. The next moment he was struck a heavy blow to the back and flung to the earth with bone-jarring impact. He lost his grip on the bow.

Dazed, Mat-ta-vish started to push to his feet. There was a *swish*, and pain lanced his head. The trees and the stars swapped places. His cheek smacked the earth. He made it to his knees just as a pair of thick arms encircled him from behind like bands of metal.

"I've got the old redskin!" his captor bellowed in his ear in the white man's tongue.

Mat-ta-vish struggled, but whoever held him was as big and strong as a bull buffalo. He tried to reach the bone-handled knife at his hip, but a second white materialized from nowhere and yanked it from its sheath.

"You won't be needin' that pigsticker, Injun."

Long ago Mat-ta-vish had learned that when dealing with belligerent whites, it was best not to feed their craving for violence. He wondered if these were drunken cowboys out to amuse themselves at his expense and decided they weren't since he did not smell liquor on their breath.

Just then a four-legged form shot out of the vegetation to his rescue. The dog snarled, its fangs white in the starlight, and bounded toward the bull holding Mat-ta-vish. "No!" he shouted in Shoshone, but the dog did not heed.

Another rider burst from the cottonwoods. He was swinging something over his head. Mat-ta-vish recognized it was a rope a few heartbeats before the loop darted at the charging mongrel like a striking snake. Dog and rope met in midair, and the dog yelped as the noose constricted around its neck and it was brought up short with a snap.

Whooping merrily, the rider spurred his horse toward the stream, dragging the mongrel after him. The dog tried to regain its footing, but the horse was moving too fast. It yipped when it struck a boulder, and Mat-ta-vish was sure he heard the *crack* of breaking bone.

Two more whites appeared. In the lead was one who sat tall in the saddle and did not rein up until his bay practically trod on Mat-ta-vish. He had white hair, this man, sticking out from under his hat and growing on his chin, but he was not old. If Mat-ta-vish had to guess, he would say the tall rider had not seen more than thirty winters.

"Do you know who we are?"

Mat-ta-vish did not respond even when the bull who was holding him shook him as a badger might shake a mouse.

"It won't do no good to play dumb. Word is, you savvy the white tongue just fine. So I'll ask one more time. If you don't answer, we'll whittle on you some until you do."

The white who had taken Mat-ta-vish's knife held it under Mat-ta-vish's nose. "Just say the word, Alvord. There's nothin' I'd like more than to carve up this red scum." This one was as lean as a sapling and spoke with a peculiar twang.

"Do you know who we are?" Alvord repeated.

"Yes," Mat-ta-vish admitted. He had long dreaded they might pay him a visit. Word of his herd had been bound to reach their ears eventually.

"Say it."

"You are the Hoodoos. My people have suffered much at your hands. The bluecoats have told us to be on the watch for you. They will put you in the room made of bars at the fort if they catch you here."

The man who had ridden up with Alvord now laughed. He was young, his face baby-smooth, and had to have been the runt of the litter when he was born.

His slicker was swept back to reveal a pair of revolvers with shiny grips. "That'll be the day. Those bluebellies couldn't catch their hind ends without help."

Alvord leaned on his saddle horn. "Where are they, old-timer?"

Mat-ta-vish would rather have his tongue cut out.

"We'll find them on our own. Your valley isn't that big. But we want to light a shuck before any of your kin show up, so do us both a favor and tell us where your horses are." Alvord waited, and when no reply came, he nodded at the man who had taken Mat-ta-vish's knife. "Go ahead, Noonan."

"My pleasure, pard."

The knife flashed, and Mat-ta-vish winced as his right cheek was opened like a ripe melon. But he did not cry out.

"I can't hear you, old man," Noonan drawled.

Again the blade glinted. Again Mat-ta-vish felt a damp sensation on his face. Blood trickled into his mouth.

Noonan shifted the knife down low. "I can keep this up all night."

Mat-ta-vish stood straighter. Long ago he had been a warrior of renown. Many coup were counted to his credit, and his advice had been sought on matters of import in council. While his sinews were not what they once were, he was still a warrior. He still had his pride.

"You're dumb as a shovel," Noonan said and set to work.

The pain was excruciating. Mat-ta-vish doubled over. The bull holding him let go, and he pitched to his knees.

"Damn it, Noonan! I don't want this heathen's blood all over my new pants!"

"New? Hell, Ben, you bought them over two months ago and ain't washed them once since. A little blood will lend the dirt some color."

"That's the most foolish notion I've ever heard." Ben had a great moon face split by bushy eyebrows and a hooked nose the size of an eagle's beak.

"No more foolish than those onions you're always eatin'."

Mat-ta-vish barely heard. Waves of agony washed over him, and he gritted his teeth to keep from crying out. It hurt worse than the time a Piegan lance had pierced his leg. Worse, even, than the time he was thrown by his pinto during a buffalo surround and nearly trampled to death before a friend had pulled him to safety.

A saddle creaked. A callused hand gripped Mat-ta-vish by the jaw and tilted his head back. "Had enough?" Alvord asked. "This doesn't need to take forever. We can get it over with pronto. All you have to do is tell us where they are." He waited, and when Mat-ta-vish stayed silent, he went on. "It's not like you can trick us. We know all about the horses you raise. The best of their kind in the territory. It would be a shame for all that prime horseflesh to go to waste."

Even through the haze of torment, Mat-ta-vish wondered how the Hoodoos had heard. Through his nephew, possibly. The boy was scouting for the army. Mat-ta-vish had given him one of his best horses, and although his nephew had promised not to tell anyone where it came from, the young were never as tight-lipped as they should be.

Alvord sighed and straightened. "Some folks are too damn stubborn for their own good."

Hooves hammered, and from the direction of the

stream trotted the white man who had roped the dog
and dragged it off. He was still dragging it, only now
it was limp and still. "Yeehaw! I haven't had this
grand a time in a month of Sundays!"

"Yell a little louder, why don't you, Curly?" Alvord was angry. "That way we can have the whole
Shoshone nation down on our heads."

Curly did not let the comment spoil his mood.
"We're miles from the nearest village, so they aren't
likely to hear. You're just jealous 'cause I'm the only
one in this outfit who knows how to have fun."

"Killin' dogs ain't hardly my notion of a frolic,"
Noonan interjected. "Give me a filly and a bottle of
rotgut any day."

The young runt who wore revolvers with shiny
grips cursed and kneed his mount closer. "We're
wastin' time with all this jawin'. Kill the damned
treaty Injun so we can get this over with."

"Simmer down, Kid," Alvord said. "I always
know what I'm doin', don't I?"

"You've never once led us astray, and that's a
fact," the Kid agreed. "But we've already been gone
a week and a half. We'll have to lay low in one of
our hidey-holes at least that long to be sure the army
has lost our trail. Then it's another two weeks to get
the herd to our buyer."

"Since when have you counted days like they were
poker chips?"

Curly chuckled. "I know why the Kid is actin' like
a wolverine with a burr up its ass. He's pinin' for
that gal he met at the Lucky Star. What was her
name again?"

The Kid's hands were a blur. He leveled both Colts
at his curly-topped companion and warned, "I'll

thank you not to bring her up ever again, Curly Means, or so help me God, I'll put windows in your skull.''

The whites froze. All eyes were on the young one. No one noticed Mat-ta-vish as, on hands and knees, he crept toward the cottonwoods. They had forgotten about him for the moment. A heated argument broke out, smothering the slight noise he made. As soon as the undergrowth closed around him, Mat-ta-vish rose into a crouch and hobbled as fast as his legs would carry him. He was weak from loss of blood, and every step was torture. But he refused to stay and be butchered. He would die on his own terms.

Mat-ta-vish wished he could save his herd. He did not like the idea of his horses being sold to fill the pockets of a greedy pack of killers and thieves, but he was in no condition to stop them even if he could.

A shout warned Mat-ta-vish his absence had been discovered. He came to a thicket, sank onto his belly, and wriggled into its depths. There he lay on his side, his heart pounding in his chest.

The brush crackled and popped. Several times the Hoodoos passed near him. But it was too dark for them to track, and they dared not risk using torches.

Once the one called Ben stopped right beside the thicket, muttering something about "stinkin' lousy Injuns," then stomped off.

Soon Mat-ta-vish heard them ride toward the north end of the valley, and his heart grew heavy with sorrow. They would find his horses in the meadow and be long gone by dawn.

Crawling into the open, Mat-ta-vish sat with his knees tucked to his chest. It helped lessen the discomfort. He began to sing his death song. But he could not stop thinking about the Hoodoos and how he would dearly love to repay them in some measure for their cruelty.

The idea that came to him made Mat-ta-vish smile despite his pain. It was not much, but it was the best he could do. Whether it would do any good depended on who found him and how observant they were.

His strength fading rapidly, Mat-ta-vish groped for a stick, and when he found one, he used it to draw in the dirt. He had loved to draw when he was younger, and one of his favorite pastimes was to paint symbols on lodges with paints he made himself. His people did not have a written tongue like the whites, but they had something similar. Something that might come back to haunt the Hoodoos.

Mat-ta-vish sang louder as he drew.

Chapter One

Charley Pickett was about to pass the sorrel's stall when it hiked its tail. Without thinking, Charley swung his broom and swatted it soundly on the rump. "Don't you dare!" he hollered. "I'm sick to death of shovelin' that stuff."

The sorrel paid him no mind.

Charley was going to swat it again, but he heard someone near the front of the stable clear their throat. Fearing the worst, he slowly turned. "Mr. Leeds! I didn't know you were back."

"Obviously not." Artemis Leeds was a broomstick of a man who always dressed in a starched suit and knee-high boots. One hand behind his back, the other tugging in irritation at his droopy mustache, Leeds frowned in disapproval. "Did my eyes deceive me, young man, or did you hit that horse for answering nature's call?"

"I was just bein' playful, sir. I didn't really mean anything by it."

Leeds came over, tore the broom from Charley's

grasp, and shook it at him. "How would you like it if I took this to your backside every time you lowered your britches?"

"I reckon I wouldn't, sir." Charley squirmed like a fish on a hook, afraid he was in for another of his employer's long-winded lectures.

"Is it too much to ask, then, that you extend the same courtesy to the stock in our care? What if the gentleman who owns that sorrel had seen you instead of me? Why, he would be outraged. He would be well within his rights to thrash you within an inch of your life."

"I'd like to see him try," Charley blurted and inwardly cringed at his stupidity. The last thing he needed was to anger Leeds more.

"Just because you're built like an ox doesn't mean you can't be whipped," the stable owner noted and shook his head. "You're much too cocky, boy. Mark my words. One of these days that mouth of yours will get you into more trouble than you can handle."

"Yes, sir." Charley hoped that agreeing would soothe Leeds's ruffled feathers, but no such luck.

"I mean it. For someone who won't see eighteen for another couple of months, you act like you're God's gift to creation. You seem to think shoveling horse manure for a living is beneath you."

"I need the job, Mr. Leeds," Charley assured him. Which was an understatement. The three dollars a week the skinflint paid was barely enough to keep from starving to death.

"Needing a job, boy, isn't the same as wanting a job. I can't help but wonder if you know the difference. Oh, you work hard enough, but your enthusiasm isn't all I had hoped it would be."

How enthusiastic could someone get about shoveling horse shit? Charley thought but kept it to himself.

"That's the trouble with the youth of today," Leeds pontificated. "They have no idea what the world is like. They think it owes them a living, when it's the other way around." He paused. "Do you know what the difference is between men like me and boys like you?"

Hot air, Charley guessed, but again he had the presence of mind not to share his opinion.

"A sense of responsibility. I was in the War between the North and the South, as I've mentioned a few times, and the lessons I learned are lessons you could stand to benefit from. Nothing is ever given to us on a silver platter. To succeed in life, we must carve our own niche. That's the only way to get ahead, to become a prosperous businessman like I am."

Charley glanced at the sorrel's droppings and bit his lower lip.

"You can't succeed at anything in life without wanting to. Without that enthusiasm I mentioned. You need to set your sights on something you desire more than anything else, then go after it, heart and soul. That's the road to success in a nutshell." Satisfied with himself, Leeds puffed out his chest and marched toward his office next to the tack room. "It's almost eight. Clean up that mess, and you can leave a few minutes early. Use them to reflect on my words of wisdom." He stopped in the doorway. "By rights I should fire you, Mr. Pickett, for hitting a horse we're boarding. But I've always had a generous nature. I'll give you another chance."

The door closed. Charley muttered a few choice

words and fetched the shovel. He scooped the pile onto the manure wagon and groaned when he saw how full it was. Tomorrow Leeds would want him to take the load out to a potato farmer who used it as fertilizer, and he would spend most of the morning up to his knees in the stuff.

Grabbing his coat, Charley stormed into the street. He was mad. Mad at what came out the hind end of horses. Mad at Leeds for paying him so little. Mad at the unfairness of it all. But most of all, he was mad at himself for leaving the good life he'd had on his parents' farm in Kentucky to go it on his own.

Many a time Charley wanted to kick himself for being so stupid. His folks had always treated him kindly. Sure, his pa had worked him to death, or so he'd thought. Looking back, though, the hours were nowhere near as long and the work nowhere near as disgusting as the work he was doing now.

Charley had been a fool, plain and simple. He had soaked up the stories in *Harper's Monthly*, the *Police Gazette,* and *Leslie*'s. He had read all the penny dreadfuls he could get his hands on and listened to the tales of travelers. He had decided there had to be more to life than growing crops and tending cows. He'd craved excitement. He'd craved adventure. So one evening, he'd snuck off while his parents were in the parlor, and here he was.

Charley stopped and looked around. The street bustled with activity, with men on horseback and wagons, carts, and buggies. But their numbers could not begin to compare to the river of pedestrians who packed the street to overflowing.

Denver was busting at the seams. The city had grown to become the grandest between St. Louis and San Francisco. It was called the city of opportunity, the city of riches, but all it had been for Charley was a city of disappointment. Scowling, he shouldered his way along the boardwalk to the next intersection and took a right. He nearly tripped over a stray pig, and kicked it. Squealing, it darted out in front of a carriage and was nearly run down. "Serves you right," he grumbled.

Peddlers and hawkers were out in force. A kid not much over twelve had set up a grinder and was calling out, "Knives to grind! Scissors and razors!"

Across the street, a black man bawled, "Charcoal for sale! By the peck or the bushel! Get your charcoal here!"

There were days when Charley thought maybe he should give up being a stableboy and take up vending. The only thing was, he never had been comfortable around crowds. Too many people made him nervous.

A boy in a bowler hawking newspapers was on the next corner. "Get your *Rocky Mountain News*! Hot off the presses! Read all about the riot in New York City! Thirty-three dead!"

Another twenty yards and Charley spied a girl peddling sweet potatoes. "Yeddy ho! Sweet potatoes, so! Best to be found!"

A lump formed in Charley's throat, and he edged into the shadow of a store. Out of habit he removed his hat and nervously crumpled it in his big hands. He would have stood there forever admiring her, but the girl noticed him and smiled sweetly.

"Charley! You're early tonight." She held out a potato on a stick. "Hungry? You can have one for free."

Charley's tongue seemed to have swollen to the size of his shoe. Shaking his head, he croaked, "No thanks, Melissa. It's awful kind of you, but you need money as much as I do."

Melissa Patterson was bone thin and had straggly blond hair. No one would call her pretty by a stretch, but to Charley she was the loveliest girl in the city, if not all of creation. He had bought a potato from her once, and she had struck up a conversation in that warm and open manner she had, and before he knew it, he was stopping every evening just to bask in a few minutes of her company. "Call it my treat, then. Friend to friend."

Charley took that as an insult. It implied he couldn't fend for himself. Fishing in a pocket for a coin, he informed her, "I pay my own way, thank you very much. Here." He accepted the potato, which was warm to the touch, and took a bite. As he was chewing, what she had just said sank in. "Am I your friend?"

"The best I have." Melissa grinned and put a hand on his arm. "And I mean that from the bottom of my heart."

Charley's face seemed to catch fire. "Seen Tony?" he asked with his mouth full.

"Two blocks south, last I knew." Melissa lowered her hand, and her grin faded. "Going to spend your night with him again, I take it?"

"He's my friend too."

"If you want my opinion, it's a one-sided friendship. He lets you tag along because he needs your muscle to keep from having his head stove in."

"He can take care of himself." Charley had long sensed Melissa didn't care for Tony, and he couldn't understand why. They were both from New York. That gave them something in common. He would have thought they would hit it right off. And at first they had. But then she'd taken to treating Tony as if he had a contagious disease.

"You worry me, Charley. You truly do. It's not the hands of a clock that count—it's the gears inside that move the hands."

Charley was sure she had a point, but it eluded him. "I don't own a clock. I don't even own a watch. The pocketwatch I had was busted on the trip out. It fell off the wagon, and a wheel ran over it."

Melissa sighed. "You've got to learn to look past the outside of things, is all I'm saying. Don't always take people at how they appear. Think of them as ponds or lakes."

All Charley could think of was how confused he was. To hide the fact, he bit into the potato.

"All you see when you look at a lake is the surface. You never see what's underneath. It could be a big old trout. It could be a water snake waiting to bite you. Remember that, and you'll go a lot farther in life."

"You know a lot about lakes and such for a city girl."

"Whatever gave you that idea?" Melissa handed a potato to a customer and accepted payment. "I'm from upstate New York, not New York City. I was raised on a farm, just like you. I'd still be there now if my mother and father hadn't died in that accident."

Charley knew the details. How her folks had been coming home late one winter's night from a church social, and how the wagon had overturned on an icy bend in the road, killing them. Melissa had been sent to live with an uncle but had run away after six months. Now here she was, alone in the world and barely scraping by, the same as him. "I never did understand why you left your uncle. From what you say, he had a nice house and plenty of land."

"Uncle Thaddeus had the devil in him," Melissa said and let it go at that.

Charley finished the potato. He wouldn't mind staying longer and talking, but he was afraid of becoming tongue-tied like he usually did. "Well, I'll be seeing you." He shuffled off.

"Darn you, Charley Pickett!"

Charley turned. She was looking at him strangely. "What did I do now? I paid you, didn't I?"

"Yes." Melissa sighed, and her thin shoulders slumped. "It was nothing. You go on ahead and have fun. I just hope I get to see you tomorrow."

"Tomorrow and every day." Charley was rewarded with a smile that warmed him to his toes. Shoving his hands into his pockets, he ambled the two blocks to the corner of Walker and McCallister. Sure enough, a familiar voice pealed above the clamor of traffic.

"Fresh water! By the glass, the quart, the gallon! Get your fresh mountain water right here!"

Tony Fabrizio's cart was filled with bottles of all shapes and sizes. He was a year or two older than Charley and wore faded street clothes and a rakish cap. With his dark hair, chiseled profile, and square jaw, he was just about the most handsome fellow Charley had ever met. Which made Melissa's dislike of him all the harder to explain.

"Sold much water today, buddy?"

"Charley!" Tony grinned and clasped Charley by the shoulders. "*Mio amico!* Do I have a treat in store for us tonight!" He pulled Charley around behind the cart. "How would you like to eat at one of the best restaurants in the city?"

"Are they givin' away free meals?"

Tony glanced both ways, then pulled open his jacket, slid a hand into a pocket, and flashed a roll of bills large enough to choke a mule. "I would say this is more than enough, *si*?"

Astounded, Charley blurted, "How in the world . . . ?"

Placing a finger to his lips, Tony said, "Never mind the how. Help me take my cart back to my place, and we will enjoy a night we will long remember." He clapped Charley on the back, bent, and began pushing the water cart south. After only a few steps, he winked and asked, "How about you do me a favor and take over? I have been on my feet all day, and they are sore."

Charley had worked hard all day too, but he didn't mind helping. The cart was light as a feather. It amused him that Tony always asked for help. His friend had a fast tongue and faster hands, but he was as puny as a kitten. "You sure tire easy."

"Think so, do you? We cannot all be slabs of muscle like you. The heaviest thing I lifted back home was a wine bottle. I am not able to throw a cow over my shoulders and walk off with it."

Charley guffawed at the image. "You're exaggeratin'. It has to be a real small cow."

For some reason, Tony found that hilarious. "You amaze me sometimes. You truly do. You were fortunate to be raised on a farm. On the streets of most cities, you would not last two days."

"I can hold my own when I have to."

"Sure you can. All I am saying is that you are too

trusting, too gullible. One of these days someone will stab you in the back unless you learn to read people better."

"How to see inside them, you mean?" Charley let go of one of the handles to scratch his chin. "Melissa said the same thing to me earlier. It's nice, the two of you lookin' after me as you do."

"How is Miss Nose-In-The-Air, anyhow?" Tony asked.

"Don't call her that. She's a sweet gal, and I like her." In fact, Charley liked her a lot, more than he could recollect liking any girl, ever. When he was curled up in the hayloft in the stable at night, he often dreamed of Melissa and himself on a farm of their own. He was always so happy in those dreams, he could bust.

"I would never speak ill of any female." Tony glanced into a store window at his reflection and adjusted his cap. "My sainted *madre* taught me that women work as hard if not harder than we do. They deserve our respect."

"Have you written your folks yet to tell them where you are?"

"Do not start with that again. I told you before. I had to leave quickly, and the *polizia* might still be looking for me. They do not take killing as lightly there as they do on the frontier."

Charley recollected the details. Tony had gotten into an argument with another man over a woman. One hot word led to another, and the two pulled knives. Tony had to defend himself, and in the fight, his rival was stabbed in the chest.

"Anyhow, you are a fine one to talk. When are you writing your parents? From what you have told me, they must be worried sick. You were *stupido* to leave them like you did."

Had it been anyone else, Charley would have walloped them for talking like that. As it was, he said indignantly, "I'll make you a deal. You don't talk about my folks, and I won't talk about yours."

"*Accordo.*"

They had gone six blocks when Tony had Charley wheel the cart down an alley and out the other side to a water trough. Grabbing an empty bottle, Tony dipped it into the trough until it was full, stuck a cork in the top, and replaced it in the cart.

"What are you doing?"

"Filling up for tomorrow. We will be out real late tonight, and I do not want to bother with it later."

Charley's lower jaw dropped. "All the water you sell is from a horse trough?"

"Why not? It is free. And this is the cleanest trough in town. The man who owns it fills it twice a day. He has his own well." Tony dipped another bottle in. It made chugging sounds as bubbles rose to the top. "Now you know why I offer my customers a discount if they bring their bottles back."

Charley picked up a bottle with a label that had a word he had never seen before: *Perrier.* "This here is supposed to be water from France." He picked up another. "This says it's from Maine. And here's one from Maryland." Charley read more of the labels. "Wait a minute. Why does this one say 'toilet water'?"

Tony shrugged. "I take it where I find it."

"But you're cheatin' folks!"

"Calm down. I make no claims other than the water is fresh. So what if it does not come all the way from France? All water tastes the same to one who is thirsty." Tony held up a hand when Charley went to say something. "I do not do this for the fun of it. I do it because it is an easy way to make money. When I find a job more worthy of my talents, I will stop." He corked the second bottle. "I am not hurting anyone, am I?"

"Well, no," Charley conceded. "But it still doesn't strike me as right."

"You are just jealous I do not spend my days breaking my back like you do." Tony grinned and tossed Charley an empty bottle. "Now get busy. The sooner we fill these, the sooner we feast on heaping plates of spaghetti."

"Those noodles that look like shoelaces?" Charley shook his head. "For me it'll be a big, juicy steak with all the trimmin's."

Tony was lucky enough to have his own apartment; rooms to rent were at a premium. It wasn't much, a small room at the back of a house owned by an elderly couple, but he had his own entrance and could come and go as he pleased.

Charley parked the cart under an overhang, and they went in so Tony could spruce up. Tony owned a large mirror and not one, not two, but *three* hairbrushes. Charley couldn't get over it. He didn't even own a comb.

"I was thinking we should dine at the Crown Royal Hotel. They have their own restaurant, and it is rated one of the best in the city."

"It also costs an arm and a leg."

Tony patted his jacket pocket. "You are forgetting, are you not? Tonight we do as we please. The cost is no object." He took a washcloth from a rung above a basin. "Here. You should clean yourself up. You have bits of straw in your hair and God knows what on your shoes."

It was indeed a night Charley would long remember. The Crown Royal was everything everyone claimed, with gilt marble and glittering chandeliers. A waiter in a crisp uniform fussed over them like a mother hen. Charley had to chuckle when he discovered that every time he drained his water glass, the waiter promptly refilled it. He drank five glasses just to see the waiter come scurrying toward them with the crystal pitcher.

The food was delicious. Charley's mouth watered simply staring at it, and the aroma of his sizzling steak set his stomach to rumbling like distant thunder. He cut a piece thick with dripping fat and forked it into his mouth. Someone moaned, and he realized it was himself.

"Quit making a spectacle of yourself," Tony joked. His plate was heaped high with stringy noodles smothered in tomato sauce and ringed by meatballs.

"This beats McGuffy's all hollow." Charley was referring to an eatery where the food bore a strong resemblance to hog swill.

Tony ordered a bottle of wine. The waiter brought long-stemmed glasses and filled them, then stood back as if waiting.

Charley knew why. He chugged his, then set down the glass so the waiter could refill it.

"Not so fast, *mio amico*," Tony cautioned. "Fine wine should be savored, not guzzled." He sipped his. "That bottle set me back fifteen dollars."

Doing the math in his head took Charley a few seconds. "That's more than I make in a month. Shouldn't you save some of your money? Or send some to your folks?"

"We had a deal, *ricordare*?"

"Sorry."

"I am Italian, my friend, and Italians are passionate

people. We live life day to day, making the most of every moment. Yes, I could save the money, but what enjoyment would that give me? I would rather spend it here and now on things I like. I would rather *live*."

At moments like this, Charley appreciated how different they were and how much more worldly Tony was. He envied him and said so.

"Pick someone more worthy. My past is darker than most. There is much I have not shared." Tony contemplated the wine in his sparkling glass. "I will never do anything great. I will never be rich or famous. The best I could hope for was to marry the woman I love, and that has been denied me."

"Land sakes. You make it sound like your life is etched in stone."

"It is. My people call it *destino*. Yours would call it fate. The threads of our lives were woven before we were born, you and I. There is nothing we can do to change them. Believe me, I have tried."

Charley had never heard his friend talk this way, and it bothered him. "You're wrong there. I may not be the smartest person on the planet, but I know we decide what we do, and no one else." Charley mulled how best to express his sentiments. "Life is like a road. Each day is a new fork. We decide which to take and which not to take. Our fate is in our lap, no one else's."

"*Interessante.*" Tony glanced past Charley and stiffened. Suddenly bending at the waist, he whispered, "Let me do the talking. Whatever happens, it is not to involve you."

Before Charley could ask what Tony meant, three men walked up to their table—burly, broad-shouldered men wearing suits and polished shoes, one with a diamond stickpin in his tie.

"Well, well, well." Stickpin's voice was like two rocks grating together. "All evening I've been trying to figure out how in hell I lost my roll. Then who should I see across the room at the most expensive restaurant in Denver? The water boy I always buy water from." He leaned on the edge of the table and glared at Tony. "You made the worst mistake of your life picking my pocket. I've beat people to a pulp for a lot less." His smile was ripe with menace. "So where do you want it? Here or outside?"

Chapter Two

Charley Pickett didn't know which shocked him more. That someone would come up to them in public and threaten them, or that his best friend, Anthony Michael Fabrizio, was a pickpocket. For just as sure as he was sitting there, he knew it was true.

Tony, though, smiled that pearly white smile of his and responded, "I have no idea what you are talking about, *signore.*"

The newspapers were full of stories about how bad crime was in Denver. Thieves, pickpockets, footpads, robbers; whatever they were called, they were thick as fleas on an old coon dog. That's why Charley had taken to keeping what little money he had saved in his right shoe.

"Spare me, punk!" the man with the diamond stickpin snarled. "Do you have any idea who I am?" He drew himself up to his full height. "I'm Walter Radtke. I run half a dozen concert halls and twice as many gambling dens. I make more money in a day than you'll ever earn in your lifetime. I'm not someone you want to mess with."

Charley saw Tony glance right and left as if he

were thinking about bolting. Right away, the two bruisers with Radtke flanked him to prevent it.

Tony's smile never wavered. "All that may be true, but it does not prove I stole your money. For all you know, it was someone else. Or you lost it."

Radtke folded his arms across his chest. "Quit playing me for a sucker. Hell, I buy water from you every day on my way to one of my concert halls. You must have been waiting your chance for weeks. And you're good. I'll grant you that. I never felt you lift it."

Charley was being ignored. He was relieved, since he would never want to rile someone like Radtke. But it also made him a little angry that he wasn't important enough to be noticed.

"I want my money, punk. All of it. If you don't hand it over right this minute, Loritz and Arch are taking you out into the alley and rearranging your bones. It's that simple."

"You would cause a scene here?" Tony gestured at the array of Denver's richest and most influential. "Unless I am mistaken, over there is the mayor with his lovely wife. At the table next to them is the president of the bank down the street. What will they think if they see your *scimmie* drag me out? It would not do to spoil their digestion."

Radtke glanced at the tables Tony had indicated, and his eyebrows pinched together. "Damn." He leaned on the table again. "You think you're smart, don't you, boy? But all you've done is bought yourself some time. You have until seven p.m. tomorrow to bring my money to the Hull Boarding House on Fremont Street. If you don't, by eight I'll have a hundred men scouring Denver from end to end. There's nowhere you can hide that I can't find you. There's nowhere you can run that my men can't hunt you down."

Tony was still smiling when the trio walked off. As soon as they were out of sight, he drained his wineglass in several gulps and sat glumly staring at the linen tablecloth. "I am in for it now. Even if I return the money, Radtke is not likely to forgive and forget. He does not strike me as the type to turn the other cheek."

"How could you steal someone else's money?" Charley asked in amazement.

"There you go again. I swear, the way you go on, you should consider becoming a priest." Tony paused. "Sorry. Make that a preacher."

"Needle me all you want. But there's right and there's wrong, and a man has to know which is which or he'll never amount to a hill of beans."

"Is that you talking or your *padre*? Your father?" Tony put a hand to his forehead and closed his eyes. "It is easy for you to spout virtue, my friend. You did not have the childhood I did. You have not been living by your wits as long as I have. It is not easy, Charley. Sometimes you must do things you are not proud of."

"I'd never steal."

Tony looked at him and smiled. "I believe you. I believe you would rather starve than do whatever it takes to survive. That is the big difference between us." He reached across and patted Charley's big hand. "But do not take me wrong. I do not think less of you. I think more. We are more alike in that respect than you can imagine. I am honored to call you my friend."

Charley thought of how his mother used to pat him on the head and tell him he was her pride and joy, and he grew all tingly. "Right or wrong, we can't let Radtke hurt you. We've got to do something."

"I am open to suggestions. But I tell you right now, I am not returning the money. I need a stake, Charley. Why, I cannot say. But I need a lot of money, and I need it soon." Tony gazed wistfully at a chandelier. "In many respects we are like driftwood. The currents of our lives carry us places we would rather not go, but which we are powerless to prevent."

Charley had no idea what his friend was talking about. He bent to his steak and tried to enjoy it, but the mood had been ruined. Twice he tried to engage Tony in conversation, but Tony had withdrawn into himself.

"If you do not mind," Tony said as he paid for their meals, "I would very much like to be alone. I will walk home by myself and see you tomorrow on the same corner."

"Whatever you want." Charley was feeling sad himself. Whenever someone he liked was upset, it upset him too. He trailed Tony out the gilded glass doors and watched until Tony reached the far end of the block. About to turn and go his own way, he saw a pair of shadows emerge from the recessed doorway of a butcher shop and fall into step a dozen yards behind his friend.

Charley was startled to realize they were the same pair who had been with Walter Radtke. Loritz and Arch. They had on hats and coats with the collars pulled high, but they didn't fool him. Pulling the short brim of his own hat low, he followed to see what they were up to. Radtke had given Tony until tomorrow night to fork over the money, but maybe he had changed his mind and decided to have Tony beaten to a pulp sooner.

Charley wouldn't let that happen. Shoving his hands into his pockets, he hunched forward so he would appear smaller than he was in case they looked back. His size had always set him apart, and they were bound to recognize him otherwise. But they never once glanced over their shoulders. They were intent on Tony and Tony alone.

Charley thought about what his friend had said about needing a stake. Tony wasn't the only one. He could use one. So could Melissa. And they were not alone. There had to be thousands who would give their eyeteeth for a chance at a better life. For most, though, their dreams would never amount to more than flights of fancy.

All those years in Kentucky, Charley had never imagined life was so hard, so cruel. His parents, he now knew, had protected him from the worst of the world. They fed him; they clothed him; they were always there when he needed a helping hand. He had never fully appreciated all they did.

Charley would very much like to go back and tell them to their faces how much they meant to him. How much he loved them. But he couldn't bear to show up on their doorstep penniless and jobless, like some tramp begging for a handout. He had his pride to think of. When he returned to Kentucky, he wanted them to be proud of him, not ashamed.

Tony had turned left into a street with fewer gas lamps. Loritz and Arch followed, pacing him. They brushed aside a fallen dove in a blue dress who had brazenly blocked their path and thrust her chest out for them to admire. She swore like a soldier but shut up when one raised a hand to cuff her.

Several more blocks fell behind them. Charley was half-convinced the pair were tailing Tony to learn where Tony lived and nothing more. Then Fabrizio stopped at the mouth of an alley and peered down it as if trying to decide whether to take a shortcut. The taller of the pair nudged the other, and they quickened their pace until they were practically running. Too late, Tony heard them. He took a few steps but was grabbed by the arms and hauled into the alley. He didn't resist.

Charley wasn't a fast runner, but he could move when he had to. When he reached the alley, the shorter man had Tony up against a wall, and the tall one was smacking his right fist against his left palm.

"—sends his regards," Charley heard him say. "To prove he's a man of his word, you still have until tomorrow night to come up with the money you stole. But Mr. Radtke figures you should have—" He looked at his companion. "What was it the boss said again, Arch?"

"Incentive, Loritz," Arch quoted. "Mr. Radtke wants we should give this guy some incentive."

Loritz grinned and smacked his fist against his palm again. "That was it. So where do you want your incentive, boy? Above the belt or below it?"

Charley barged into the alley. "Lay a hand on him, and you'll answer to me." He had never been in a fight in his life, but he could not stand there and do nothing. "Let him go, and there will be no hard feelin's."

"Who the hell?" Loritz blurted. "Oh. It's the hick. Mind your own business, stupid, or we'll show you why the city is no place for bumpkins."

Tony amazed Charley by saying, "Do as they tell you, Charley. I am the one Radtke wants to get even with. Leave me. I know what I'm doing."

"I won't desert a friend."

"You must, for both our sakes." Tony tried to wave him away, but Arch pinned his arms to the wall. "Please, Charley. You will only get us in deeper. I have everything under control."

Arch laughed. "Sure you do, jackass." He punched Tony in the gut. Not with all his might, but enough that Tony sputtered and gasped.

"I warned you." Charley moved closer. Loritz swore and flicked a looping right cross, which Charley blocked. He swung at Loritz's jaw, but Loritz ducked, sidestepped, and hit Charley twice in the gut. Charley stepped back, surprised there wasn't much pain. Setting himself, he raised his fists as he had seen boxers do at the county fair. "I don't go down easy."

"We'll see." Loritz was taller than Charley but nowhere near as big in the chest. Skipping from side to side, he jabbed a few times without trying to connect, testing Charley's reflexes. "I'm about to stomp you into the dirt."

"You do, and you're a daisy," Charley blustered, then had to defend himself from a barrage of blows. He blocked some but not all and was rocked onto his heels by an uppercut.

"Quit it!" Tony hollered at Loritz. "Let him go, and I will give you the money I have left. It is in my pocket."

Loritz stepped back. He was not even breathing heavily. "You should have thought of that at the Crown Royal Hotel. Your pal here asked for trouble, and now he's going to get it." Again Loritz waded in, in earnest this time.

Charley tried. He truly did. But the man was older and had a lot more experience. For every two punches Charley countered, one slipped through. He was taking a terrible beating, but it still didn't hurt anywhere near as much as he had thought it would. His years behind a plow had lent him muscles to spare, and they absorbed the worst of the punishment.

"End it, Loritz!" Arch urged. "The boss will be upset if we get hauled in by the law, and the last thing we need is him mad at us."

Loritz feinted high to the face, and when Charley hiked his forearms to ward the blow off, Loritz drove his left knee into Charley's groin.

To Charley it felt as if he had been smashed with a sledgehammer. There was no denying the pain; it washed over him in excruciating waves that brought him to his knees.

"Say so long to your teeth." Loritz drew back his fist.

"No!" The cry came from Tony. Simultaneously, he tore his right arm free and whipped it out and down. Cold steel glinted dully in the dark. A stiletto had appeared in his hand. He slashed the blade across Arch's throat, and Arch jerked back, a scarlet mist spraying from his severed jugular. Again Tony cut him. Arch backpedaled, but he had nowhere to go except against the opposite wall.

Loritz sprang to help. From under his jacket he flashed a short-barreled revolver that he cocked as he drew. Fast as he was, though, Tony was faster. The stiletto sliced deep into Lortiz's knuckles, and he howled and dropped the six-gun. "I'm getting the hell out of here!" He never went anywhere.

Tony thrust the blade to the hilt into Loritz's ribs, and Loritz oozed to the ground without another sound.

"Good God!" Charley bleated. "You've killed them!"

"Would you rather I let them put you in the hospital?" Tony stared at the blood dripping from his stiletto. "I am a dead man, Charley. A judge will sentence me to have my neck stretched. Or else Walter Radtke will have me cut into little pieces and fed to coyotes in the foothills." Tony squatted and wiped the blade clean on Loritz's jacket. "It is the old ways all over again. I came here to start over. Instead, all I have done is dig my own grave."

Charley struggled to his feet. His oysters, as his pa always called them, were throbbing. But Tony needed him, and he would not let his friend down. "Quit talkin' like that, and put your pigsticker away. We'll waltz out of this alley like we don't have a care in the world. Smile some. Laugh some. Act like this never happened, so anyone who sees us won't suspect."

Wrapping his right arm around Tony's shoulders, Charley strolled to the street. No one paid the slightest attention as they blended into the ebb and flow.

Tony was unusually quiet. He never spoke once the whole time they followed a roundabout route back to Tony's apartment. At the iron gate that opened onto the gravel path to the house, he paused.

"This is as far as you go. I will pack up and be gone by noon. San Francisco is nice, I hear. They do not have much snow. And there are Italians. My own kind. A lot more than here."

Charley couldn't stand the notion of Tony leaving. To lose one of the two people who made Denver bearable was enough to make him want to rip the gate from its hinges. "Maybe we can think of a way you can stay."

"Be serious. *Signore* Radtke will know I am to blame. He will report me to the police, and a warrant will be issued for my arrest. I must get out of Denver while I can."

"What about your cart and your bottles?"

"Keep them. You can earn more selling water than you ever will cleaning horse stalls. Or maybe give them to that girlfriend of yours. Potatoes are only in season a short while. She will need a new means to support herself."

"Promise me one thing. Promise me you won't leave without saying good-bye. It would hurt something awful." Wheeling, Charley hurried away before he made a fool of himself.

Normally, the city's nightlife held an allure Charley found fascinating. But tonight he plodded along, overcome by sorrow. There had to be something he could do to help Tony. But his mind, like his legs, had never been very fast, and he could not come up with anything.

Charley let himself into the livery through the rear door. He climbed the ladder to the hayloft and walked over to his blanket. Spreading it out, he lay on his back with his hands under his head and gave the problem more thought.

Sleep came grudgingly. Charley tossed and turned, his mind plodding like a tortoise. It had to be four in the morning when he finally dozed off, and he was supposed to be up by six to open the stable. He was relying on the crowing of a rooster down the street to wake him, but fatigue took its toll.

Faint pounding roused Charley from a vague dream. When he opened his eyes and saw shafts of sunlight streaming through cracks in the plank wall, he scrambled down the ladder and raced to the wide double doors. Lifting the heavy bar, he lugged it to one side.

"About time, young man."

Charley was so relieved it wasn't his employer, he smiled and declared, "Mr. Parmenton! Off on your buggy ride early today, are we?"

"Early?" Parmenton consulted a pocket watch. "It's three minutes past seven, I'll have you know. I could have been to Cherry Creek and back if I had left at six. Prepare my buggy and be quick about it."

Most mornings Leeds was there by eight, but today he was late. Charley had time to feed the horses, sweep the center aisle, and shovel droppings into the manure wagon. He was spreading straw when in stormed the stableman.

"It's an outrage, I tell you! This sort of thing can't go on!" Mr. Leeds shook a newspaper as if he were throttling it. "How can we expect decent people to move to Denver with atrocities like this happening all the time?"

"Sir?" Charley had seldom seen Leeds so fired up.

"Haven't you heard? There was a double murder last night! Right in the street! Two unsavory characters no one will ever miss were stabbed to death. But if the Kansas City and St. Louis newspapers pick up the story, it will tarnish Denver's image no end." Leeds shook the newspaper at Charley. "And why in thunder are you standing there loafing? Didn't you notice the manure wagon is full?"

"You told me to never leave the stable unattended."

Leeds puffed out his cheeks like an agitated chipmunk. "Don't throw my own words back at me. Hitch up the team and run the wagon out to Klimek's. Don't dawdle either, if you know what is good for you."

For once, Charley didn't mind. It would give him more time to ponder. The smell was atrocious, as always, but the view, as always, was spectacular. To the west rose emerald foothills, footstools for the towering Rockies. Snow mantled a few of the highest peaks, but in a few weeks the last of it would melt off, and the peaks would be bare until winter. To the south was Pike's Peak, and to the northwest loomed Long's Peak, which was higher but nowhere near as famous.

Once across the bridge, Charley had the road virtually to himself. Farmland stretched for as far as the eye could see. Thanks to an extensive irrigation system, the arid land was being transformed into an Eden.

Ziven Klimek had been a potato farmer in the Old Country, so it was only natural he took it up again in the New World. His sprawling farm was the largest in the territory, and Klimek ran it with European precision. Field after precisely arranged field radiated outward from the sprawling house Klimek had built for his new, and considerably younger, wife.

Charley never knew exactly where the old farmer wanted the manure delivered. One trip it might be a plot to the north, the next trip a field to the east. Finding Klimek was a chore in itself, as the man, for all his years, had the energy of a yearling and never stayed in one spot too long.

Today Charley was lucky. He had passed through the gate and was only a quarter mile in when a booming hail caused him to bring the team to the halt. "Howdy, Mr. Klimek!"

The potato farmer had his shirtsleeves rolled up to his elbows and his thumbs hooked around his suspenders. "Master Pickett! What have you brought Ziven today?"

"The usual." Since manure was all Charley ever delivered, he couldn't fathom why Klimek always asked the same question. "Where do you want it dumped?"

"Ziven show you." Klimek swung up onto the seat with an agility belying his years. He pointed. "That way. And do not let your wheels get too near the water ditch."

"How have things been?" Charley asked to make small talk.

"Life is good. Ziven grow corn now. Sugar beets too. You ever taste sugar beets, Master Pickett?"

"My ma used to grow them in a garden out back of the house. She also had cauliflower and cabbage, and the tiniest peas you ever did see." Charley smacked his lips, his mouth watering. "There's nothing more delicious than a sugar beet though, when it's cooked just right."

Klimek nodded vigorously. "True, true. You watch. Sugar beets will be big. Bigger than potatoes. Bigger than corn. Bring Ziven lots and lots of money."

"You like making money, don't you, Mr. Klimek?"

"What kind of question is that? With money a man can do anything. Without money a man can do nothing. It not matter of 'like.' It matter of 'need.' You understand need, Master Pickett?"

"I'm beginning to," Charley acknowledged.

Klimek encompassed his farm with a sweep of his brawny arms. "This is rich land. Good land. One day many farmers will be here. Many families with

children. No more Indians on warpath. No more
murders like last night. No more badmen like those
Hoodoos."

"Hoodoos?" Charley had heard the word before
but couldn't recall where.

"The horse stealers!" Klimek rasped. "Master Pickett not hear? They kill three cavalry troopers a while
ago. Kid Falon, he kill two himself. But you wait.
They get caught, they get hung." He rubbed his
palms together in glee. "Soon all badmen gone. Soon
everyone live safe."

Charley was thinking of Kid Falon. It was said the
Kid was a genuine two-gun terror. Falon had four-
teen gunfights to his credit, and that didn't count
Indians and Mexicans. A fellow Charley met in a
saloon claimed to have seen Kid Falon draw and was
willing to swear on a stack of Bibles that the Kid was
as fast as Wild Bill Hickock, the prince of the pistol-
eers. Charley had his doubts, since Wild Bill was generally considered the premier shootist alive and
according to *Harper's* had slain well over a hundred
men.

Klimek was still talking. "Government must stop
Hoodoos. Must stop all outlaws. Pay more bounty.
Use army. Anything."

"The government is offering a bounty for the
Hoodoos?"

"Where have you been, Master Pickett? Bounty
was one thousand dollars. After soldiers killed,
bounty now seven thousand. Highest in territory."

Seven thousand dollars. Charley had never had more
than thirty dollars to his name his whole life long,
and that only on one occasion, after he scrimped and
saved for years to go West. Seven thousand was
enough to last years. It would be a great stake. Not

just for him but for Tony . . . and for someone else besides. An idea took root, and Charley grinned at his brainstorm.

"Why so happy, Master Pickett?"

"You've just given me the greatest idea I've ever had. The answer to all my prayers and then some."

Ziven Klimek was no fool. "If that idea be what Ziven think, forget idea. You no sheriff. You no gun shark. You horse-shit boy. Go after Hoodoos, and they will kill Master Pickett dead, dead, dead."

Chapter Three

"Yeddy ho! Sweet potatoes, so! Best to be found!"

Charley Pickett heard Melissa at the same instant he saw her. Not as many people were out and about in the middle of the day, and traffic was light. He brought the manure wagon over next to the board-walk, wrapped the reins around the brake, and hopped down. He was so worried, he forgot himself and gripped her by the arm. "Melissa! Have you seen Tony?"

Melissa had not noticed him and about jumped out of her skin. "Charley! Goodness gracious. Don't sneak up on a person like that!" Relaxing, she smiled and did not ask him to remove his hand. "What are you doing here? Has Mr. Leeds given you time off?"

"I'm on an errand." Charley stepped back in disappointment. "Tony is leaving for San Francisco today. By noon, he told me. It's almost that now. I stopped by his place, but his cart was gone, and his landlady said he had given notice and bid her good-bye."

"Tony is leaving?"

"You don't have to sound so happy about it. He's the only real friend I have." Charley quickly added,

"Besides you, I mean. I know the two of you don't get along, but I'll miss him something awful."

From behind them came a chuckle. *"Buon giorno. Is the world coming to an end and no one told me, my friend? You look as if you swallowed a scorpion."*

"Tony!" Charley was so happy, he lifted his friend. "I was scared to death you were gone! Where have you been?" A battered valise at Tony's feet sobered him, and he put Tony down.

"I went to the stable to say so long, as I promised. But Leeds said you were not back from the potato farm. He is mad at you, by the way. He says he could unload ten manure wagons in the time it takes you to unload one." Tony doffed his cap to Melissa and gave a courtly bow. "So I came to ask your *amica* if she would relay my regards for me. And here you are."

"I don't want you to go."

Tony smiled. "You know why I must. Already I hear Radtke has men out searching. The police are not after me yet, but they are slow about such things."

"The police?" Melissa covered her pot with a lid. "What have you done that involves them?"

"Nothing that need concern you." Tony picked up his valise.

"Wait!" Charley's idea was bubbling in him like lava in a volcano. "What if you could get your hands on the stake you want? What if all of us could end up with more money than we thought possible? Stick around awhile and hear me out."

Tony surveyed the street. "Start talking. I must be gone within the hour."

"Not here. Somewhere we can have peace and

quiet." Charley had never been much good at expressing himself and would need time to convince them.

"There is a tavern a few blocks west. The owner knows me, and I trust him. He will give us a private room at the back. "

Charley looked at Melissa. "This concerns you too. Please say you'll come with us."

"I've never set foot in a tavern in my life. My mother always said they were no place for a proper lady."

Tony muttered something that Charley didn't catch. "Please, Melissa," he urged. "Just this once. Do it for me. I'll protect you, if it comes to that. But it's important, or I wouldn't ask."

"My mother would roll over in her grave, but all right. For you, and you alone." Melissa gave Tony a sharp look. "Would you mind answering my question about the police? I've never been arrested, and I don't intend to start."

"At the tavern," Tony said.

Charley was eager to be off. "Hop in the wagon, and I can have us there in no time."

"What about my potatoes?"

Tony was already heading for the wagon. "For God's sake, woman. Bring your precious pot if you must. I can not stay out in the open like this, or I am a dead man."

Melissa gave in, but she took forever taking the pot off the tripod and folding the tripod. "Where do I put my utensils?" she asked, staring at the manure-encrusted bed.

"Under the seat will be fine." Charley helped her, then boosted her up and climbed on. He was so big, there was barely enough space for the three of them.

Melissa was wedged between them, her hands folded in her lap. She wouldn't look at Tony, and he wouldn't look at her.

Charley set the team in motion. "This is the greatest day of our lives," he announced to whet their interest, but neither took the bait.

The tavern was a seamy little building set back from the street. Melissa balked at entering until Charley took her arm and assured her he would be by her side the whole time. A swarthy Italian came up to them and huddled with Tony, then pointed down a dark hallway.

The small room smelled of odors far worse than manure. Melissa scrunched up her nose and started to back out, but Charley ushered her to a bench against the left wall: the only item of furniture.

Tony stepped to the other wall, dropped his valise, and squatted. "All right. Here we are. Now what is so *importante* you risk my life?"

Both of them looked at Charley, who suddenly had a pickle in his throat.

"We're waiting," Melissa said impatiently.

Charley licked his lips. "Last night Tony and me were talkin' about how we need a stake. How if we had enough money, we could make something of our lives. Pick ourselves up off the street and become respectable."

"I've had the same dream," Melissa said. "There's no future in hawking. You never make enough to get ahead. It's hand to mouth, with more lean times than flush. But good jobs for women are few and pay pennies. And I refuse to become one of *those*."

Charley's confusion must have shown, because Tony laughed and said, "She will never offer herself for money." His next comment, spoken almost in a whisper, was odd. "I pity the fool who tries to touch her."

Melissa came off the bench with her bony fists bunched. "You promised never to bring that up again. So help me, I'll sock you on the nose if you don't get over yourself. Just because you're so good-looking doesn't mean every female you meet will swoon at your feet."

"What are you two talkin' about?" Charley asked.

"It's between your friend and me." Flames danced in Melissa's eyes. "He knows, and that's all that counts. So what will it be, Mr. Stallion? Will you act your age and drop it?"

Tony was tight-lipped with anger.

"So far I've kept this strictly between us. But I won't if you persist." Melissa was madder than Charley had ever seen her. "What is it with men? My uncle and you are a lot alike, only he was worse. I'll hold my peace. But this is the last time, you hear me?"

Charley saw Tony's expression undergo a puzzling change. It went from angry to serene to an undeniable sorrow. Sadness so deep, Charley felt sad just looking at him. He was glad when Tony shook himself and smiled.

"Consider the matter dropped." Tony seemed to develop an interest in his shoes. "Now, can we get on with why we are here? Every minute I remain is another minute my life is in danger."

Melissa unclenched her fists and sat back down. "Suppose you get on with your grand revelation, Charley."

"Huh?" Charley never had been able to follow two trains of thought at once. Having one derailed so abruptly threw him, and it was a few seconds before he exclaimed, "My brainstorm? Sure enough. Wait until you hear." He leaned forward with his forearms on his knees. "What would you say if I have a way for each of us to end up with more than two thousand dollars in our pockets?"

"I would say the altitude is getting to you," Tony cracked. "They say Denver is over a mile high."

"Go on, Charley," Melissa coaxed. "I've endured this much. I might as well hear the rest."

Here it was, the moment Charley had been leading up to. He could scarcely contain himself. "Ever heard of the Hoodoos?"

"Do you mean those horrible horse thieves up in Wyoming?" Melissa responded. "The ones who steal horses from Indians and sell them to whites in Nebraska and Kansas or wherever? The newspaper carries stories about them all the time." She tilted her head. "Why?"

"They went too far and killed some troopers not long ago, and now the government has posted a bounty on their heads. Seven thousand dollars, dead or alive." Charley waited for them to catch on and be filled with the same excitement he felt, but they stared at him as if he were a block of wood. "Well? Don't you see? That seven thousand dollars can be ours."

For the first time, Melissa and Tony looked at one another without a trace of hostility. Both burst out laughing. Tony rocked on his heels, while Melissa covered her mouth with her hand and tittered with abandon.

"I don't rightly see what's so hilarious." Charley was miffed. "Seven thousand dollars is nothin' to laugh at. We'd split it three ways. I could buy a farm somewhere. Tony would have enough to make a start in San Francisco. And Melissa, well, you could use your share toward the millinery you talked about ownin' one day."

Melissa had stopped tittering. "I would get an equal share? Be an equal partner? For real? You would take me with you and let me help out?"

"That's fair, isn't it? You could do the cookin' and stuff like that. But I'd never put you in danger. Once we catch up to the Hoodoos, Tony and me will take over and do what needs doing."

"I would insist on pulling my weight," Melissa said. "I've never freeloaded in my life. An honest day's pay for an honest day's work, my mother always said."

Tony stood up. "Listen to the two of you. Talking about shares and what's fair. As if we will ever see any of that money." He snorted. "Even if by some miracle we found them, the Hoodoos aren't about to throw down their guns and give up. We would be dead before we lifted a finger."

"Not if we do it smart," Charley insisted. "Not if we can take them by surprise. One by one, say, when they're least liable to expect anything."

"You are *matto*, my friend. Insane. I have read the newspapers. Their leader is Brock Alvord, a most clever desperado. The rest are deadly killers, Kid Falon most of all. The newspapers say he murdered his first man when he was ten, and he has been killing ever since. Your effort to help means a lot, but you must be practical. Besides, we could not find the Hoodoos if we hunted for them forever."

"I know someone who might be willing to help," Melissa offered. "He's had a lot of experience tracking and hunting and the like. But we'd probably have to offer him a share of the bounty."

"Who is he? What does he do?" Charley supposed they could divide the money four ways instead of three. It would still leave him with enough for a sizeable down payment on a good piece of land.

"His name is Enos Howard. He used to shoot buffalo for a living. He buys potatoes from me now and then, and from what he's told me, he's been all over, from Montana to Mexico."

Tony was skeptical. "If this Howard is so good, why did he give up hunting buffalo?" He shook his head in amusement. "Will you listen to me? I am as crazy as you two. Why are we still talking about this?" He picked up the valise.

"Wait!" Charley blocked the doorway. "What harm can it do to go see Howard? If he's as good as Melissa says, he could be just what we need." Charley turned to her. "Do you know where this hunter lives?"

"I know where we can find him at six tonight. A saloon on Sixteenth Street. He always goes there after he eats his potatoes."

Tony tried to slip past Charley to reach the latch. "I wish you both the best. But there is a mule train heading west in an hour, and I have paid to ride with a mule skinner on one of the wagons."

"You would pass up a chance at close to two thousand dollars?"

"I cannot spend the money if I am dead." Tony set down his valise again. "Tell me. These Hoodoos. How long have they been stealing and killing?"

"Five years or better, or so I've heard." Charley didn't see why Fabrizio was making such a fuss.

"Haven't you wondered how they can go on stealing and killing for so long? Why hasn't a marshal or a sheriff arrested them? I will tell you. Because the marshals and the sheriffs are scared of them. They are *cattivo,* these Hoodoos. Vicious. They kill for the thrill of killing. Kid Falon once shot a man for snoring too loud. It should teach you something."

"It does. We better buy guns before we head out."

Tony's eyes narrowed. "You are doing this on purpose."

"Doing what? All I want is for us to have enough money to do the things we've always dreamed about. We're sure not going to earn enough shovelin' hay or sellin' potatoes or trough water. A chance like this comes along once in a lifetime. We should take it before someone else beats us to it." Charley paused. "Six o'clock isn't that far off. Can't you lie low until then? I'd like you to be there when we talk to Enos Howard."

"The mule train leaves in an hour."

Charley glanced at Melissa for support. "Talk to him. Show him he's makin' a mistake he'll regret the rest of his life."

"Me?"

"You're smarter than me, Melissa. Heck, you're both smarter than me. I know that. So he'll listen to you. Tell him it can be done. Tell him it's worth the risk to stick around a day or so, or as long as it takes for us to get ready."

Melissa gazed at Tony but said nothing. Tony gazed at Charley for the longest while, then sighed.

"If it means this much to you, I will tell the mule skinner to go on without me, and I will catch up with him later. I can always take a stage to Santa Fe and get there before they do."

"I knew you would change your mind!" Charley whooped for joy. "Wait and see! Both of you will thank me before this is done!"

They separated after agreeing to meet in front of Kincaid's Beer and Billiards on Sixteenth Street at ten minutes to six. Charley pushed the team as fast as he could, but he still didn't arrive at the livery until twelve thirty. Mr. Leeds was waiting out front, and to say he was in fine spirits would be a lie.

"Let me guess. You couldn't find Klimek's potato farm and wound up going all the way to Canada? Or did you decide to take a tour of Kansas City and St. Louis on your way back?"

"Neither." Charley hopped down and began stripping the harness.

"That's it? No feeble excuses for why you're so late? A wheel didn't break? A horse didn't throw a shoe? The earth didn't open up and swallow you and the wagon whole?"

"Nope. I stopped to talk with a couple of friends."

Leeds made a sound that came out as a "Harrummph!" Then he opened his mouth, closed it, and opened it again. "As the Lord is my witness, I don't know what to make of you, Charley Pickett. You squander my time, and when I confront you, you freely confess. You're either one of the most honest young men I've ever run across, or else you're a simpleton."

Charley had a thought. "You've lived here a good long while, haven't you, Mr. Leeds?"

"How does that pertain?"

"I was just thinkin' that you must know a lot about a lot of people, given how you keep up with the latest news and all."

"I try. Every citizen owes it to himself to stay well informed. It wouldn't hurt if you kept up with things too. You're never too young to do your part to make your community a better place to live."

Charley hadn't meant that at all. Afraid Leeds was about to launch into one of his long-winded spiels, he quickly asked, "Ever heard of a man called Enos Howard?"

Mr. Leeds scratched his chin. "Howard? Howard? Where have I heard that name before?" He snapped his fingers and nodded. "Of course! The buffalo hunter. The one involved in that fracas with the Blackfeet on the upper Missouri River. The Battle of the Chalk Cliffs, I believe it was called."

"I've never heard of it." Charley didn't stop working. He knew the moment he did, Leeds would stop talking.

"Not many have. Let me see. It happened about '66. Or was it '65? A bunch of buffalo hunters were jumped by a Blackfoot war party. Two were killed outright, and the rest ran for their lives. The Blackfeet chased them clear to the bluffs overlooking the Missouri. With their backs to the chalk cliffs, the buffalo hunters used their Sharps rifles to keep the Blackfeet at bay. Howard was hailed as a hero because he picked off a Blackfoot chief at a range of three-quarters of a mile, and the rest took that as a sign of bad medicine and rode off."

"Three-quarters of a mile?"

"I keep forgetting that although you're a country boy, you're green as grass when it comes to life on the frontier. And while I'm a city dweller myself, I've learned a few things over the years. Among them, that a skilled marksman with a Sharps can hit a man-sized target from a mile away or more."

To Charley, it bordered on the preposterous. He had done a lot of hunting in Kentucky and could drop a buck at two hundred yards. But a mile? That had to be another of those outlandish tall tales frontiersmen were so fond of spreading. "What else do you know about Enos Howard?"

"Let's see. There was an item in the newspaper about the time he tried to break Buffalo Bill Cody's record for killing the most buffalo in a certain span of time, but Howard fell short, as I recall. Then he was involved in a shooting match with Jesse Comstock. It had something to do with seeing which of them could shoot the most bull's-eyes. Howard lost, I believe, and nothing much was heard about him again until he showed up in Denver a year or so ago. He's been here ever since, generally making a nuisance of himself." To demonstrate, Leeds raised an imaginary glass or bottle to his mouth and mimicked drinking.

To Charley, it didn't sound promising. A drunk would be of no use on a manhunt.

"Now, is there anything else you would like to know?" Leeds asked. "The history of Denver, perhaps? Or maybe I should recite the Declaration of Independence?"

"You're pullin' my leg," Charley said. "But there is one more thing you can do for me. You can let me go early tonight. Say, about five thirty?"

Mr. Leeds did a marvelous imitation of someone who had swallowed a chicken egg, shell and all. "Is there no limit to your gall, young man? Give me one reason why I should agree."

Charley was about to lead the team to their stalls. "The credit is all yours."

"Honestly, there are moments when I can't decide if you are sincere or, as you just so quaintly phrased it, pulling *my* leg."

"Weren't you the one who told me I should set

my sights on something I desire more than anything else, then go after it, heart and soul?" Charley quoted. "Well, it so happens I've found something, and I'm takin' your advice."

"Indeed?" Mr. Leeds was flattered. "In that case, I'll gladly give you the evening off. But I expect you to make up the extra time on your day off. That is, if you want a full week's pay."

The hours crawled by. Charley was so preoccupied, he didn't hear four men enter the stable. He was in the tack room repairing a bridle when one coughed. He rose to go see what they wanted, but the bridle slipped off his lap to the ground, and in the time it took for him to bend and retrieve it, Mr. Leeds came out of his office to greet them.

"May I help you gentlemen? I'm the proprietor. Artemis Leeds, at your service. My livery has some of the finest horses, buggies, and carriages for rent anywhere in Denver. By the hour or the day, at affordable rates."

The quartet wore suits and bowlers. At first glance they looked like businessmen, but something about them reminded Charley of Loritz and Arch. Maybe it was how they carried themselves, like coiled springs. Or maybe it was their hard features. One wore a vest with mother-of-pearl buttons and a gold watch chain dangling from one of its pockets. He had blond hair and blue eyes and carried a polished cane with an ivory knob at the top. The others were slabs of muscle with thick necks and knuckles as big as walnuts.

"My associates and I are not here to rent anything, Mr. Leeds," said the fancy dresser with the gold watch chain. "We are searching for someone. The

word on the street is that you have a farm boy working for you. Pickett. Charles Pickett. We would very
much like a word with him, if you don't mind."

Charley's mouth went dry. He thought for sure
Mr. Leeds would point to where he was, but his employer responded, "Haven't you any manners, sir?
Or don't people introduce themselves where you
come from?"

The man with the cane raised it. For a moment
Charley thought he was going to strike Leeds, but
instead he rested the knob on his right shoulder and
smiled an oily smile. "I am Ubel Gunther. My friends
and I work for Walter Radtke. Perhaps you have
heard this name?"

"Who hasn't? He's very rich and very powerful."

Ubel's smile widened, but Mr. Leeds wasn't
finished.

"It's well known that your Mr. Radtke has his dirty
fingers in every illegal and illicit enterprise in Denver. Were I to make a list of the ten most detestable
men in the city, he would be at the top."

A lantern-jawed husky with shoulders as wide as
Charley's took a step toward Leeds but stopped
when Ubel motioned with the cane. "Watch that temper of yours, Hans. Remember our instructions."
Ubel pushed his bowler back on his head using the
knob of his cane, then said softly, "Where is the farm
boy, stableman?"

"How should I know? I sent him on an errand,
and he never came back. Young people today have
no sense of responsibility. Why, when I was his age,
I would have been grateful for a job like this."

"Spare me your life's story." Ubel regarded Leeds
a few moments. "I trust you wouldn't lie to us. We

wouldn't like that. Not one bit." Ubel glanced around the stable.

Instinctively, Charley crouched down, although it was unlikely Gunther would spot him there in the shadows.

"Since the farm boy isn't here, we won't take up any more of your time. But we'll be back." Ubel turned to go. "It is in your best interest to keep our visit to yourself."

Mr. Leeds did not move until they were out of sight, then he uttered the first swear words Charley had ever heard him say. Charley went out.

"I trust you heard everything? How on earth did you make an enemy of a man like Walter Radtke?"

"It wasn't easy," Charley said.

"This is serious. Radtke is not anyone to trifle with." Mr. Leeds looked at him, and Leeds was worried. "Take some more of my advice, and make yourself scarce. Otherwise, as surely as the sun rises every morning, your days are numbered."

Chapter Four

Nebraska Panhandle

The rider was tall, and any woman who saw him would say he was uncommonly striking. He rode well, but not as one born to the saddle. From a distance he could easily be mistaken for a cowboy since he wore cowboy garb, from the Stetson atop his neatly combed black hair to the spurs attached to his boots. But up close, an observer would notice everything was new and showed none of the wear and tear of a true cowhand's work clothes.

He had piercing green eyes, this rider, and he constantly scoured the countryside, searching. Several times that day he took a map from his saddlebags, spread it out across his saddle, and reassured himself he was where he wanted to be.

Confirmation came in the form of a well-worn trail that wound off across the prairie to the northeast. Churned by countless hooves, the ground had been worn bare. The rider followed it for over an hour, until he came on a crudely painted sign. Drawing rein, he read it twice, his eyes crinkling in amusement.

O. T. QUARREL RANCH

No trespassing. No drummers. No preachers.
No Injuns except Sioux. Rustlers will be hung
at our convenience. All others welcome.

"That's comforting to know," the rider said to the
claybank, and gigged it on along the trail.

At any moment the rider expected to see the ranch
house. But he had forgotten where he was. Distance
meant little to men accustomed to vast open spaces.
A Westerner thought nothing of traveling hundreds
of miles to visit the nearest town. A rancher could
ride for a week and still be on his own spread.

O. T. Quarrel had one of the largest spreads in
Nebraska. His brand was famous from Montana to
New Mexico for quality stock, whether cattle or
horses. The men who rode for him were notoriously
loyal to the brand, a fact the rider reminded himself
not to forget once he arrived.

The sun was balanced on the western rim of the
world when the rider finally spied the ranch house.
It was modest but sturdily built and surrounded by
a long bunkhouse, a stable, and sundry outbuildings.
As the rider drew near, the clear peal of a triangle
signaled the call to supper.

The rider slid his right hand under his slicker to a
Smith and Wesson snug in its shoulder holster. He
worked it up and down a few times. As he passed
the stable, the corral caught his interest. All fifteen
horses in it were pintos, or paints as they were
known.

Next to the mess was a hitch rail. Beside it was a
bench on which sat a battered washbasin, a used bar
of lye soap, and a towel in dire need of a washing
itself. Dismounting, the rider looped the reins around

the rail, removed his hat, and dipped his comb in the brown water. He was running it through his hair when spurs jangled; someone was approaching from the ranch house.

"Howdy, stranger. Nice duds you've got there."

The speaker looked as if he could tote an anvil under each arm and not feel the strain. His face was as rugged as the land and seamed by years of toil. Tufts of grey hair stuck from under his hat.

"I bought them in Cheyenne."

"Do tell. Then I take it you're not ridin' the grub-line, not if you've got money to spare." The ranch-man studied the rider. "We don't get many visitors to these parts. Are you bound somewhere special?"

Replacing his Stetson, the rider turned. "I thought it's against range etiquette to pry into another's affairs."

"I'm entitled. I own this spread. O. T. Quarrel is my handle, but most hereabouts call me Quarry." Quarrel thrust out a callused hand with fingers like railroad spikes. "You could say I have a vested interest in pryin' where others shouldn't."

"William Shores." The rider shook. "You can call me Bill."

Quarrel washed his hands in the dirty water and wiped them on the dirty towel. "Let's go in. I don't want to keep the boys waitin' any longer than I have to."

Seated at the long table were over twenty punchers ranging in age from barely old enough to shave to alkalied old-timers. They were waiting, some with forks and knives in hand, for the big augur to arrive. As soon as Quarrel stepped through the doorway, many cheerfully called out greetings.

Shores entered, and the good-natured yells died. He smiled, but no one repaid the courtesy.

"This way." Quarrel moved to the head of the table. A puncher in the chair to the right got up and moved down to an empty one. Quarrel tapped the vacated chair. "Why don't you have a seat, and we'll get acquainted after we eat?"

The meal was typical ranch fare: fried steak and gravy, sourdough biscuits, beans, vinegar pie, and dried peaches. Shores followed the example of the punchers and heaped his plate high. A long day in the saddle had him famished, and he wolfed down his portions as hungrily as everyone else.

O. T. Quarrel had two helpings of everything. At length he pushed back his chair, lit an old corncob pipe, and squinted at Shores through the smoke. "Now then, suppose you tell me what brought you to my spread?"

Fishing in a pocket for his identification, Shores handed it over.

"William E. Shores," Quarrel read loud enough for everyone at the table to hear. "United States Department of Justice."

A gangly cowpuncher spooning sugar into a cup of coffee looked up. "What in tarnation is that, Quarry?"

Shores answered for himself. "The Justice Department was created about a year ago to help the attorney general enforce federal laws. The department also provides legal counsel in federal cases."

The puncher's grin was several teeth shy of a full set. "Just what we need. More government."

His comment was greeted with general mirth and scorn. Shores let it subside before saying, "I'm a federal agent with authority to arrest anyone guilty of breaking federal law."

Another puncher made a show of gazing around the room. "Anyone here see a federal law runnin' loose? I wouldn't want to step on it and break it."

Shores failed to see the humor, but the cow crowd cackled.

Quarrel lowered his pipe and grinned. "Don't take them serious, Mr. Shores. They're good hands. They'd do to ride the river with, every last one. They're just havin' a little fun at your expense."

"I've been around cowboys before."

"You don't say? I noticed you sit a horse right smart. So even though your clothes brand you a dude, I reckoned there was more to you than met the eye."

"I was born in Texas," Shores revealed. "Brazos, to be exact. Spent a lot of my childhood on horseback. But when I was eleven, my parents dragged me off to Chicago. I became a Pinkerton. Four months ago, I was contacted about becoming a federal agent." Shores shrugged. "Here I am."

"A Pinkertonian, huh? They're not held in high regard in these parts. A pair showed up here a while back huntin' a bank robber. They put on airs like you wouldn't believe, but both combined weren't worth their weight in spit." Quarrel paused. "Who are *you* huntin', Mr. Justice Department Agent?"

"I'm after the Hoodoos," Shores announced.

Total silence ensued. No one looked at him except O. T. Quarrel. "What makes you reckon you'll find them here?"

"I never said I would," Shores responded, "but I hope to learn something equally as valuable. The information I need to track them to their hideout and put an end to their reign of bloodshed and terror."

A puncher across the table snickered. "Hellfire, mister. You make them sound like they're the worst hombres who ever rode the high lines."

"Not all that long ago they murdered several troopers from the Second Cavalry. One of the troopers made the mistake of recognizing Kid Falon and decided to go for the marshal. Unfortunately, Curly Means overheard them and told the Kid." Shores took a sheet of paper from a pocket and unfolded it. "Three weeks prior to that, the Hoodoos murdered an old Shoshone by the name of Mat-ta-vish. Four months earlier, they shot two Arapahos who tried to stop them from stealing horses from an Arapaho village. Before that, it's believed they stole a herd from the Pawnees. You name a tribe, odds are they've lost horses to the Hoodoos."

"Any Sioux on that list?" Quarrel asked.

Shores ran a finger down the sheet. "No. Flatheads, Nez Perce, even the Blackfeet once."

"Notice anything?" Quarrel asked. "Except for the troopers, who brought it on themselves, all those on your list are redskins."

"What are you saying?"

"You won't find any Injun lovers in this room, Mr. Shores. We've all had run-ins with hostiles at one time or another. We all know someone who has lost kin to a red arrow or tomahawk." Quarrel blew a puff of smoke into the air. "Did you happen to notice my sign on your way in? I shoot any Injuns I find on my spread, except Sioux."

"So you don't care that the Hoodoos go around stealing and killing as they see fit?" Shores couldn't hide his resentment.

"Not when they're stealin' from and killin' Injuns, no." Quarrel set his pipe down. "Brock Alvord is nobody's fool. He's been rustlin' for years and never been caught because he steals from the red man and sells to the white. He knows that if he stole stock from me or any other rancher, we'd hunt him to the ends of the earth and treat him to a hemp social. But no one out here gives a damn what he does to redskins."

"Indians should have the same rights whites do," Shores declared.

The room rocked with hoots and jeers. "Pilgrim, you're tryin' to sell your tonic to the wrong crowd!" a cowboy hollered. "We'd all as soon every last Injun was pushin' up tumbleweeds as breathin'." He glanced at his employer. "Except the Sioux, of course."

Folding the paper, Shores shoved it into his pocket. "I can see I won't get anywhere by appealing to your sense of civic duty."

"Our what?" The toothless puncher pulled his shirt out from his chest and peered down under it. "I'm not sure I have one of those."

Laughter shook the rafters.

William Shores faced O. T. Quarrel. "Very well. Let's get to it. In Cheyenne I ran into a cowhand who told me an interesting story. He claimed the Hoodoos paid you a visit a while back and sold you a fine herd of pintos for your remuda. Fifteen in all, rustled from Mat-ta-vish after they murdered him." Shores nodded at a window. "The same fifteen pintos right out there in your corral."

"That's not true," Quarrel said.

"You're a liar."

Chairs went flying as seven or eight cowhands

leaped to their feet. But the cowboys froze when the federal agent's Smith & Wesson blossomed in his hand, trained on the man they rode for.

Quarrel, as calm as could be, motioned at his would-be defenders. "Simmer down, boys. This gent doesn't have enough sense to bell a cat, but he's my guest, and we'll treat him accordingly." He smiled at Shores. "Put your nickel-plated hardware away, mister. All I'd have to do is snap my fingers, and you'd be perforated with more holes than a sieve."

It was no idle threat. Shores replaced the Smith & Wesson but kept his hand inches from it on the table. "How can you sit there and tell me you didn't accept stolen stock when I saw the pintos on my way in?"

"All I meant was that I didn't buy them for my remuda. I bought them for the Sioux."

Shores remembered the sign and the comments by Quarrel and the puncher. "You've lost me."

Quarrel picked up his corncob pipe and puffed a few times. "I was one of the first, Mr. Shores. There was nothin' here before me except prairie dogs. And the Oglala Sioux. This was their territory, and they drove off every white who tried to plant roots. But I wanted this land, wanted it from the moment I set eyes on it. So I hired an army scout to arrange a parley with the Oglala."

"That took nerve," Shores had to admit.

"When a man wants somethin' bad enough, he'll do anything to get it. I offered the Sioux their weight in trade blankets and trinkets. I offered them knives, rifles, ammunition. I offered all the money I had and more each year for the rest of my life. But they weren't interested. All they wanted were horses."

"Pintos?" Shores deduced.

"Injuns are mighty fond of bright colors. They love

blue beads and red blankets and paint horses. So they agreed to let me stay for fifteen paint horses." Quarrel chuckled at the recollection. "I don't mind admittin' I about pulled out my hair findin' that many. I sent riders as far south as Texas, as far north as Canada. But I found the fifteen."

"That was decades ago."

The rancher nodded. "Fifteen paints that first year and fifteen more every five winters for as long as I live on their land. In another month, or moon as the Sioux call them, another fifteen are due."

Shores digested this. "But you don't need to give them the horses. The Oglalas drifted north years ago. They're up on the reservation in the Black Hills. As far as the United States government is concerned, this land is yours, free and clear."

"I gave my word, Mr. Shores. It doesn't matter where the Oglalas are. I'm still here. I'm obligated to live up to my promise."

Shores glanced out the window and did not say anything else for a while. "Why hire the Hoodoos? Why not send punchers out to find the paints you needed?"

The lines in Quarrel's face deepened. "I never hired Alvord's bunch. He's been around awhile, Burt has. He knows how I got my start. He heard I'd need more paints soon. So he took it on himself to rustle some and showed up here to offer them to me for top dollar."

"You knew they were stolen, yet you bought them anyway? By rights I could arrest you as an accessory."

"You could try," a puncher declared.

Shores ignored him. "All I'm interested in are the

Hoodoos. Tell me where to find them, and I'll forget the rest."

Quarrel's pipe was going out, and he tapped it a few times. "You give me too much credit, government man. I've known Brock since the early days, true, but we've never been friendly. He's always been a hellion. Me, I like the straight and narrow. He's not about to confide his secrets."

"You can't tell me where the Hoodoos lie low? Or whether any of them have a wife or a family stashed away somewhere?

"Sorry."

Shores reached into his slicker and produced a different sheet of paper. "Do me a favor. Mat-ta-vish drew these in the dirt right before he died. His daughter thought they might be important, so she copied the drawings onto the back of an old buffalo hide." He slid the paper across. "I sketched them as best I could."

O. T. Quarrel gave them due consideration. "I'm not much on Injun symbols. If the Shoshones don't know what they mean, it's a cinch I wouldn't."

"Damn." William Shores sat back, defeated. "I came all this way for nothing."

Colorado-Nebraska border

Eli's was part tavern, part general store, and all sod from roof to floor. The proprietor, Eli Brandenberg, had been on his way to the Rocky Mountains to prospect for gold when one of his mules came up lame. Insult was added to misfortune when the wagon train he was with had decided to go on without him. The wagon master had found tracks of unshod ponies and concluded a hostile war party was in the area. The rest of the emigrants took a vote and decided they were unwilling to slow their pace to a crawl and heighten the risk of losing their scalps for Eli's sake.

After four days of being on his own, after being drenched by the most violent thunderstorm Eli had ever experienced and losing the canvas on his Conestoga to hail the size of walnuts, after running into a friendly band of Pawnees who offered to trade half an antelope for half a bottle of whiskey, and after a second mule broke a leg in a prairie dog hole, Eli decided enough was enough. He built his soddy, piled his belongings inside, and hung a sign over the door.

That had been a decade ago.

Eli prospered. He made annual treks to Denver for supplies, then charged five times what he paid when he resold the items to frontiersmen and Indians. He charged emigrants ten times as much.

Most days Eli had to himself. His old coon dog would doze by the counter while Eli indulged in his favorite hobby: picking lice off himself and crushing them between his fingertips. He loved how they squished.

This day, five riders arrived shortly after noon. Eli recognized them right away. They had visited him before and never caused trouble, so he had no qualms about serving them a couple of bottles of redeye along with their food. First, though, he took his coon dog and hid it in the storeroom behind the soddy.

Along about two in the afternoon, a couple of buffalo hunters rode up. There was no mistaking their profession. They wore buffalo coats and buffalo hats and had greased their hair with buffalo fat. Whenever Eli stood too close, he caught a whiff of an odor that reminded him of the south end of a northbound buffalo. They paid for a bottle and sat at the other table.

Eli didn't pay much attention to which of the five long ropes asked the hunters if they wanted to sit in on a friendly game of cards. He thought maybe it was Curly Means, who was the friendliest cuss around when he was sober and there weren't any dogs in the vicinity.

Engrossed in his lice-picking, Eli wasn't paying a lot of attention to the gum-flapping. The buffalo hunters were on their way east after an extended stay at a boarding house in Denver where the ladies "were as plump as ripe plums and as sociable as schoolmarms," as one boasted.

Only Brock Alvord, Kid Falon, and Curly Means joined in the game. Big Ben Brody leaned his chair against the wall and was soon snoring loud enough to be mistaken for an earthquake. John Noonan was sharpening a bone-handled knife he had acquired somewhere.

All seemed well until Eli heard Kid Falon say, "If you two stunk any worse, I'd swear I had my head up a buffalo's ass."

"This from a runt who took his last bath in horse piss," a buffalo hunter rejoined, and both hunters laughed.

The Hoodoos weren't nearly as amused. Particularly Kid Falon, who, as Eli recollected, prided himself on taking a bath once a month whether he needed it or not.

"I'd take that back, you bucket of fat, or learn to breathe dirt."

The hunter so addressed pulled his heavy coat aside to display a Remington revolver. "I'd be a heap more polite, midget, when addressin' your betters."

Eli tried to head off trouble. He scurried around the counter and loudly exclaimed, "Gentlemen! Gentlemen! There's no call for insults. We're all here to have a good time, right?"

Kid Falon looked at him with eyes as cold as winter snow. "My notion of a good time is blowin' out the lamps of jackasses who prod me. Are you volunteerin'?"

"No, never," Eli hastily assured him.

"Then go on back to squishin' your seam squirrels and leave us men to conduct our business." Kid Falon pushed his chair back. "Now then, gents. What was that about you bein' better than me?"

"Don't push us, boy," the second hunter warned. "We're not greeners. We've tangled with Comanches and come out on top. We've outfought the Sioux and put the fear of dyin' into a Blackfoot war party. And we've beat the tar out of more blowhards like you than there are blades of grass outside that door."

"Is that a fact?"

Brock Alvord and Curly Means rose and stepped away from the table, Brock saying, "Don't expect us to take the big jump over this, Kid. That leaky mouth of yours will earn you windows in your skull one day."

The hunter with the Remington developed an interest in Falon. "Why did he call you 'Kid'?"

"Most folks do."

Curly Means was grinning from ear to ear. "His Christian name is Alphonse Rudolph Falon. Which shows that his ma and pa had a better sense of humor than most, or they were drunker than an Irishman on St. Patty's day when they named him."

The second buffalo hunter put two and two together. "You're Kid Falon?" His complexion grew several shades lighter.

"I didn't know who you were when I called you a runt," said the first.

Never for a second taking his icy eyes off the hunters, the Kid slowly stood and pushed his chair back with the sole of his boot. "Whenever you're ready to dance, start the fiddlin'."

"Hold on!" The hunter with the Remington was ready to eat crow. "We're not loco. We ain't about to tangle with the likes of you. If it's all the same, we'll back on out and leave you be. What do you say? No hard feelin's?"

"I hate cowards," Kid Falon said.

"Please, Kid."

"Those were your last words, bucket of fat."

Eli was watching for it. Like everyone else, he had heard tales about the Kid's speed. About how the Kid was chained lightning and then some. And here he was, about to witness it for himself. But just as the Kid's hands moved, Eli blinked. The next he knew, his soddy thundered to two shots, and the buffalo hunters were flung to the dirt floor, chairs and all, bullet holes smack between their eyes.

Kid Falon never gave them another glance. He sat back down and began replacing the spent cartridges. "Drinks for everyone, Eli. The bucket of fat has a poke on him, so he's buyin'."

"Right away." Eli scampered to obey, delighted at the thought of the story he could share with all those who stopped by his place from then on. His only regret was that the buffalo hunters hadn't been emigrants.

Chapter Five

Denver
Colorado Territory

"Maybe this is the wrong place, Melissa. Or maybe he's left town." After an hour of waiting for Enos Howard to appear, Charley Pickett had to be sure. He went to the bar and asked the bartender if he knew anyone by that name.

"Do I ever," the man replied while pouring a drink for another customer. "That ornery coot practically lives here. If everyone sucked down rotgut like he does, the whole country would be bone dry inside of a week."

"We were told he's usually here by six o'clock, but it's past seven." Charley was afraid Tony would walk out if Howard didn't show up soon.

The bartender wiped drops from the counter. "Every now and then he's late. Usually because he's sleeping off a binge the like of which would kill you or me."

"You make it sound like all he does is guzzle the stuff."

"That about sums Enos up. I never met anyone so

anxious to drink themselves into the grave, and I see more than my share of drunkards."

Charley glanced at the corner table where Melissa and Tony were waiting. Tony was staring at the wall clock, which wasn't a good sign. "You wouldn't happen to know where Howard lives, would you?"

"As a matter of fact, I do. I felt sorry for the old bastard one night and lugged him home when he was so booze blind he couldn't take two steps without fallin' on his face." The bartender mentioned the address.

"Well?" Tony impatiently demanded as Charley came hurrying back. "Did I miss my ride with the freight wagons for nothing? Was she wrong?" The glance he cast at Melissa wasn't flattering.

Melissa hadn't spoken two words to Tony the whole hour, but now she made up for lost time. "Don't look at me like that. This is where he comes, I tell you. Kincaid's. I remember it real well because he went on and on about how it carries his favorite brand of whiskey. He told me to my face he never drinks anywhere else." She stabbed a finger at Tony. "For this to work out, we have to try to get along. I'm willing to bury the hatchet for the time being if you are."

"Sounds good to me," Charley piped up. He would love for the two of them to stop bickering. In light of Melissa's comments earlier at the tavern, he had been wondering about the cause of their spat, and he did not like where his thoughts were leading him.

"Maybe you are willing to bury the hatchet," Tony told Melissa, "but a gentleman by the name of Walter Radtke will not. Every moment I stay, my life is in danger."

Charley suddenly realized he had yet to tell his friend about Ubel Gunther's visit to the stable. He deemed it best to do so later, when they were alone. If Melissa found out Tony had killed those two men in the alley, she might rethink her decision to join the hunt for the Hoodoos. And Charley dearly wanted her along.

"What exactly is that all about anyway?" Melissa asked.

Charley knew Tony wouldn't answer, which was bound to make her mad, so he declared, "Enough of this sittin' around. I found out where Enos Howard lives. What say we go there and see if he'll listen to our proposition?"

Tony was on his feet and heading for the door before Charley stopped speaking. He held it open for them, and once outside, he pulled his cap low and turned up his collar.

The address was on the western outskirts of the city. They had to ask a Mexican leading a donkey if they had the right street since there were no street signs and the streets weren't so much streets as dirt tracks. The Mexican asked who they were looking for, and when they told him, he laughed and pointed.

Melissa said, "That can't be it."

But it was. In the center of an otherwise empty lot stood the sorriest excuse for a shack Charley had ever set eyes on. Whoever built it hadn't been too particular about how. Some of the planks overlapped, while others had gaps between them. The roof was only half done, and a faded strip of canvas with holes in it had been draped over the rest. A door, half shut, hung on a rusty hinge.

"Someone lives in that hovel?" Tony was skeptical.

Charley walked to the door. As he raised his fist,

a terrible odor nearly made him gag. It was like the stink of rancid sweat, only ten times worse. He knocked and called out, "Mr. Enos Howard? We'd like a word with you, if you please."

There was no answer. Charley knocked again, louder, and when that still failed to elicit a reply, he pushed on the door. It scraped across an uneven floor until the bottom snagged on a warped plank half an inch higher than the rest. "Mr. Howard?" The smell was worse, compounded by the reek of alcohol. Covering his mouth and nose, Charley stepped inside. "Are you home?"

A hideous rumbling caused Charley to spin to the right. It took a few seconds for his eyes to adjust to the murk and to distinguish a bulky form sprawled on a cot. The noise was repeated, a snore so loud it seemed to shake the walls. Charley inched closer. His foot bumped something that skittered across the floor, and, glancing down, he discovered the floor was littered with empty liquor bottles. And with smears and stains better left unexamined.

"Mr. Howard? Sorry to bother you, but we need to talk." Charley poked what he hoped was a shoulder. Howard mumbled something, then snored louder.

Tony filled the doorway. He, too, had a hand over his nose and mouth. "Forget it, *mio amico*. This is a waste of our time."

"Is Mr. Howard in there?" Melissa wanted to know. She was trying to peer over Tony's shoulder. "Should I come in?"

"No!" Charley didn't want her amid such filth. Angry they had put their hopes in a hopeless drunk, he poked Howard's shoulder again, a lot harder. "Mr. Howard! Wake up, damn you!"

Without warning, there was an explosion of movement. Charley abruptly found his neck in the grip of iron fingers and the razor edge of a Bowie pressed against his throat. Foul breath fanned his nose. A craggy face filled his vision, half of it hidden by an unkempt beard. Howard wore an old buffalo coat so worn and filthy no self-respecting moth would touch it.

"Who the hell are you, pup? And what in hell are you doin' in my livin' room?"

Charley figured the buffalo hunter had to be drunk. The shack only had one room, livable or otherwise. But he dared not try to answer with the knife pricking his skin. He was saved by a holler from outside.

"Mr. Howard? It's me. Melissa Patterson. The girl who sells you sweet potatoes all the time."

"Missy?" Howard lowered the Bowie and gave Charley a rough push. Like a great grizzly rousing from its den, he lumbered to the doorway. Tony stepped back, his right arm held at an odd angle from his body. Howard ignored him. "Missy! What in blazes are you doin' here?"

Charley stepped outside just as the buffalo hunter embraced Melissa in a great hug. She giggled and returned it, apparently not minding his stink or how he rubbed his bushy beard against her cheek. An intense emotion welled up in Charley, an emotion he had never felt before, one that made him want to take a plank and beat Enos Howard over the head.

"Speak up, gal. Why the visit? And who are these two cubs you've brought along?"

"Acquaintances of mine," Melissa said. "I've told them what a marvelous frontiersman you are, and how you're just the man we need for a certain daring enterprise from which we all stand to benefit."

"You don't say?" Enos Howard opened his coat

and slid the Bowie into a beaded sheath. His clothes were threadbare buckskins with most of the whangs missing or cut partway off. Knee-high boots completed his wardrobe. One had a hole in it, and the other was cracked at the heel. He fixed bloodshot eyes on Charley and Tony. "You two don't look as if you amount to much, but sometimes mighty puny spools hold a heap of thread."

"Wonderful," Tony said. "Simply wonderful."

Howard's brows knit. "What's that supposed to mean, hoss? Are you one of those city loons who go around talkin' to himself all the time?" Reaching under his coat, he scratched an armpit. "If'n we've got us some palaverin' to do, I need my throat muscles lubricated. Which of you wetnoses has a bottle?"

"I don't drink," Charley informed him.

"Never?" Howard cocked his head and squinted at Charley as if Charley were a six-legged jackrabbit. "Don't tell me you're a Bible-thumper? I knew a coon once who got religion and gave up all the earthly vices that make this world worth livin' in. Liquor. Women. Gamblin'. You name it. Walked around all day like he had a ramrod shoved up his ass."

"I don't think that's any way to talk with a lady present." Charley didn't like this buffalo hunter much.

"What? 'Cause I said 'ass'?" Howard winked at Melissa. "How about you, little Missy? Does it frazzle you to hear a feller mention the one part of your body you use more than your feet?"

"I find it cute how you talk."

"Cute?" Howard roared with laughter and clapped her on the back so hard she nearly pitched onto her face. "You sure can tickle my silly bone, gal. You're almost as hilarious as those temperance ladies."

"Thank you. I think."

Howard smacked his lips and gazed longingly off toward the center of the city. "I must have overslept. What say we go to Kincaid's for my nightly libations? Your treat. You can explain what this is all about along the way." He held out his arm like a gallant gentleman, and, giggling, Melissa took it.

The new emotion bubbling in Charley bubbled more fiercely. He hastened to Melissa's side. "Is it true you used to be one of the best buffalo hunters on the plains?'

"On the continent," Howard amended, yawning. "Buffalo Bill himself told me I was as good as him any day of the week and twice as good on Sundays."

"But you never broke his record," Charley commented, pleased to take the frontiersman down a peg.

Howard's face clouded. "Heard about that, did you, pup? Cody claims to have kilt over four thousand bufflers in a year and a half. Four thousand two hundred and eighty, to be exact. If'n you ask me, he's exaggerated the tally more than a handful. He always did sling bullshit better than anyone who ever lived. To listen to him, he pisses champagne and craps gold ore."

Now it was Charley who clouded over. "I won't ask you again to watch your tongue around Miss Patterson."

"I don't hear her complainin'," Enos said and nudged Melissa. "Better watch yourself, Missy. This pup has taken a shine to you, or I'm the Queen of England."

Charley's anger mounted. "Quit callin' me a pup."

"Or what? You'll huff and puff and get me all afeared of you? Mercy me, whatever will I do?"

To Charley's dismay, when Howard cackled, Melissa laughed, too. "Since we might be workin' together, we shouldn't bandy insults."

"Work? Hell, son, if that's why you came lookin' for me, you're a loon. I haven't done a lick of work in nigh on a year or better, and I don't aim to do any for as long as I can avoid it."

Melissa was as puzzled as Charley. "Then how do you make ends meet? How can you afford to buy potatoes and whiskey?"

"Anyone else, I'd tell them to go bite a porcupine, but since it's you, Missy, I'll let you in on my secret." Howard lowered his voice. "Antlers, dearie. Deer antlers, elk antlers, antelope antlers, you name it. There's this Chinese feller who's willin' to buy every one I find."

Charley had been through Denver's Chinese section a few times. It always fascinated him. A number of the buildings were exactly like the buildings in China, and everywhere he looked there were Orientals. Many worked on the railroad. Most had come to Denver by way of San Francisco.

"Wong is some kind of medicine man," Howard was saying. "He grinds up the antlers, mixes 'em with herbs and whatnot, and sells the stuff to his own kind for whatever ails them."

"You must shoot a lot of animals to get so many antlers," Melissa mentioned, and she did not sound happy about it.

"Hell no, Missy. Dear and elk and the like shed them once a year. I've got me an old Injun who spends all his time lookin' for antlers up in the foothills. I give him a bottle for every sackful he brings me. Then I take the sack to Wong."

"How much do you earn?" Tony inquired.

"Enough to keep me in redeye for weeks at a stretch." Howard licked his lips, then stroked his beard. His fingers trembled slightly. Swearing under his breath, he shoved his hand in a coat pocket.

Charley recognized the symptoms. Back in Kentucky, he had a neighbor who was uncommonly fond of liquor and, when in need of more, always came down with a powerful bad case of the shakes. "How would you like to make enough money to keep you in redeye for the next ten years?"

"Did somebody sell you a map to one of those lost Spanish mines?" Howard chortled.

Melissa cleared her throat. "We're thinking of collecting the bounty on some wanted men and splitting it four ways. Equal shares for everyone, including you—provided you'll throw in with us, of course."

"Manhunters? *You?*" Howard erupted in a fit of glee. When he stopped, he glanced at Charley and Tony and began laughing anew so hard it brought tears to his eyes. "Lordy! I haven't enjoyed a belly-buster like that in a coon's age. Talk about flashes in the pan! What makes you lunkheads think you've got what it takes to be bounty chasers?"

Since Tony saw fit not to defend their honor, Charley took it upon himself. "We'd only need to collect bounty once. The men we plan to track down have a high-enough price on their heads that we can split it and still have plenty."

"Who are these badmen, pray tell?"

"Maybe you've heard of them. They're called the Hoodoos."

Enos Howard acted like he had walked into a stone wall. He nearly tripped over his own feet, he stopped so suddenly. Utterly dumfounded, he gawked at Melissa, then Tony, then back at Charley. His mouth moved, but no words came out until, "The *Hoodoos*? Brock Alvord's wild bunch?"

"The bounty on their heads is up to seven thousand dollars. I don't know about you, but that's more money than I've seen my whole life long." Charley thought to add as incentive, "We'd each get one thousand seven hundred and fifty dollars."

"You'd each get kilt, is what you'd get. Boy, that's about the dumbest notion I've heard since who flung the chunk! What idiot came up with it?" Howard looked at Melissa, then at Tony, neither of whom met his gaze. Slapping his thigh, he exclaimed, "Don't this beat all! It's true what they say. You never can tell which direction a pickle is goin' to squirt."

Charley was trying to fathom how pickles were mixed up in it when the buffalo hunter nudged him.

"It was you, wasn't it, hoss? You're the grubber who thought this silliness up. The Hoodoos! You might as well go up against a pack of rabid wolves. The result would be the same."

"They're men, aren't they? They put their britches on one leg at a time like the rest of us, don't they?" Charley was mad again. "I didn't expect this kind of talk from a buffalo hunter with your reputation. Why, you must have fought all kinds of men and beasts when you were in your prime."

"First off, we call ourselves buffler *runners*, not hunters. Second, who in hell says I'm not *in* my prime?" Howard drew himself up to his full height. "I'll have you know I can whip my weight in wildcats and beat a griz in a rasslin' match. I am a two-legged twister, half-wolverine, half-snapper, and all grist and gristle. You won't find another like me anywhere west of the muddy Mississippi."

Tony rolled his eyes skyward. "And you say Buffalo Bill Cody likes to exaggerate?"

"Don't rile me, pup," Howard warned. "I'm hell with the bark on when I'm riled. Why, once I kilt seven Blackfeet with nothin' but my Bowie and my bare teeth. They caught me in a box canyon, and I was plumb out of bullets so I lit into 'em man-to-man. I took two arrows in the shoulder and another in the leg, but when I was done, that canyon was runnin' red with Blackfoot blood."

Charley saw his opening. "Then huntin' the Hoodoos should be a piece of cake for a man like you."

"Those Blackfeet didn't have guns," Howard shot back. "And I was in a spot where they couldn't get at me all at once." Clasping Melissa's arm, he resumed walking. "I've got to tell you, Missy, these acquaintances of yours have marbles between their ears."

"It's impossible then?" Melissa asked him

"Nothin' is ever impossible, potato gal. One day Alvord's luck will run out. A war party will catch the Hoodoos with their pants down. Or a sheriff will get up a posse that don't know how to quit. Or an army patrol will be in the right place at the right time."

Melissa nodded. "So it's only impossible for us, is that what you're saying, Mr. Howard?"

"It's Enos. And don't be puttin' words in my mouth. I could track the Hoodoos clear to Canada if'n I was of a mind. Then all I'd have to do is keep my distance and pick 'em off one by one with my Sharps. At the Battle of the Chalk Cliffs, I dropped a Blackfoot chief at a range of a mile and a half, and I can do the same with the Hoodoos."

"I heard it was three-quarters of a mile," Charley said.

"Who was there, whelp? You or me?" Howard bared his yellow teeth like a dog about to bite. "Why, those Blackfeet were so far off, they weren't no bigger than ants."

Melissa plucked at his coat to get his attention. "I'm confused, Enos. First you say it can't be done. Then you say exactly how it *can* be done. Which is it? Because if it can, I'd like you to consider our proposal. The money means more to me than you can imagine."

Howard glanced down at his hands. They were shaking worse than before. Perhaps to disguise the fact, he tugged on his beard. "I truly would like to help you out, Missy. I'll cogitate on it some over a drink. But I ain't makin' no promises."

Charley wondered if Howard really would consider it, or whether he was only interested in the liquor. Little else was said until they reached Kincaid's. They took a corner table.

Rubbing his hands in anticipation, Howard bawled, "Tom! A bottle of your best for me and my pards! And glasses for these younguns!"

"You're not that old yourself," Charley remarked. Forty, maybe forty-five, would be his guess. Howard looked older though, thanks to the battering his skin had taken from the sun and the wind.

"Old enough to know not to grab a sidewinder by the tail or a bull by the horns," was Howard's rebuttal. "I was your age once. And just like you, I couldn't find my common sense without a magnifyin' glass."

Tony wasn't trying to hide his growing irritation. "You're full of wisdom, aren't you, buffalo runner?"

"I have enough not to poke my head where it can get chopped off. Or to sass someone who can carve me up into tiny pieces."

"I would like to see you try," Tony said flatly.

To forestall violence, Charley changed the subject. "Why did you give up huntin' buffalo, Enos, when you were so good at it?"

"That's Mr. Howard to you, pup. And why I do what I do is none of your damn business."

"Would you tell me?" Melissa asked, placing a hand on his.

The frontiersman turned red, jerked his hand loose, and hunched in his chair. His arms were shaking. The bartender had barely set the bottle down when Howard snatched it up and glued his mouth to it. He chugged greedily, gulping a third of the whiskey in the bat of an eye. The color and the tension slowly drained from his features, and he sat back, smiling contentedly. "The Almighty's elixir of life," he said softly, tapping the bottle.

Tony shook his head in disgust and turned away.

It wasn't hard for Charley to guess what his friend was thinking: that Enos Howard was as worthless as teats on a bull; that Howard would be of no help whatsoever even if he agreed to help; that, in short, Tony had prolonged his stay in Denver for nothing.

Out of the blue, Melissa bluntly asked, "Enos, does why you drink have anything to do with why you gave up hunting buffalo?"

Howard was about to guzzle more. He glared at her over the bottle, his lips wrapped around the mouth.

"You can hit me if you want," Melissa said. "But I'm your friend, and I'd like to help you if I can."

The frontiersman was a long time answering. He lowered the whiskey without taking a sip and sat with his beard bowed to his chest and his eyes half closed. "I hate you, gal," he said at last. "You're trickier than these two put together, but a hell of a lot more honest."

"If you'd rather not talk about it, I'll understand."

Charley was anxious to hear what Howard had to say. Just then the front door opened; he glanced toward it and was seared by a bolt of lightning. It was none other than Ubel Gunther and two of the three men who had been with Gunther at the stable. Charley was sure they must know he and Tony were there, but they walked to the bar without once looking at their table. Careful to keep his back to them, he whispered to his friend, "Those are some of Radtke's men!"

Tony had been glumly contemplating the floor. Now he took a swift look and shifted in his chair so his back was to them, too.

"What's goin' on?" Enos Howard asked much more loudly than he should.

"Quiet!" Charley whispered. "If those gents spot Tony, they'll kill him."

The buffalo hunter's eyes lit like candles. "You don't say?" He grinned at Tony. "What did you do, boy? Accidentally spit on their fancy shoes?" He swigged whiskey, exhaled loudly, and rose. "So you think I'm worthless? Think I couldn't lick a ladybug if she had one wing tied behind her back?" Melissa began to say something, but Howard held a hand up. "Don't deny it, Missy. I can see it in their eyes. And here's where I prove them wrong."

Charley watched, thunderstruck, as Howard walked

to within half a dozen feet of Ubel Gunther and let out with a war whoop like those Charley had always imagined Indians made.

"Look out, world! I'm a he-bear from the high country, and I am on the prod! Who wants to put me to the test?"

Ubel Gunther turned partway around, his elbow on the bar. "You've had too much to drink. Sit back down before someone takes that bottle away from you and hits you over the head with it."

Enos Howard deliberately took a long swallow and smirked. "I'd sure like to see someone try. How about you, pretty boy?"

Chapter Six

The last thing Charley Pickett wanted was for the buffalo hunter to draw attention. Ubel Gunther hadn't noticed Tony or him yet, and Charley wanted to keep it that way. Gunther must have descriptions of them both.

It might be sheer coincidence Gunther was here. Right before Howard stood up, Charley had seen the bartender slip a poke across the counter to Gunther, who'd slid it under his jacket.

The two men with Ubel were ready to tear into Enos. They moved toward him but stopped when Gunther barked a command in a language Charley thought was German. The owner of the general store in the town near his parents' farm had been German, and a nicer man Charley had never met.

Now that Charley thought about it, he realized Walter Radtke must be of German extraction too. Maybe everyone who worked for Radtke was.

"My name is Ubel Gunther, not pretty boy." Gunther addressed Enos. "Go spout your drivel elsewhere. Or better yet, go take a bath. You stink worse than swine."

Enos was upending the bottle and sloshed some of

the whiskey over his chin when he suddenly jerked it down. "Now, that there was an insult if ever I heard one. And in this country, when a man airs his tonsils the wrong way, he answers for it. So set the tumbleweed to rollin'."

The gauntlet had been thrown. The men with Ubel were eagerly awaiting the word to pounce. But all Gunther did was stand there.

"Are you implying I am a foreigner, you drunken lout? I'll have you know my grandparents came to America seventy years ago. I was born here. I am an American citizen, the same as you."

"Too bad the midwife didn't drop you on your noggin." Enos wagged the bottle at him. "Do you have any grit, pretty boy? Or are you fixin' to talk me to death?"

Ubel said one word, just one, and his associates, as he had called them at the stable, were on Enos before Enos could blink. One swung a right cross that, had it landed, would have dropped Howard like a rock. But much to Charley's amazement, the buffalo hunter ducked, raised his right foot, and stomped on his attacker's instep. The man yelped and hopped backwards, swearing in German.

The other tough assumed a boxer's stance and waded into the buffalo hunter with his fists flying.

Enos Howard was a marvel. He dodged. He weaved. He sidestepped. Charley had a hard time keeping up with who was doing what, they moved so fast. But he had the impression not one of the tough's blows landed. Suddenly Howard spun, grabbed a chair, and flung it at the German's legs. The man went down in a tumble.

"If you want something done right," Ubel Gunther said. Hefting his cane, he stalked forward.

Howard's Bowie leaped from its sheath. "I'm goin' to carve that walkin' stick of yours into kindlin' and then do the same to you."

The metallic click of gun hammers being thumbed back brought the fight to an end. The bartender had taken a shotgun from under the counter and was aiming it squarely at Howard. "That'll be enough. Enos, I've warned you before about actin' up in my place. Put that pigsticker away, or I'll splatter your innards all over this room."

"Tom!" Enos sounded stricken. "I thought we were friends."

"We are, you dunce, or you'd see I'm doin' you a favor. These men work for Walter Ratdke, who doesn't take kindly to having his men rousted. Remember that fella found hacked into fifty pieces last winter?"

Howard's disappointment was no sham. "I ain't scared of Radtke, and I ain't scared of pretty boy or his cane. Bring 'em all on, and I'll buck 'em out in gore."

"You heard me," Tom said.

It was back down or be shot. Enos backed down. Instead of returning to their table, though, he moved to another on the other side of the saloon. "There. Happy now?"

"Delirious." Tom lowered the shotgun but didn't put it away. To Gunther he said, "This was none of my doin'. Be sure to tell Mr. Radtke that."

"You are not responsible for the antics of every cretin who enters your establishment." Gunther bowed toward Enos Howard. "Another time, perhaps, *schwein*?"

"I can't wait, pretty boy."

With a twirl of his cane, Gunther departed. The

two toughs limped at his heels, their hatred of Howard transparent.

All smiles, Enos came back across the room. "Still think I'm not worth my weight in spit?" he demanded. "I swatted that pair like they were bedbugs." He swilled some whiskey, then patted the bottle. "I trust I've proven myself."

Tony had faced his chair around now that Gunther was gone. "All you've proven is you have mush for brains. Baiting them served no purpose."

"Didn't it?" Howard sneered. "I kept their attention on me, didn't I, so they wouldn't spot you and the farm boy here? I did you a good turn, but you're not man enough to admit it."

"You didn't do it just for us," Tony responded.

"True. There's nothin' more fun than a good brawl. Last one I was in, up Wyoming way, we broke every piece of furniture in the saloon. Cost every coin I had to my name, but it was worth it."

"I thought you were wonderful, Enos," Melissa gushed. "But I'm still waiting to hear why you gave up buffalo hunting."

Howard's exuberant mood evaporated like dew under a hot sun. "Maybe another time, Missy. Right now we've got somethin' more important to jaw about."

"We do?" Charley said.

"As sure as I live and breathe." Howard polished off another finger of coffin varnish and belched. "When are we headin' out after the Hoodoos?"

Nebraska Panhandle

Agent William Shores of the newly created United States Department of Justice had made camp out on the plain. O. T. Quarrel had offered him the use of a bunk, but Shores had declined. His superiors were counting on him to wrap things up in short order, and he had no intention of letting them down. He prided himself on his ability to perform his job effectively and expeditiously, and he would treat this case as he had every other throughout his career.

Shores rode until close to midnight, then made a cold camp. He considered making a fire but opted not to. He was in flat, open country, and a fire would be seen from a long way off. Supposedly, there weren't any Sioux in the area, but why tempt fate?

His saddle for a pillow, Shores wrapped himself in a blanket and lay on his side. His rifle was close at hand. He heard a coyote yip. Not far distant, another answered. Much closer, something snorted, and there was the thud of receding hooves. It was the same every night. Constant animal sounds, often sounds Shores couldn't identify. Grunts and snarls and roars that made sleep next to impossible.

William Shores was not fond of the West. He would rather be sleeping in his four-poster bed under his own roof than on the ground in the middle of the godforsaken prairie. He wasn't a country boy. Far from it. His childhood in Texas had been spent mostly in town, and his later years in Chicago had ingrained into him the belief that city life was the only life.

It was a question of what a person was comfortable with. Shores liked the convenience of walking into a restaurant and ordering a meal rather than having to hunt it, shoot it, butcher it, and cook it. He would rather deal with heavy traffic than a war party. And given his druthers, he would rather have to contend with a stray dog rummaging in his garbage than a stray grizzly interested in devouring him.

Shores rolled onto his back and stared at the stars. He had only himself to blame for his current assignment. When the assistant director had called him in and asked if he had much experience with horses, he'd bragged that as a kid he had ridden nearly every day and was as at home in the saddle as he was in a trolley. Now here he was, chasing his own tail all over the wilds, trying to find five of the worst killers alive.

On that cheerful note, Shores dozed off. He slept fitfully, awakening at the slightest noises, until about four in the morning, when he gave in to fatigue and slept the sleep of the dead. A feeling of warmth on his face roused him. The sun was half an hour high. He had wanted to head out before dawn.

"Damn," Shores said and sat up. The first thing he saw was his hobbled claybank, munching grass. The second thing he saw was an Indian.

Shores came up out of his blanket as if fired from a catapult. His hand automatically rose to his Smith & Wesson, but he didn't draw.

The Indian made no threatening moves. Hunkered on his haunches, his thin arms folded across his knees, he grinned and said, "How do, Brother John." He was naked except for a breechclout and moccasins and had long grey hair that hung down to his waist. His oval face was ridged with lines, the stamp of seventy- or eighty-plus years. A quiver hung across his back. At his feet lay an unslung bow and a tomahawk. "How do, Brother John," he said again as Shores stood gaping.

"Who are you, Indian? What in heaven's name are you up to?"

The old Indian went on grinning. "In Red Fox tongue him be *Ainga-bite-waahni-a*. In white tongue him be Red Fox." His English was heavily accented. "I come far find you, Brother John."

Shores scanned the prairie. He saw no other Indians. A paint horse was thirty yards out, grazing. "Why were you looking for me? And why do you keep calling me Brother John? My name is Bill. Bill Shores."

"As you say, Brother John." Red Fox slowly unfurled, the bow in his left hand, the tomahawk in his right. He stuck the handle of the tomahawk under the top of his breechclout. "Red Fox hunt you. Know you hunt badmen, Brother John."

"Didn't you hear me? My name is Bill. Not John." Shores had a hunch the old Indian wasn't in full control of his faculties. "What badmen are you talking about?"

"Hoodoos, Brother John."

"Will you quit calling me that?" Shores couldn't get over how the old Indian had snuck up on him as slick as could be. Had it been a Sioux, his throat would be slit and his scalp would be hanging from a coup stick. Which reminded him. "What tribe are you from? And what's your interest in the Hoodoos?"

Red Fox touched his scrawny chest. "Red Fox be Sho-sho-ne. Uncle to White Dove. Brother to Matta-vish."

Shores understood now. "You're after the men who killed him."

"White Dove say Great Father send Brother John. Say you hunt *gizhaa* men. I help. We hunt. We kill."

"How old are you?"

Red Fox looked at Shores as if to say "why do you ask?" But he answered, "Red Fox be seventy-eight winters. I born winter ice break on river, four children drown."

Shores recalled hearing somewhere that Indian tribes measured years in "winters," with each winter known for a notable event. "I don't know how to tell you this without hurting your feelings, so I'll come right out with it. You've come all this way for nothing. Go back to the reservation. I don't need your help, Red Fox. You'll only get yourself killed, and the Great Father would be mad at me for letting you come along." He smiled to show he had only the old Indian's best interests at heart and bent to pick up his saddle blanket.

Red Fox didn't move.

Shores threw the blanket on the claybank. He was conscious of the Indian's eyes boring into his back as he saddled up, tied on his saddlebags, and stepped into the stirrups. "Give my regards to White Dove." He applied his spurs, traveling west.

Presently hooves drummed, and the paint came up alongside. "Brother John go wrong way."

Sighing, Shores reined up. "Pay attention. I'm not in the habit of repeating myself. *You cannot come with me.* Return to the reservation where you belong. I'll deal with the Hoodoos in my own time and my own way."

"Hoodoos that way." Red Fox pointed southwest.

"And how would you know that?" Shores was trying hard not to lose his temper. He never had liked Indians all that much. Comanches had tortured and killed his grandparents when he was seven, and he would take the horrid images of their butchered bodies to his grave.

Red Fox spoke each word slowly, trying to be as precise as he could. "*Gizhaa daiboo-a* steal many horses from Mat-ta-vish. Take horses wooden lodge of White-Who-Likes-Lakotas. Then *gizhaa daiboo-a* go that way." Again Red Fox pointed southwest.

The full import of what the old Indian was saying hit Shores with the jolt of a sledgehammer. "Wait a minute. Are you saying you can track the Hoodoos from the point where they left the ranch?"

Red Fox grunted. "Come get Brother John first. Make Great Father happy."

Gazing heavenward, Shores silently mouthed "Thank you." To the Shoshone he said, "I'm willing to let you join me on two conditions. One, you must do as I say at all times. Two, you will not take revenge on any of the Hoodoos without my permission. Do we have a deal?"

"Brother John not want Red Fox kill *gizhaa daiboo-a*?"

"Not unless I expressly say you can," Shores stressed. "What do those Shoshone words mean? You've used them several times now."

"*Gizhaa daiboo-a* mean not-good-white men." Red Fox lapsed into deep thought for all of a minute. "We have deal, Brother John. But Red Fox say this. If *gizhaa daiboo-a* try kill us, Red Fox kill *gizhaa daiboo-a*."

"Sounds fair to me," Shores said. Especially since he would scrupulously avoid placing the old Shoshone in a life-or-death situation. "Let's shake on it." He thrust out his hand.

Red Fox stared at the proffered hand, then at Shores. "Brother John speak with straight tongue?"

"I am not Brother—" Shores began but stopped. *What was the use?* he asked himself. The old Indian would go on calling him that stupid name no matter what he said. "I always speak with a straight tongue."

"Then no need shake." Red Fox jabbed his heels against the pinto, and their trackdown commenced.

William Shores had never spent more than five minutes in the company of an Indian his whole life, and for a while he felt distinctly uncomfortable. It helped that the Shoshone was a tame treaty Indian, but even so, he couldn't stop thinking about his grandparents and the legion of other incidents he had read or heard about.

The other's silence eventually got to him. "Were you and your brother close?" Shores asked to break the monotony.

"We brothers," Red Fox responded, his tone implying it was all the answer needed.

Shores didn't give up. "How did Mat-ta-vish get so good with horses?" The general consensus was that Red Fox's sibling raised some of the best horse-flesh anywhere. Quarrel rated the paints so high, he had mentioned to Shores that he would gladly keep them for himself if it weren't for his pact with the Sioux.

"Horses children," Red Fox said.

"Sorry?"

"Mat-ta-vish raise children, raise horses, all same. Mat-ta-vish love children, Mat-ta-vish love horses. Mat-ta-vish love all but *daiboo-a.*"

"All but white men." Until that moment, Shores had felt sorry for Mat-ta-vish. "And here I am, risking life and limb to bring your brother's murderers to bay. Life is one irony after another."

Red Fox looked at him. "Why you do this, Brother John? You not know Mat-ta-vish."

"It's my job. It's what the Great Father pays me to do." But there was a lot more to it, Shores ruefully reflected.

The Department of Justice was the newest kid on the government block. And as with most new kids, it had to prove itself before the other kids would accept it. So Attorney General Akerman had devised a strategy to prove the department was worthy of respect. His plan involved sending agents across the country to locales infested by various criminal elements. Elements, be it noted, which had garnered a lot of attention in the press. In Missouri it was a gang of bank robbers. In Georgia it was a small band of Southerners who refused to accept the South's defeat. In New Jersey it was a corporate ring swindling millions of dollars with sham raffles. In Wyoming and adjacent territories, it was the Hoodoos.

A lot was riding on Shores's shoulders. As the attorney general had put it at their last meeting, "I couldn't care less about a bunch of stolen horses. But there's more at stake here than stopping the thieves. We're building up the department's reputation. We're showing we've got what it takes, as common parlance would have it. By the end of the year, there won't be a person in the country who hasn't heard of us. And when they think of us, William, I want them to think of us with pride."

There were moments when Shores had the impression he had been set adrift in a rowboat without oars and expected to make his way upstream against the rapids. But he was nothing if not tenacious, and he wouldn't give up until the Hoodoos were in custody or dead.

For hours Shores and his newfound ally pressed steadily on. The sun was directly overhead when Shores mentioned they should stop to rest the horses.

"Paint fine," Red Fox said.

And it was, Shores had to admit. But the claybank

was a stable rental, and he must not wear it down if he could help it. Then there was the little fact that Shores had gone without breakfast, and his stomach wouldn't stop growling. "We'll rest awhile anyway." He went to draw rein.

"Not here, Brother John. There."

Shores looked where the Shoshone pointed but saw nothing to recommend the spot. It was just another grassy tract in an unending sea of grassland. But he humored the old man and in a few moments drew rein at a buffalo wallow.

"Less chance Lakotas, Blackfeet, whites see us." Red Fox rode into the wallow and dismounted by sliding off the right side of his paint.

Shores climbed down and walked the claybank to relieve some of the soreness in his leg muscles from all the time he had spent in the saddle recently. He frankly couldn't wait to wrap this assignment up and return to Washington, D.C. He missed being shuttled everywhere in a carriage, missed the private club he went to each evening for a cigar and a glass or two of brandy.

Red Fox squatted. "Brother John like Red Fox?"

The query was unforeseen. To stall, Shores loosened the claybank's cinch. As a Pinkerton, he had learned the best way to fend off unwanted questions was to answer a question with another, so he responded, "Why ask me a thing like that?"

"Many whites not like Indians. Say only good Indians, dead Indians. Brother John think same?"

"If I did, would we be having this ridiculous conversation?" Shores hedged. "My people have another saying. Judge a man by his actions, not by his words." He moved to the rim so he could keep watch, although he didn't really need to; the wallow was only about a foot and a half deep. But hopefully it would keep the old man from being a nuisance.

Shores gazed to the northeast and saw no sign of anyone on their back trail. To the east were specks that might be antelope. He shifted to gaze to the west and nearly jumped out of his skin.

Red Fox was a yard away, hunkered on his heels.

"Is there something you want?" Shores snapped, embarrassed at being caught off guard.

"Tell Red Fox about Great Father. Washakie say Great Father friend. Say Great Father help Shoshone. But Great Father make Shoshone stay reservation."

Washakie, as Shores had learned on his arrival at the Wind River Reservation, was a Shoshone chief of immense influence who always did all in his power to maintain peaceful relations with whites. "You're living on the land Washakie said your people want to live on. I should think you would be grateful."

"Reservation like fence. Keep Shoshone in. We told where go, when can hunt. Not like before white man. Shoshone go anywhere, do anything." A wistful smile spread across the old warrior's face. "Red Fox happy then."

"Those days are gone. More and more whites will come. More and more towns and settlements will spring up. There will be more ranches, more farms. But the Great Father will protect your tribe and not let anyone take the land he has given to you." Or so the official line went. As a dinner guest of the Indian Agent at the Wind River Agency, Shores had been dished an earful about the Indian problem and its solution.

Red Fox abruptly stood up. "Brother John hear?"

"Hear what?" Shores pivoted in a circle. The specks that might be antelope were still there. He saw nothing else.

"Buffalo."

It was Shores's understanding the big herds were a lot farther south at this time of year. "Are you sure?" He hadn't seen hide nor hair of the great shaggy beasts since leaving Cheyenne.

"Sure." Red Fox extended an arm.

They were specks at first, no larger than the antelope, and partially hidden by the immense dust cloud they were raising. But as they rapidly drew near, they swelled in size.

So, too, swelled the accompanying thunder of hundreds, possibly thousands, of hooves.

Shores grinned. He was ten the first time he ever set eyes on a buffalo, at the time, and still living in Texas. A farmer had come into town and mentioned seeing an old, decrepit bull out near his cornfield. Shores and several other boys had rushed to the spot and found the buffalo on its side, wheezing like a bellows. Shores would never forget how huge it was: six feet at the shoulder and twice that in length, with curved horns that could shear through a person like a hot knife through butter.

"Brother John?" Red Fox said.

Shores recalled how one of the boys had beaned the buffalo with a rock. He and the others had joined in, as boys that age were wont to do, and spent the next half an hour stoning the buffalo to death. When it finally stopped breathing, they congratulated one another on their mighty feat and ran off to tell their parents. That weekend there was a church social. Buffalo meat was the main dish.

"Brother John!"

Shores looked up. The herd was a lot closer and moving a lot faster than a herd normally did. It dawned on him they were stampeding—straight toward the wallow.

Chapter Seven

Colorado-Nebraska border

Eli Brandenberg was worried. The Hoodoos had stayed overnight at his place, something they had never done before. Kid Falon had spent much of it drinking and now was in a surly mood. Eli had to walk on eggshells around the little gunsman, which didn't sit well with Eli's nerves.

Then there was the grave business. Eli took it for granted the Hoodoos would do their own burying. But no. Brock Alvord had called him over after sunset, slid two dollars across the table, and said, "For the diggin'."

Eli honestly couldn't believe what he was hearing. "You expect me to bury those buff boys?"

Kid Falon, who had been about to deal cards, glanced up. "Do you have a problem with that, you louse-ridden soddy?"

"No problem at all," Eli lied, smiling to give the impression that burying bodies was something he did every day of the week and twice on Sundays because he loved it more than breathing. "It's just that they're both mighty big, and I'm kind of puny. I could use some help draggin' them out."

Brock Alvord might be a horse thief, but he wasn't near as mean as the men who rode under him. "Ben, Noonan, give him a hand."

It never ceased to amaze Eli how Alvord could boss around the likes of the sidewinders who rode with him, and they never seemed to mind. Kid Falon was the worst of the bunch, but the others weren't daisies. Big Ben Brody, who hailed from Arkansas, was a bear in human guise. Brody wasn't all that handy with a six-gun but he had been known to wrap his huge arms around gents he wasn't fond of and crush them in a hug. John Noonan, the quiet one of the bunch, was from the backwoods of Missouri, and a deadlier man never lived. He was good with a pistol, rifle, and knife. It was said he had a habit of making love to women whether they wanted to make love or not. Curly Means had the sunniest disposition this side of St. Louis but would shoot a man in the back as quick as look at him. Curly also had a thing about dogs. It seems that when he was a boy, a dog had bit his leg clear down to the bone and left a scar that never healed. Ever since, Curly had amused himself by killing every stray dog he ran across, usually by dragging them by the neck until they were dead.

That men like these took orders from Brock Alvord was all the proof Eli needed that Alvord was as tough as they came. But there was more to it than that. Alvord had brains. He was smarter than most outlaws. His notion of stealing horses only from Indians was a stroke of genius, in Eli's estimation. Then there was the business of their hideout. Everyone knew they had one, but no one knew where it was. Some claimed the Tetons. Others that it was off on the prairie somewhere.

But all that hardly mattered to Eli as he spent hours raising blisters on his hands. The ground was hard as rock, and once below the sod he had to chip away with a pick to make any kind of progress. He dug until well after midnight, then rolled the bodies into the holes and covered them.

Now here it was, eight the next morning, and Eli was fixing breakfast for his unwanted guests. His palms hurt like hell. Whenever he gripped the big wooden spoon to stir the hominy, he flinched. He was also making johnnycakes. He had eggs stored away, but he would be damned if he would share them. The same applied to his bacon.

The Hoodoos had spread out their bedrolls and slept on the floor. They were up early, although Big Ben Brody had refused to stir until Brock Alvord had upended a glass of water over his head. Brody came up wet and sputtering. Eli thought he would tear into Alvord, but all Brody did was grin.

"Sometime this year with that food!" Kid Falon barked. "We're expectin' company, and we want to be done when they get here."

This was news to Eli. It explained why they'd stayed the night. But he would just as soon they mounted up and went elsewhere. Having them around was like having a pack of wild dogs move in. He never knew but when one of them might take it into their head to bite him.

Curly's smile, it seemed, was carved into his handsome face. Strolling to the door, he opened it wide and breathed deep of the crisp morning air. "Do you know what's better than bein' alive?" he asked.

When none of the Hoodoos replied, Eli took it on himself to say, "No. What?"

"Nothin'." Curly laughed and pushed his hat back on his thatch of curls. "When the time comes to have my wick blown out, I'll be one mighty sad hombre."

"You make it sound like a foregone conclusion," Eli commented.

"Just because I steal horses for a livin' doesn't make me stupid," Curly said amiably enough. "Wildcats like me don't generally die in bed with their boots off. I reckon when my turn comes, I'll go out with a smokin' hogleg in my hand and a song in my heart."

Eli grinned. That was another thing about Curly: He could say the strangest things.

"I envy you, Brandenberg."

"Sure you're awake?" Eli joshed. He didn't see where his life was so great. Oh, he had a roof over his head, and he never went hungry, but that's the most that could be said. "My life would bore you silly."

"That it would," Curly agreed. "But you're not always lookin' over your shoulder. You can go anywhere you want without havin' to worry a lawman is goin' to walk up behind you and put a gun to your head."

Brock Alvord came to the counter. "That's not the worst of it," he threw in. "You don't have every Indian in four territories after your scalp. And now that the bounty on our heads is so high, manhunters will be crawlin' out of the woodwork."

Kid Falon heard that last comment. "How do we know this soddy won't try to collect the bounty for himself?"

"Why don't we let Eli answer that?" Alvord said.

Eli had the johnnycakes heaped high on a plate, and he turned from the cookstove to carry them to the table. "It don't make me no nevermind what other folks do. You boys have never done wrong by me, and I believe in lettin' every man skin his own skunk."

"I don't trust you," Kid Falon declared. "I have half a mind to put a slug in you just so you'll know what you'll get if you ever cross us."

Brock Alvord rubbed his white Vandyke. "You'll do no such thing. Eli's is one of the few places we can come where we don't have to sleep with one eye open. Throw down on him, and you'll answer to me."

Never in a million years would Eli have believed anyone could talk like that to Kid Falon and get away with it, but all the Kid did was scowl and slump in his chair. Eli suspected that Brock Alvord better be mighty careful. There might come a time when the Kid refused to back down when he was on the prod, and Alvord would be in trouble.

Curly Means sniffed a few times and hurried over. "Those cakes sure do set my mouth to waterin'. You missed your callin', Eli. You should have been a cook."

John Noonan produced his new bone-handled knife, jabbed the tip into a cake, and took a bite. "They'd be better with honey."

"I'm plumb out," Eli said, when in reality he had some stashed in a cabinet. "Sorry."

Big Ben Brody stuffed two of the cakes into his mouth and chomped like a starved griz on a slab of meat. "My ma used to make cakes like these," he said, crumbs dribbling over his lower lip. He looked at Alvord. "How soon you reckon before those red-skins get here?"

Eli started. "Indians are comin' *here*?" If there was one thing he was scared of, it was hostiles. He couldn't abide the thought of being taken alive and tortured to death. The things some of those heathens did were horrible beyond mention.

"Don't wet yourself," Kid Falon growled. "They're friendlies. They got wind of our offer and had a whiskey peddler set up a get-together."

"Offer?" Eli said, returning to the cookstove for the hominy.

It was Brock Alvord who answered. "We get the word out through scouts and whiskey Indians and the like that we'll pay one hundred dollars for information on herds worth stealin'."

So that was how they did it, Eli thought. Out loud he said, "Indians turn against their own kind like that?"

"Peel off their skin, and they're no different than whites," Brock said. "Down Arizona way, Apaches sign up as scouts to fight their own tribe. Indians are always squabblin' among themselves. The Arapahos hate the Shoshones, and the Shoshones hate the Sioux, and everybody hates the Blackfeet." Brock smiled slyly. "How do you reckon we found out about that Crow herd we stole not long ago? A Shoshone told us."

"No wonder you've never been caught, Mr. Alvord. You're as smart as a tree full of owls," Eli complimented him.

"My grandpa used to say that brains in the head saves blisters on the feet. And my pa was always goin' on about how a man can make more money

usin' his head than his back. I learned from them."
Brock helped himself to a cup from a shelf and filled
it with piping-hot coffee. "They'd roll over in their
graves, though, if they knew how I'd turned out. Pa
had high hopes of me bein' a lawyer or a doctor."

"My pa wanted me to be a store clerk like him,"
Kid Falon said. "He used to slap me silly whenever
he caught me playin' with an old revolver I bought.
One day he slapped me once too often, and I shot
him in the belly." The Kid laughed. "You should
have seen the look on his face when he died!"

Eli shivered, and not from the breeze wafting in
through the open door. He went to close it and felt
his heart leap into his throat. A stocky warrior was
just outside, a Henry rifle cradled in the crook of an
elbow. The warrior had painted himself yellow and
wore what appeared to be a small stuffed prairie dog
in his hair. "Brock! We've got company!" Eli hastily
backpedaled behind the counter.

The Hoodoos acted as surprised as Eli. The Kid
stood, his hands over his Colts. John Noonan and
Big Ben also pushed to their feet. Curly Means was
ladling hominy onto a plate and stayed in his chair.

"Sunset!" Brock Alvord declared, offering his hand
white-man fashion. "We didn't figure to see you
until noon."

Eli had no idea which tribe the warrior was from.
His gut balled into a knot when Sunset entered, but
that was nothing to the flip-flops his stomach did
when four more Indians followed.

"What's this?" Brock said. "I thought there were
only goin' to be you and your cousin."

Sunset moved so the other warriors could file to
the counter. All were carrying rifles, and all had
knives. "My cousin and his brothers come. It is not

safe for just one or two of us. Whites shoot at Indians on sight.''

"Can you blame them?'' Kid Falon asked in ill-concealed contempt. He might have said more, but Alvord motioned for him to hush up.

"Have a seat,'' Brock urged the yellow warrior. "We'd be happy to have you join us for breakfast.''

Sunset said something in his own tongue to the other warriors, then took the seat Alvord indicated. He sat stiffly, as one unaccustomed to chairs, and placed the Henry across the chair's arms.

"Have a cake.'' Brock handed him one.

After a nibble to test the taste, Sunset smiled and inhaled the johnnycake. Eli had more ready and set them on the counter. He stepped back quickly when a warrior's bronzed hand almost brushed his. Being that close to them made him want to curl up into a ball and scream.

"Now then.'' Brock Alvord turned a chair around and straddled it. "Suppose we get down to business. Sam Crotchet let on that you might know where we can get our hands on a herd.''

The name jarred Eli's memory. Crotchet was a crusty old whiskey peddler who had been arrested twice for selling watered-down firewater to Indians but never learned from his mistakes.

"Maybe so,'' Sunset said. "Crotchet say you pay one hundred dollars to learn where horses are.'' He slid a palm toward Alvord.

"Not so fast. That's not how this works. I wasn't born on crazy creek. You give me the information, and if I think you're talkin' straight tongue, I'll give you the money. But not before.''

"What stops you from cheating me?''

"That works both ways,'' Brock observed. "Look.

Crotchet told me you can be trusted. That you don't hate whites like a lot of Cheyenne do. But if you're worried about being buffaloed, we'll call this off right now."

Sunset digested that before replying. "I have heard of you, Hoodoo. For five winters you steal many horses from many tribes. I never hear you cheat anyone."

"I'm not stupid. The first time I did, word would get out, and soon there wouldn't be an Indian this side of the Divide who would want anything to do with me or my boys. So long as I'm honest, I'm trusted."

A second johnnycake proved too much for the Cheyenne to resist. He ate slowly, thoughtfully, smacking his lips when he was done. "Very well. I will trust you. But if you trick us, my cousins and I will count coup on you."

Kid Falon snickered and went to say something, but again Brock Alvord shushed him. "Let's hear about this herd. Who owns it? Where can we find it? And most important, how many horses and what kind?"

"This many." Sunset held up all his fingers and thumbs six times. "War horses, not travois horses. They belong to a Crow."

Eli wasn't much on Indian lore, but he did know they took powerful good care of their best horses, the mounts they used when they went on the warpath. Some warriors went so far as to bring their favorite war horse into their lodge at night so it couldn't be stolen or set on by meat eaters.

"This Crow have a name?"

"To the whites he is Looks With His Ears. He belongs to the Kicked In The Bellies band." Sunset then went on to relate where the band could be found. "They will stay there another moon, maybe two, then move on. You have until then to steal the herd."

"Tell me about the horses."

Eli didn't listen to the rest. He was more interested in what the other Cheyenne were up to. Indians were big eaters, and these four were typical. They gobbled down the rest of the johnnycakes and held out their hands for more. "I ain't got any," Eli informed them more gruffly than he should have, and one scowled and fingered his rifle. "Hold your britches though."

Some years ago, Eli had made jerked venison that didn't turn out right. The meat had a rancid taste. He had stuffed it in a cabinet and forgotten about it, but now he took out the strip of deer hide the jerky was wrapped in and placed it in front of the four moochers. "Help yourselves."

The meat had mold on it, but that didn't stop the Cheyenne from biting off big chunks and chewing hungrily. Grunting, they grinned at Eli to show their gratitude, and he grinned back, thinking they had to be the biggest idiots ever born.

Brock Alvord and Sunset were talking and smiling. Eli assumed the palaver was going smoothly. So he was all the more stupefied when Sunset suddenly yipped like a coyote, leveled his Winchester at Brock Alvord's chest, and fired. How Sunset missed, Eli might never have known had he not seen Kid Falon's Colts streak above the table and blast in unison.

The Kid's reflexes were so unbelievably swift that, having seen Sunset start to level the Winchester, he had drawn and fired before the warrior could squeeze off a shot. The slugs from his pearl-handled Colts cored Sunset's sternum and smashed him and his chair back a yard, spoiling his aim.

The yip had been a signal for the other Cheyenne. They spun, firing as they whirled, working their rifle levers rapidly.

Big Ben Brody yelped and flung himself, and his chair, out of the hail of lead. Curly Means and John Noonan met it head on. Apparently they had expected treachery, because they were on their feet before the warriors turned, Noonan fanning his six-gun, Curly firing from the hip. Eli saw Noonan jolted by a bullet. Kid Falon and Brock Alvord were also blazing away, and it abruptly dawned on Eli that he was in the line of all that lead.

Eli dived for the floor and felt a searing pain in his right shoulder. He cried out, and his cry was echoed by one of the Cheyenne. Bodies thudded as more shots boomed. Then quiet descended.

"Stinkin' vermin," Kid Falon spat.

Cautiously rising, Eli peeked over the counter. The three warriors had been shot to ribbons. The Kid and Curly were reloading. Noonan was examining a wound low on his left side. Big Ben was on his knees, swatting at the clouds of smoke that hung in the air like acrid fog.

Brock Alvord looked fit to explode. He stormed over to Sunset, sank onto a knee, and gripped the Cheyenne by the throat. "*Why?*" he raged, shaking him. "Why the hell did you do that?"

Sunset wasn't long for this world. Scarlet ribbons trickled from his mouth. Feebly, he attempted to draw his knife, but Brock angrily stomped on his wrist, pinning his hand.

"Answer me, damn your hide!"

Eli knew what the Cheyenne would say before Sunset choked it out.

"The bounty."

Livid with fury, Brock stood, thumbed back the hammer to his six-gun, and shot Sunset in the forehead. He thumbed back the hammer a second time, but it clicked on a spent cartridge. Beside himself, he hiked his boot and stomped on the Cheyenne's face again and again and again. When he stepped back, breathless, it was a pulped ruin.

"You know what this means, don't you?" Curly Means said. "We can't trust anyone from here on out."

Eli straightened and was spiked by agony. He touched his shoulder, and his fingers came away sticky with blood. Dizziness assailed him, and he staggered around to a chair and oozed into it, his legs so much mush. "I've been shot!" he bleakly exclaimed. He envisioned being planted next to the buffalo hunters and groaned.

Curly ambled over. "How bad is it?" He had a folding knife in his left hand. Opening it, he carefully cut Eli's shirt to expose the wound. "You must have been born with a four-leaf clover in your mouth."

"I'm done for, and you poke fun?"

"Hell. You'll outlive me and the rest of the boys put together. The slug missed the bone and went out your back without leavin' much of a hole. You're not bleedin' that bad either. You were lucky."

Eli didn't feel lucky. He felt like he had been kicked by a mustang.

Noonan's wound was a lot worse, but he dabbed at it with his bandanna, tucked his shirt back under his pants, and said, "I'm ready when the rest of you are."

"Ready for what?" Eli said weakly, but no one was listening. The Hoodoos were gathering up their saddles and their effects, and Big Ben was shoving the few johnnycakes left into his saddlebags. "You're leavin'?"

Brock Alvord walked over. "I'm sorry, Eli. There might be a whole war party nearby. We can't stick around and chance bein' trapped in here." He patted Eli's good shoulder. "I'm sure you understand."

Eli did no such thing. "What about *me*? I can't fight off a war party by my lonesome! You owe it to me to stick and help out."

Kid Falon's right Colt blossomed out of thin air. "Foolish talk like that can get you planted. We don't owe you a blessed thing, soddy."

Brock shook his head. "Put that away." He reached into a pocket and counted out one hundred dollars in United States notes. "I was fixin' to give this to Sunset, but his loss is your gain. It should make us even." Throwing his saddle over his back, he jangled out on the heels of his *compañeros*. They weren't letting any grass grow under them.

Eli sat there. He trembled all over but not from fear. Throwing the bills onto the table, he struggled erect. "No sir! No sir!" Rage made him reckless. Clutching his shoulder, he shuffled to the doorway.

Over under the lean-to beside the corral, the Hoodoos were hastily preparing to ride out. Their horses were some of the best they had stolen in recent years, animals that could go forever and a day and not tire.

"Wait!" Eli stumbled toward them. "Take me!"

Kid Falon laughed. Big Ben Brody shook his head.

"Let me ride with one of you!" Eli grasped at a straw. "Drop me off at the first town you come to."

"Pitiful," the Kid said and forked an Appaloosa.

"Don't do this to yourself," Brock Alvord said in mild reproach. He was astride a magnificent blue roan.

"Do *what*?" Eli shouted and moved to block the lean-to entrance so they couldn't abandon him. But it was twenty feet wide, and he was only one man. He snatched at Big Ben's reins and had them ripped from his hand. He tried to seize Noonan's bridle and was brushed off.

"You boys should be ashamed of yourselves," Curly Means said. Grinning, he bent down with an arm extended. "Come on, soddy. You can swing up behind me. I don't mind."

"Thank you," Eli blubbered, tears filling his eyes. "Thank you, thank you, thank you." He reached out with his left arm.

Instead of taking hold, Curly placed his hand against Eli's face and shoved. Eli fell backward, collided with a bale of straw, and cartwheeled. He landed on his wounded shoulder. The pain that spiked through him was nearly unbearable. He heard their rough glee and made it to his knees.

Four of the five were already trotting southeast.

"You brought that on yourself," Brock Alvord said. "Ridin' double with one of us will slow the rest. We can't have that, Eli."

"But the Cheyenne!" Eli was crying and wanted to stop, but he couldn't help himself.

Brock gave the prairie a quick scrutiny. "Maybe there aren't any more. Get inside and bar your door. If none show by up nightfall, you're safe." He touched his hat brim and wheeled the roan.

"Not you too!" Eli begged and wrapped his hand around Alvord's stirrup.

"Try to be nice to some folks and look at what they do."

Eli never saw the boot that slammed into his cheek. He fell heavily and tasted dirt in his mouth. Dirt and the bitterest of bile, composed of equal parts rage and hate. His vision blurred by tears, he watched Brock Alvord ride away and gave voice to his turmoil. "I'll get even if it's the last thing I do!"

Chapter Eight

Charley Pickett was elated when Enos Howard announced he would help track down the Hoodoos. His high spirits were crushed, however, by the next statement out of the buffalo hunter's mouth.

"I sold my horse a while ago, so you'll have to buy me one. I'll need supplies too. Ammunition, for starters. It's been a year since I squeezed the trigger. I need to practice to get my eye back in." Howard paused. "What's wrong, cub? You look like you just swallowed a cactus."

"I don't have the money to buy you a horse," Charley confessed. "Heck, I don't even have a horse of my own." Charley looked at Tony. "You must have enough. Care to chip in for the cause?"

"I was wondering when you would get around to asking." Tony pulled out his wad of stolen bills. "I am willing to contribute it to the cause, but it will not be anywhere near enough."

Howard swilled whiskey and wiped his mouth with the back of a hand. "Seems to me that you younguns don't have this very thought-out. What did you reckon, that horses and food would fall out of the sky? To outfit us right, we need about eight hundred to a thousand dollars."

Charley's brainstorm came crashing down around him in tiny shards. "That's an awful lot of money."

Howard broke it down. "A good saddle horse costs about two hundred. Saddles run from thirty to sixty, dependin' on whether you want a good one or one that will leave your hind end so sore at the end of the day you can't sit down. Cartridges cost from fifty cents to a dollar a box." He stopped as if struck by a thought. "How many of you have a rifle and a revolver?"

None of them answered.

"No one? What do you figure to do? Throw rocks at any hostiles we come across?" Howard tittered. "Add guns to the cost. Plus bridles, saddlebags, blankets, coffee, flour, butter, sugar, cheese. Hell, I could go on and on." He tugged at his beard. "There's somethin' I'm missin'. Somethin' important." He began to raise the bottle to his mouth, grinned, and waved it in the air. "Tarantula juice! I reckon twenty bottles should do me. And a crate to pack 'em in so they won't break.

"How much money do you have?" Charley bleakly asked Tony.

"Two hundred and two dollars."

Howard made a clucking sound. "You pups are pitiful." He indulged in more whiskey; over three-fourths of the bottle was gone. Suddenly he snapped his fingers. "I know! We can rob a bank!"

"That's the dumbest idea I've ever heard," Melissa admonished.

"Folks do it all the time. It's how many a coon has raised a grubstake. And if'n it will make you feel any better, we won't take all their money. Only as much as we need."

Charley shook his head. "You're missin' the point. We want to hunt a gang of outlaws, not *become* outlaws."

Howard sat back. "Suit yourself. We should forget this silliness and go on about our own business then. Without horses and whatnot, we're not going anywhere unless we sprout wings and fly." He flapped his arms a few times and laughed. "Dang. I must have left mine in my shack."

"I have money," Melissa said quietly.

Everyone faced her.

"I've been saving every spare penny since I left home. I don't intend to sell potatoes my whole life, you know. My dream is to open a millinery. Here, or in St. Louis maybe. With all the latest fashions, the newest dresses—"

"All that fofarraw is fine and dandy, Missy." Howard cut her short. "But what's more important is how much you have squirreled away. Because if it's not enough, I'm walkin' out that door and robbin' the first bank I see."

"The last time I checked, I had a hundred and sixty-four dollars."

Howard snorted. "That settles it." He stood and turned to go.

"Sit back down!" Charley commanded and smacked the table to emphasize his point. "We're not robbin' banks, and that's that!"

"Then you can kiss all that bounty money goodbye." Offended, Howard walked over to the bar.

Charley was crestfallen. "I'm sorry. I guess I put the cart before the horse. I barely have seventy dollars to my own name."

"Don't be so hard on yourself." Melissa covered his hand with hers. "I admire a man who's looking to get ahead."

"Thanks." Charley's neck grew hotter than a burning brand. He was content to sit there forever with her touching him.

For a long while no one said anything. Then Tony commented, "I'll catch the noon stage to Santa Fe tomorrow. Two months from now, I'll be in California. What will you do, my friend?"

Charley hadn't thought that far ahead. He would continue working at the stable for the time being.

"You know," Melissa said, and her own voice sounded peculiar. "Everyone says that two people can make a go of it better than one."

A keg of black powder blew up in Charley's chest. His skin prickled, and he thought he would stop breathing. She couldn't mean what he thought she meant. He was going to ask her to explain, but a shadow fell across the table and the stale smell of an old buffalo coat filled his nostrils.

"I've had a talk with myself," Enos Howard announced, "and I've decided to chip in enough to make up the difference." He finished the last of the whiskey. "On two conditions."

"Chip in what?" Charley asked suspiciously.

"Don't fret. I'm not fixin' to rob anything. But I know how to get my hands on a right smart amount, right quick."

"How?"

"That's my secret." Howard's confidence was both inspiring and troubling. "But if I chip in more, I expect more. I want two thousand dollars of the bounty, and when it's all over, I get to keep my horse, the pack animals, and whatever supplies are left. Agreed?"

Charley did the arithmetic in his head. He had never been a wizard at large sums, so it took a bit. His share would come to a little over sixteen hundred, which was still plenty. "Sounds fair to me."

"What I would like to know," Tony said to Enos, "is why you changed your mind so suddenly about coming along. And why you are being so helpful. Most *strano*."

"I have my reasons." Howard held out a hand. "Do we shake on it or not?"

They shook.

From there, events proceeded quickly. Almost too quickly for Charley. He gave his notice to Mr. Leeds, who insisted on knowing all the details. Charley expected Leeds to tell him they were loons, but not only did the stable owner wish them well, he offered to sell them three horses at a special price of one hundred and thirty dollars each, which was twenty dollars less than what Leeds could sell them for to most anyone else. They were older horses but not so old as to be worthless.

Charley cheerfully accepted.

Next, Leeds took him into the tack room, and they searched along the back wall where Leeds kept harness and tack that had seen a lot of use. Two saddles and several bridles were added to Charley's growing collection, along with four saddle blankets that Leeds had been ready to toss. They were frayed and worn but would suffice.

Falling asleep that night was next to impossible.

Charley lay on his back in the hayloft staring at the rafters and wondering what on earth he had let himself in for. He was willing to bet the Hoodoos wouldn't surrender without a fight, if they surrendered at all. But he had never fired a weapon at another human being in his life. All he ever shot was game for the supper pot.

Then there was the bigger issue, the one that had Charley's conscience gnawing at him like a chigger boring through flesh. He never should have invited Melissa along. Not on so dangerous an undertaking. It wasn't too late to tell her she couldn't go. That was the sensible thing to do. But heaven help him, he liked the idea of being with her day in and day out for however long it took to find the outlaws. They could talk about things, get to know each other better.

Who am I kidding? Charley thought. He was usually so tongue-tied around her that he was afraid to speak out of fear of making a fool of himself. Fortunately, she jabbered enough for both of them, and she seemed to really like him, which amazed him no end. The girls in Kentucky had been friendly, but only a couple had ever showed him much interest, and the few times he had gotten up the nerve to ask a girl to go out with him, he'd run into the same problem he had with Melissa. He couldn't string more than three intelligent words together for the life of him.

Charley made a mental note to keep an eye on the buffalo hunter. Enos was old enough to be Melissa's pa, yet he was always putting his arm around her shoulders and generally being more familiar with her than he had a right to be. If Howard persisted with that behavior out on the prairie, Charley would put a stop to it.

Then there was Tony. Charley was as sure as sure

could be that Tony had no interest in Melissa. Not in the way he did anyhow. The way they sniped at each other, and the comments dropped by Melissa, led him to believe something had happened between them. Something he might not like. Part of him wanted to corner Tony and demand an explanation. But Tony was his best friend—his only friend, when it came right down to it—and he was reluctant to put their friendship in jeopardy by making accusations which might or might not be true.

Sleep snuck up on him, and Charley slept soundly until the crow of the rooster interrupted a dream he was having in which Melissa and he were doing things that would have made him blush if he'd thought about doing them when he was awake. He was only halfway down the ladder when someone pounded on the wide double doors.

"Open up! Are you awake in there, boy? Or are you a layabout who wastes his days in bed?"

Charley and the others had agreed to meet at the stable at eight a.m. It couldn't be much after six. He removed the long bar and opened a door. "Make more noise, why don't you? You probably woke up everyone within ten blocks."

Enos Howard glanced both ways, then quickly stepped inside. "Took you long enough. What did you do, come by way of Arkansas?"

"You're early." Charley left the door open so that Melissa and Tony could walk right in when they arrived. But the buffalo hunter closed it. "What's with you? You're actin' like someone is after you."

"Let's just say we don't want any grass to grow under us." Howard had a rifle with him, an old Sharps. "As soon we have our horses and supplies, we need to light a shuck."

"What have you done?" Charley asked. "You promised not to do any robbin'."

"And I'm a man of my word. But money don't come easy. I had to shake the trees some to get the apples to fall."

"How much do you have?"

"Not enough by itself. But with what Missy and you and the Italian have, it should do us." Howard flourished more money than Charley had ever seen anyone hold in their hand at one time. "Five hundred dollars."

Whistling in surprise, Charley reached for it, but Enos slapped his hand. "Keep your paws off. I rustled it up, and I'm holdin' on to it until we work out how it should be spent." Enos shoved the money back in his pocket.

Charley felt slighted. It wasn't like he was fixing to steal it or anything. "I've got something to show you," he said testily.

The three horses Leeds was letting them have were in stalls at the rear. Piled nearby was the gear. Enos examined each of the animals and the saddles and bridles and snorted. "So you reckon this liveryman is doin' you a favor? Hell, these nags are only a couple months shy of bein' turned into glue. And this tack is older than I am."

"If you think you can do better, you're welcome to try." Simmering mad now, Charley went to the front. He was sick and tired of Enos treating him like he was wet behind the ears. Maybe he was, in some respects, but that didn't give Enos call to harp on it like he did.

Soon Leeds arrived. Charley introduced them and girded for an outburst from Enos, but the buffalo hunter stunned him by acting as gracious as a parson at a church social.

"I want to thank you for helpin' us. It's fine gentlemen like you who are the salt of the earth. A lot of people are only out for themselves, and they don't give a hang who they step on."

"All too true," Leeds said solemnly. He looked Enos up and down. "You're not quite what I expected. I remember reading about your fight with the Blackfeet at the chalk cliffs. It was the talk of the territory."

"That it was," Enos declared with pride. Then his features darkened. "So was my try to break Buffalo Bill's record and that shootin' match I had with Comstock. Everywhere I went, I was looked down on."

"You did your best. What more could be asked?"

Enos clapped Leeds on the shoulder. "That was a darned decent thing to say. Most folks weren't as charitable. Every saloon I went in, someone would haze me. It got so I couldn't stand it anymore. So I came to Denver."

"Few barbs hurt worse than laughter," Mr. Leeds sympathized.

"Now who's talkin' truth?" Enos said sadly.

Charley was amazed they were hitting it off so well. Leeds was a teetotaling churchgoer, Enos a natural-born hell-raiser. They couldn't be less alike if they tried, yet there they were, smiling and jawing like they were the best of friends. Intent on their banter, he didn't realize someone else had arrived until he heard a low cough.

"Charley Pickett! I realize I'm not much to look at. But you could at least have the courtesy to say good morning."

"Melissa!" Charley sprang to help with her effects. Crammed into a carpetbag were all her worldly possessions. She also had a shoulder bag that she held on to. "I didn't see you there. You're early too."

"I couldn't sleep." Melissa had no sooner stepped inside than Enos enfolded her in a hug. In his exuberance, he lifted her clear off the floor. "Missy! I was afeared maybe you would change your mind!"

Mr. Leeds was horrified. "You intend to take a woman along?" He made a passionate appeal for them not to do so, citing a host of reasons: that manhunting was no fit occupation for a woman; that she would be exposed to constant danger; that if she fell into the hands of hostiles, they would mistreat her in the worse way imaginable; that she must endure heat and dust and insects and wild animals.

Melissa let him have his say, and when he was done, she thanked him sincerely but stated that she could not afford to let the opportunity pass. "I need the money, Mr. Leeds. You know yourself that jobs for women are too few and pay too little. I stand to make as much in a couple of months as would take me ten years or better to earn."

"Money is never easy to come by, young lady, I'll grant you that. But there has to be a safer means to acquire it."

"Name me one way I can make as much in as short a time, and I'll forget about going after the outlaws," Melissa challenged him.

For a few seconds Charley was scared Leeds would come up with one. He was being selfish, he knew, but he dearly wanted her along. He had high hopes they would grow a lot closer. But he need not have worried.

"I cannot think of one," Leeds said. "So if you

insist on taking part in this perilous enterprise, I pray the Good Lord keeps you safe from harm." Leeds then surprised Charley by hugging her.

The hinges to one of the double doors creaked, and in came Tony. He was dressed in his usual city clothes and carrying his valise. "*Buon giorno.* Against my better judgment, I am here."

Again Mr. Leeds was introduced. He excused himself to go into his office but only after taking Charley aside to remark, "Not that I don't enjoy squandering time that could be spent working, but need I remind you of the rather nasty gentleman with the cane? He promised to come back, if you'll recall. It might be prudent for you and your friends to be gone when he does."

Charley hadn't forgotten. The fix Tony was in was always at the back of his mind, spurring him to get done and get out of there. "So, where do we commence?" he asked his fellow would-be manhunters. "With the rest of the horses we need? Or with the supplies?"

"What kind of tomfool question is that?" Howard said. "All the supplies in the world won't do us a lick of good if we don't have horses to tote them." Chewing on his lower lip, he gazed down the street. "I suppose you expect me to go along and help you out?"

"Talk about tomfool questions." Charley gave him a taste of his own verbal abuse. "Of course you're taggin' along. You're the only one of us who knows what he's doin'."

"Which is not saying a whole lot," Tony muttered.

Enos removed his heavy coat. "Where can I hang this that no one will steal it?"

Before Charley could reply, Tony said, "Who would want to?"

The buffalo hunter rounded on him. "Is there somethin' botherin' you, boy? Speak up, and we'll hash it out. Because I don't take sass off anyone. Ever. And I don't want to upset Missy by stompin' you into the dirt."

"I do not like being threatened."

"Then you should be a sight more careful about whose tail you step on. Enos glowered and fingered the hammer of his rifle.

Charley stepped between them. "Will you two cut it out? You're worse than a pair of brothers. We're on the same side, remember? The sooner you two simpletons realize that, the happier all of us will be." He still thought they might tear into one another, but Melissa came to his aid.

"His sentiments are the same as mine. Tony, have you forgotten the favor Mr. Howard did you by distracting Radtke's men? And Enos, if you're going to arch your back and spit every time anyone ruffles your fur, you'd best bring forty bottles instead of twenty to keep your mouth plugged."

Enos let out with another of his belly-shaking laughs. "Gal, if you don't beat all! You're right. It's the little things that get stuck in our craw and fester and sore. But for you're sake, I'll swallow as many of 'em as I can."

Charley hung up the smelly buffalo coat in the tack room. It was the first time he had seen Enos Howard go without it. As they hurried down the block, he noticed that Howard was as nervous as a squirrel on a porch full of cats. Enos continually glanced every which way, his head tucked to his chest like he was trying to slide his chin down to his navel. Once again, Charley wondered about the money Enos had scrounged up.

It turned out, though, that the buffalo hunter was worth his weight in money saved. He was a world-class haggler. When they found an item they needed, Enos leaped into the fray and badgered the clerk into lowering the price. It didn't always work. Maybe eight times of out ten. Enough to stretch their dollars a lot further than Charley had figured.

General store by general store, stable by stable, they acquired what they needed. Their horses weren't the best. Fact was, the animals weren't much above the bottom of the barrel. And some of the others things, like the moldy cheese and the stale bread and the knives with spots of rust on the blades, weren't items most people would stoop to accept. But they got it all at a discount, thanks to Enos, and that was what counted.

Their second-to-last stop was Olinger's Guns and Gunsmithing. Mr. Olinger was a pleasant old fellow who nodded knowingly when Enos said, "We need us some hardware, old-timer. Artillery that will blow the brains out of anything inclined to do us harm but won't bankrupt us in the bargain."

Crooking a finger, Olinger took them into a back room. There, in glass cases and on wall racks, were guns he had been unable to sell for one reason or another. A few were outdated flintlocks. Some were percussion firearms. A lot were foreign-made.

"I discount all these," Olinger said.

"Even the nickel-plated ones?" Charley had seen one he liked.

"Guns, like clothes, have their fashions. What is popular one year might not be popular the next. All anyone wants of late are the latest Colt revolvers and Winchester rifles. Nothing else will do. So the foreign models go wanting." Olinger paused. "Just the other day I tried to sell a cowboy an excellent Merwin and Hulbert pistol, but he shook his head and told me if it isn't a Colt, it isn't worth carrying."

"I never realized there were so many kinds." Melissa was beside a case of derringers.

"Few do, young lady," Olinger responded. "Schofield, Bacon, Prescott, Uhlinger, Brooklyn Firearms—they all offer outstanding firearms, but I'd warrant hardly anyone has ever heard of them."

Charley sure hadn't. "If that's the case, why carry any?"

"Some I've taken in partial trade. Others because there's always that one customer in fifty who doesn't want to buy what everyone else buys." Olinger opened a case and removed a finely engraved pistol. "Some I stock because they're works of art."

It took over an hour. Olinger patiently showed them gun after gun. Enos haggled over each and every one. In the end, each of them had a rifle and a revolver and some extras besides.

Enos was pleased. As they were leading their new horses back to the stable, he crowed, "The king of hornswogglers, that's me! I ain't met a coon yet I can't talk down in price! I'm a fox and a badger rolled into one! Slick as axle grease and trickier than a politician!"

"And modest too," Tony said.

Enos was about to tear into him, but he abruptly dipped his chin to his chest and slouched along like he was having the worst day of his life.

Charley looked in the direction that Howard had been staring and spotted a burly policeman. The policeman hadn't noticed them. Soon they arrived at the stable and finished loading packs and throwing on saddles.

Mr. Leeds came out to see them off. "I wish, for her own sake, that you would reconsider taking Miss Patterson."

"Hell's bells, friend, don't dampen our spirits right out of the chute!" Enos had donned his buffalo coat and was his usual boisterous self. "We're goin' off on a grand adventure! She'll have herself a larrupin' time the likes of which these greeners won't forget the rest of their lives."

"Just so they live through it," Leeds commented. "Bring them back alive, Mr. Howard."

"I'm not about to make any promises I can't keep, hoss. It's not up to me. It's up to the Almighty. And he's mighty fickle, if'n you ask me." Laughing, Enos spurred his sorrel mare.

With that, the four manhunters rode out of Denver. Charley came last, leading the pack animals and wondering what in the name of all that was holy he had gotten them into.

Chapter Nine

Nebraska Panhandle

To William Shores it seemed as if a million buffalo were stampeding toward the wallow in which he was crouched beside Red Fox. His first impulse was to dart to the claybank and burn the breeze, but as he spun, Red Fox gripped his arm.

"No, Brother John. Buffalo catch. Buffalo kill."

Shores tore loose but stayed rooted where he was. The old warrior was right. Outrunning them wasn't an option. The herd was bearing down on them faster than he would have thought possible. The rumble of their hooves was a continuous tremendous din. A huge cloud of dust blanketed them like fog, a cloud so thick that Shores could see only the foremost hairy ranks.

"There be smarter way," Red Fox declared. Vaulting onto the rim, he spread his thin arms wide.

"Get down here, you fool! You'll be trampled!" Shores snatched at the Shoshone's ankle, but Red Fox stood firm.

"Watch, Brother John. Watch and learn." Red Fox threw back his head and began to sing.

To Shores it was utter lunacy. Even if the buffalo could hear the old man over the drumming of hooves, which was doubtful, they weren't about to stop. To them he was nothing, a frail human twig to be crushed under their heavy hooves. They would plow Red Fox under their grinding hooves, and his bones would join the bleached legion already dotting the prairie.

Again Shores tried. "You'll get yourself killed!"

Red Fox sang louder.

The claybank was snorting and prancing. Fearful it would bolt, Shores seized hold of the bridle. The Shoshone's paint showed no alarm whatsoever, but Shores grabbed its rope reins anyway. It would serve the old man right to be stranded afoot in the middle of the prairie, but Shores couldn't bring himself to let that happen.

Shores tried not to think of the buffalo or their wicked, curved horns. When he was a boy growing up in Texas, he had had occasion to see what those horns could do. Buffalo had been a lot more numerous back then, and the big herds had pushed far to the south. An uncle who was enormously fond of buffalo steak had taken Shores hunting a couple of times. Shores didn't get to do much other than camp chores, but on their second outing, another hunter, a neighbor of his uncle's who always liked to joke and laugh, had made the mistake of getting too close to a wounded bull and paid a fatal price.

The horrid image was seared into Shores's memory: the sight of the man thrashing about in a pool of scarlet, screaming and blubbering, his forearms pressed over what had once been his stomach. One of the bull's horns had shredded the flesh like wet paper, creating a cavity large enough to fit a watermelon in, and the neighbor's innards had come oozing out.

In another heartbeat, the herd was on top of them. Shores almost cried out as a hedgerow of broad, massive heads swept toward the north side of the wallow. Too many to count, an unstoppable force no man or beast could withstand. Red Fox would be smashed aside. Then it would be his turn.

But at the instant of certain death, at the moment when Shores believed Red Fox would fall under a grinding array of battering hooves, the herd parted as cleanly and completely as the Red Sea had for Moses, and instead of breaking over the wallow like waves on a shore, the buffalo parted to the right and the left, missing Red Fox, and swung wide.

All Shores could do was gape. He stifled a mad urge to shuck his Winchester from its saddle scabbard and blaze away. It sobered him to think that in the greater scheme of things, man amounted to no more than the specks of dust that floated before his eyes. Specks which were part of the choking cloud that swallowed him like the Biblical leviathan swallowed Jonah. In the blink of an eye, he couldn't see his hand holding the reins or the buffalo nor Red Fox. He couldn't hear the Shoshone either for the near-deafening din.

Something brushed against him, and Shores jerked back, thinking it was a buffalo. But it was only the claybank, as terror-struck as he was. Dust choked his nose, his lungs. His eyes watered uncontrollably. He erupted in a coughing fit, his pounding heart fit to burst.

Then, as spectacularly as it had begun, the stampede swept to the south. There had not been thousands. Several hundred at the most. The rumbling of the herd's passage gradually faded, and the dust slowly thinned.

Shores straightened. His ears were ringing, and his mouth had gone bone dry. He tried to swallow and swallowed dust. Wheezing, he touched a hand to his chest, overjoyed to be alive.

A second hand was placed next to his. "Brother John all right?" Red Fox was caked with dust. So much so, not a single patch of bare skin showed, and his grey hair was now brown. Yet he was having no trouble breathing.

"I'm fine," Shores croaked, swatting at his clothes. "I kept your horse from running off." He handed over the reins.

Red Fox's teeth were a bright flash of color. "Climb on. We ride fast or be rubbed out."

Shores thought his ears must be clogged. "What are you talking about? The buffalo are gone. You saved us from the stampede."

"But not save from cause." Red Fox hurried to the south rim. "Come, Brother John. Please."

Confused, Shores stumbled after him. He'd swear the dust had seeped into his joints and muscles, making him as sluggish as a snail. "Listen, you're not making any sense. We should rest a bit, clean ourselves off. I have a canteen, and I'm willing to share the water."

"Not drink water if dead."

"I wish you would stop talking in riddles. Granted, you're handicapped by not knowing English that well, but I'm willing to take the time to listen if you'll take the time to express yourself clearly."

Red Fox gazed to the north and immediately swung onto the paint. "You not hurry, you die."

Shores was losing his temper. "And just who in the hell is going to kill me?"

"Them." The old Shoshone pointed.

Approximately two hundred yards out were eight warriors. Six were armed with bows and arrows, two with rifles. They wore their hair differently than Red Fox and were considerably stockier and more muscular.

"Who are they?" Shores asked.

"Some call Lakotas. Some call Sioux. Same, same. Sioux fight Shoshones, Shoshones fight Sioux. Only one thing Sioux hate more."

"What's that?"

"White men."

Piercing whoops accented the old warrior's point. Shores forked leather and applied his spurs. In Cheyenne he had been assured the Sioux were much farther north this time of year. Apparently someone had forgotten to tell the Sioux. He glanced back to gauge whether the warriors would try to overtake them right away or chase them into the ground and was amused to see one of them nocking an arrow to a bow. The range was far too great. Or so he assumed until the shaft left the string and arced in a precise trajectory that ended with it embedding itself in the earth less than five feet behind him.

"Damn." Shores had heard tales about Indian prowess with a bow. Claims they were taught to use one when they were barely old enough to hold it. Claims a grown warrior could unleash ten to twenty shafts in the span of a minute. Claims of incredible accuracy when firing from horseback. He had chalked them up to the usual frontier penchant for hot air, but after the attempt he had just witnessed, he was willing to admit he might have been hasty in his judgment.

Another shaft was loosed, this time at Red Fox. It

missed, although not by much. The Shoshone reacted by laughing and taunting their pursuers.

After that, the Sioux concentrated on trying to narrow the gap. Shores and the Shoshone concentrated on increasing their lead. They did, but not by much.

Shores remembered hearing that grass-fed mounts lacked the stamina of grain-fed animals, and he was optimistic his claybank could outlast the mounts of the hostiles. As for the paint, if it tired and lagged, Shores didn't know what he would do. He needed Red Fox's help in tracking the Hoodoos, but he would be damned if he would sacrifice his life for an old Indian. Hell, he doubted he would do it for another white man. Not if it meant falling into the clutches of dusky demons who delighted in inflicting unspeakable tortures.

Red Fox's cry brought Shores out of himself. He didn't know what to make of the forms dotting the prairie ahead. Then it hit him: They were buffalo. The herd had stampeded itself out and was milling about.

Red Fox smiled and shouted something, but Shores didn't catch what the old man said. He thought the Shoshone would veer east or west, but to his consternation Red Fox reined toward the center of the herd.

Madness, Shores thought. Then he realized that by mingling with the buffalo, they might shake the Sioux. But it had to be done just right, and the chance of a mishap was high.

Red Fox started whooping and hollering and waving an arm. Shores followed suit. But the buffalo were slow responding. They had just run miles and were tired, which made them less prone to spook . . . until a bull snorted and bobbed its immense head, and, like a shaggy, churning wave, the entire herd galvanized into motion and resumed stampeding.

Shores and the Shoshone were in among them within moments. Shores had buffalo to the right, buffalo to the left. Their driving hooves hammered the ground like anvils, almost drowning out the grunts that came from all sides. Their musty, sweaty scent was overpowering.

A horn came perilously close to ripping open the claybank. Shores had never been so scared. Not even when he was eight and he'd gone down into the root cellar and was confronted by a coiled rattlesnake. Not even when he was twenty and a criminal he had cornered in a darkened room pulled a knife on him. He was so scared, he couldn't think, couldn't do anything other than ride and hope to God he made it out alive.

Dust was everywhere once again. Shores glimpsed Red Fox grinning that inane grin of his. He glanced down into the dark eye of a buffalo and saw the eye blink. It made his skin crawl. Why, he couldn't say. Maybe it was fear. Or maybe it was being so close to creatures he had no business being this close to. Their size, their power, their *strangeness* chilled his soul.

Shores lost track of how long they ran with the herd. It seemed hours but couldn't have been more than five or ten minutes. Then Red Fox yipped and motioned and reined to the east, toward where the herd was thinner. His breath catching in his throat, Shores did likewise. He had to trust the old Indian's judgment. This was far beyond the realm of his own experience, far beyond anything he had ever done or ever contemplated doing.

The buffalo let them pass unhindered. None of the great shaggy heads turned to rend and rip.

Shores glanced back but couldn't see the Sioux for

the dust. Which meant they couldn't see him either. He glanced toward Red Fox, but now the Shoshone was also lost amid the billowing cloud.

Panic nipped at Shores, but he fought it down. They had been veering east, so he continued east. At least, he hoped it was east. It was hard to be completely sure.

Tense seconds ensued. Shores was about convinced they had become separated, when the dust parted and he saw Red Fox galloping through the last of the buffalo. Another few moments, and Shores was in the clear. They raced eastward for another half a mile without slowing, then drew rein.

The herd still thundered south. Nipping at its heels like a pack of wolves, visible at random moments, were the Sioux.

Red Fox smiled and made a comment in his own tongue.

"What?" Shores asked.

"Stupid Sioux," Red Fox said and laughed.

Shores didn't share the old man's glee. Their search had barely begun, yet twice this day he had been delivered from what he took to be certain death. *What next?* he wondered. And couldn't suppress a shudder.

Denver, Colorado Territory

Artemis Leeds had just finished renting a buggy to a handsome young couple who wanted to take an afternoon ride along Cherry Creek. He was out in front of the stable, watching to gauge how the young man handled the rig, when something jabbed him in the side hard enough to make him wince.

"I told you we would return."

"Mr. Gunther, I presume," Leeds said without turning. "Do us both a favor and leave before I report you to the police."

"For what? Talking to you?"

"You and I have nothing to discuss." Enough people were passing by that Leeds was confident Gunther wouldn't lay a hand on him. He had half a mind to march off to the Chief of Police and lodge a formal protest, but instead he turned and entered the livery. "I don't care to have you set foot on these premises again."

Leeds thought that would be the end of it. He heard hinges creak and turned to find Gunther's two associates closing the double doors. Gunther, smirking, had that polished cane of his across one shoulder. "Didn't you hear me?"

"Oh, my ears work fine, stableman. It is you who did not hear me yesterday when I said I need to find the boy who works for you. But I will give you one more chance. Where is he?"

"He never came back," Leeds bluffed. "If he has the nerve to show up after all this time, I'll fire him. I can't abide shirkers."

"And I can't abide liars." Gunther strolled closer. "You see, an acquaintance of ours has gotten word to us that he saw the boy and several others in this very stable this morning. I would have come sooner, but I was off looking for one of your employee's friends, an Italian named Anthony Fabrizio. You know him too, do you not?"

"I don't keep track of all of Charley Pickett's wayward acquaintances." Leeds saw the man called Hans lift the heavy bar. "What does he think he's doing? It's not closing time. Put that down!"

Hans paid no attention.

"You do not seem to appreciate the seriousness of the situation," Gunther said. "My employer, Mr. Radtke, is most determined to find Fabrizio and Pickett. *Most determined.*"

"You say that like it should be important to me."

Gunther took another step. "It never ceases to amaze me how some people refuse to listen to what others are saying."

"I've heard every word you've said."

"Ah. But did you *listen* to them? I have given you fair warning, stableman, but you won't heed. You have only yourself to blame for what happens if you do not answer my next question truthfully." Gunther paused. "Where is Charley Pickett?"

Leeds had put up with all he was about to. "For the last time, how should I know where the boy is, you overbearing, arrogant son of a—"

Gunther swung his cane. The *thunk* of the ivory knob striking Leeds's jaw was quite loud. Leeds collapsed, groaning, and sprawled on his side. "Hans, Oscar, pick him up," Gunther directed, and his two beefy subordinates seized the stableman's arms.

Leeds was conscious, but barely.

"Now then," Gunther said. "We will try this again. I didn't hit you hard enough to break your jaw, although I easily could have. You need your mouth to talk. You don't, however, need your knees."

Never in his life had Leeds felt such pain. He cried out, or tried to, but Hans clamped a thick hand over his mouth. Tears filled his eyes, more from frustration and outrage than the blow.

"When you are ready to tell me, you have only to nod." Gunther hefted the cane. "Bear in mind, I can do this the rest of the day if I have to. I can break every bone in your body one by one. Or do far worse. You *will* talk, whether you want to or not. Hold out as long as you can, but the information my employer needs will be mine. So, what will it be?"

Leeds would be hanged if he would cooperate. But neither did he care to be hit again. "What will you do to Charley when you find him?" he stalled.

"He is not our main interest. It is Fabrizio we want most. He stole from Mr. Radtke and must be made an example of. A man in Mr. Radtke's position cannot allow a slight like this to go unpunished."

"You won't harm Charley?"

"Your devotion to your stableboy is commendable but misplaced. Are you aware that he and Fabrizio are killers? Yes, that's right. The two men murdered in an alley the other night, both of whom worked for Mr. Radtke, were killed by your precious stableboy and his friend. And Mr. Radtke is a firm believer in an eye for an eye, a tooth for a tooth."

Leeds refused to believe it. He could never imagine Charley killing anyone. Tony, maybe, but he didn't know the other boy that well. "How do you know it wasn't the buffalo hunter who's to blame?"

Gunther blinked. "Who?"

"That buffalo hunter friend of theirs. He's as wild and woolly as they come. And he carries a Bowie knife." The newspaper article, Leeds remembered, had mentioned that the men in the alley were stabbed. He thought that by confusing Gunther and the others, he might induce them into lowering their guard, and he could break free. He had a derringer in his office, and he was not averse to using it.

Gunther appeared shocked. "The lout from Kincaid's! He baited us deliberately! And I never caught on."

"What?" Leeds was having difficulty focusing with so much pain coursing through him.

"I was played for a fool." Gunther's whole body shook with the severity of his anger. "The others must have been at Kincaid's too. They will pay for this insult." He poked his cane against Leeds's chest. "For the last time, stableman. Will you tell me where they are?"

Leeds held his chin high. "Do your worst. I'll never break."

But he was wrong, dreadfully wrong, and two hours later, when the handsome young couple who had gone for a buggy ride along Cherry Creek returned, they found his broken, bloody body with a pitchfork stuck in its chest.

Kincaid's normally did light business until six, when most of the regulars began flocking in. The time was five minutes till by the bronze clock above the mirror, and Ralph Kincaid was towel-drying the last of a batch of glasses he had washed in the kitchen basin when he sensed rather than heard someone come up behind him. "Eddy, is that you? I expected you to deliver those Saratoga chips this morning." Kincaid turned. "You!"

Ubel Gunther had one hand in a pants pocket and was twirling his cane with the other. "We need to have a few words, Mr. Kincaid."

Kincaid glanced at the two slabs of muscle flanking Gunther and debated trying to get past them to reach his shotgun out under the bar. "The kitchen is off limits to the public," he said, hoping his voice did not betray his nervousness.

"Surely you jest. Mr. Radtke has a one-eighth inter-

est in your establishment, does he not? Which would
make me a fellow employee." Gunther grew somber.
"How much can you tell me about that buffalo
hunter who had the audacity to pick a fight with
me yesterday?"

"Enos Howard? He's harmless except when he's
drinkin', and he's generally always drinkin'."

"Let me be the judge of how harmless he is."
Gunther came closer. So did the other two. "Share
with me all you know about him. Or must I have
Hans and Oscar persuade you?"

Ralph Kincaid was no fool. "Where should I
begin?"

Walter Radtke's office was a monument to luxury.
A mahogany desk was the centerpiece. The rest of
the furniture was black walnut and rosewood. Plush
wine red carpet covered the floor. A serpentine-back
sofa with a half-lyre armrest sat against one wall. It
too was red.

Red was also the color of Walter Radtke's face
when he was mad, and he was mad now. His jaw
muscles twitched as he stared at his top lieutenant.
One of his huge hands wrapped around the base of
a gilded desk lamp, and he started to lift it as if to
throw it but then set it back down. "No one does
what they did to me and gets away with it. No one."

"They must be miles out on the prairie by now,"
Ubel Gunther said.

"I don't care if they're halfway to St. Louis!" Radtke slammed his hand onto his desk. "If word of this
insult got out, my competitors would see it as a sign
of weakness. A man in my position cannot afford to
give that impression."

Gunther placed the tip of his cane on the carpet

and leaned on it. "Eventually they will tire of their silly hunt."

"Which could be weeks from now. And you have no guarantee they will return to Denver. They could go anywhere." Radtke shook his head. "No, waiting for them is not an option."

"Then what?"

Radtke drummed his fingers. "I want you to take Hans and Oscar and two others and go after them. Find them. Kill them."

"As always, I will obey. But I must point out that tracking is not among my many skills."

"Hire a tracker. Frontiersmen are as common as flies in this city. There is bound to be one competent enough. Pay him well to get the job done, and spare no expense in buying provisions and the best horses. You should overtake them with no difficulty."

"Just so I am clear on this, you want the girl killed too?"

Radtke thought before answering. "Her we can put to better use. A year in one of my boarding houses will teach her to choose her friends more carefully." He jabbed a finger at Gunther. "The thing I want most, the thing you must bring me without fail, is Tony Fabrizio's head in a sack. I want it as a keepsake."

Gunther smiled. "You don't want the heads of Pickett and Howard?"

"Them?" Radtke hissed in contempt. "Do as we usually do. Chop them into small pieces and leave the pieces for the coyotes and the vultures."

"Consider it done."

Chapter Ten

Eastern Colorado Territory

Charley Pickett was in heaven. For two whole days he had basked in Melissa Patterson's company. He had eaten with her, slept near her. They had talked more than ever before, with her doing nearly all the talking. He had tried to say more but couldn't stop his tongue from tying itself in knots.

The third morning dawned bright and crisp, the sky a cloudless azure crown. Which was quite a contrast from the day before, when, late in the afternoon, storm clouds had rolled in from the mountains and dumped inches of rain on their heads in less than half an hour.

"Let's hope there's not another gully washer today," Charley commented. "That last one soaked me to the"—he was going to say "skin" but at the last instant thought it might not be appropriate to say to a woman, so he changed it to—"hide."

Enos Howard guffawed. "That drizzle was nothin', pup. Why, I've seen storms that turned the heavens blacker than the bottom of a well, with thunder that shatters your eardrums and so many lightnin' bolts they fry the air you breathe."

"Do you ever tire of your tall tales?" Tony Fabrizio asked. It was his turn to lead their two pack horses, and he was securing the last of their packs.

"Do you ever tire of breathin'?" Enos responded and bobbed his chin. "Tie that rope tighter, you citified dandy, or the first rattlesnake we come across, those packs are liable to go flyin' hell-bent for everywhere."

Charley had hoped that once they were out on the prairie, Tony and Enos would stop bickering. But the pair got along about as well as a dog and a cat; they were forever scratching and snapping. "When will we get to see some buffalo?" he asked to divert their anger.

"Maybe never," Enos said. "Time was, this plain was choked with 'em. You couldn't take a step without steppin' in buffalo shit. But that was before we started killin' 'em off in droves."

Melissa, already on her horse, twisted in her saddle. "Do you ever feel guilty, Enos, about being a buffalo hunter?"

"How many times must I tell you, gal? I was a buffalo *runner*."

"What's the difference?" Melissa posed the question Charley was set to ask. "You shot buffalo."

"It makes a difference to those of us who have done it for a livin'." Enos forked his own mount, and they moved out. "We worked in crews. I was always the runner, or the shooter, as you'd call it, and had two to three skinners under me who took care of the butcherin'. And I mean to say, they had a hard time keepin' up. No one dropped buffs like me."

"Except Buffalo Billy Cody," Tony said.

Charley anticipated an outburst, but Howard surprised him.

"Yeah, well, soon that will be forgotten. Along with that shootin' match I lost to Jesse Comstock. When men talk about me from now on, they'll do it with respect."

Melissa responded. "So that's why you changed your mind. To redeem yourself."

"You have no notion of what it's like to be a laughingstock, Missy. Of havin' men point at you and whisper behind your back. It's enough to make a fella crawl into a bottle and never come out."

"So you're hoping if we collect the bounty on the Hoodoos, it will restore your reputation."

Enos took a plug of tobacco from his possibles bag and bit off a chaw. He chomped awhile before saying, "Whoever corrals the Hoodoos will be famous. Not just a little bit famous like that idiot who discovered Long's Peak by mistake, but a lot famous, like Carson and Hickok and men like that."

Charley had listened to their exchange with great interest. He marveled at Melissa's ability to see right through Howard and divine his intentions. She was smart, that girl, a lot smarter than he was. Which was fine by him. His grandpa liked to joke that a man should marry a woman who was twice as bright, and that way they would come out even. But now that he gave it more thought, he saw how it could work against him. After all, what would an intelligent girl like Melissa ever see in a country bumpkin like him?

Charley wasn't fooling himself. He wasn't the catch of the century. He was big and strong and as loyal as the year was long, but that was basically all he had going for him. He would never be a bank president. He would never be up to his armpits in money. The best anyone who married him could hope for was that he would keep food on the table and clothes on their backs.

Tony was speaking. "I misjudged you, Howard. I thought the only reason you came was the money."

"That too," Enos said with a grin. "But it's the chance to wipe my slate clean that counts more." He spat tobacco juice and wiped his chin with his sleeve. "Just so long as I fight shy of Denver from here on out."

"I knew it!" Charley declared. "That five hundred dollars was ill-gotten gains."

"How did you get the money, Enos?" Melissa asked.

Howard chuckled. "Before I was a buffalo runner, girl, I tried my hand at a lot of things. Trappin'. Scoutin'. Guidin'. Even prospectin'. One time, down Durango way, I found what I thought was the richest gold strike since Hector was a pup. Turned out to be pyrite, though. Fool's gold, folks call it. I have several pokes of the stuff."

Tony yanked on the lead rope to keep the pack animals moving. "Why hang on to worthless ore?"

"Because not everyone knows it's worthless. A greener can't tell fool's gold from the real article. So now and then I would sell nuggets to pilgrims fresh off the stage from back East." Enos's right cheek bulged as if he had an apple in his mouth. "Last night I made the rounds of a few saloons until I found me a tipsy fella willin' to part with enough money to buy my claim in a genuine gold mine."

"Land sakes!" Melissa declared, but she didn't sound especially scandalized. "You swindled him."

"That I did, Missy. For the paltry sum of five hundred dollars, a certain gent from Boston is now the proud owner of the west slope of Long's Peak."

Enos, Melissa, and Tony laughed. But not Charley. Cheating people was not something he took lightly. His parents had taught him that the only way to get ahead in the world was by working hard and doing right. "Swindlin' isn't anything to laugh at."

"That it's not, pup!" Enos said. "Swindlin' should be held in the respect which it deserves."

"Respect?" Charley scoffed.

"Sure. Swindlin' is what our country is based on. We swindled it away from the Injuns, didn't we? And we've been swindlin' one another ever since."

"That's the silliest thing you've said yet."

"Is it? Then answer me this, boy. What do you call it when the government takes land to build a railroad whether the people who own the land like it or not? A swindle. What do you call it when a bank can charge twenty-four percent interest on a loan? A swindle. Or when a merchant gets cigars for two cents and sells them for ten cents? Another swindle. Or how about when a man buys land for a dollar an acre and sells it for twenty an acre, as all those speculators did in Denver?"

"A swindle," Charley conceded when Enos waited for him to answer.

"Exactly. Swindlin' is what Americans do best. So don't look down your nose at me for takin' advantage of that Yankee. If God didn't want people swindled, He wouldn't have made them so stupid."

Tony nodded. "For once he and I agree, my friend. It is why I feel no shame over selling trough water to those who took it for granted it was something else."

Enos cackled. "There's more to like about you than

I figured, Fabrizio. Any man who will swindle another is all right in my book."

Charley was hard-pressed to decide which upset him more: that they thought it was all right to cheat people, or that Melissa was grinning as if all this talking of swindling were great fun.

"Say! Lookee there!" Enos had risen in the stirrups and was staring to the southeast. "Just what I need."

Charley looked. Off in the distance were some antelope. They had been seeing more and more of the elusive animals the farther they went. Usually the antelope bounded off before they came close. These were about five hundred yards away and so far were content to stay and graze.

Enos slid off his horse and handed the reins to Charley. "Hold on tight. Some of these nags might spook when Clarabelle goes off."

"You named your rifle?" Melissa said.

"Why not? Lots of runners do. It was good enough for Davy Crockett, wasn't it? He called his Old Betsy." Enos caressed his Sharps. "Mine is named after a fallen dove I took a shine to in St. Louis. The greatest gal who ever lived. She could go all night and half the next day and still have enough steam in her engine for a wild night on the town."

Charley coughed and nodded at Melissa to remind Howard yet again that there was a lady in their midst. But he'd have done better taking a sledgehammer to Howard's thick skull.

"Yessir," Enos said fondly, "Clarabelle was a real peach. I wanted to take her for my wife. I visited her every chance I got and asked her every time, but she kept tellin' me I could do better. Damn her and her hard head anyhow." He scowled.

"What happened?" Melissa inquired.

"She came down with consumption and died on me. I wanted to die too. Instead, I bedded every other gal in the boardin' house in Clarabelle's honor."

"I'm sure she would have appreciated that," Charley said and was disappointed no one seemed to realize he was poking fun.

Enos nodded. "That she would, boy. Clarabelle had a zest for life no woman has ever matched. She could see beauty in little things, like the flutter of a moth at the window or the warblin' of a bird. Sunsets about put her in deliriums of joy." His eyes were misting over. "She was one of a kind, a marvel of nature, and I miss her every hour I draw a breath."

"How romantic!" Melissa gushed.

"In the Old Country we would say you were struck by the lightning bolt," Tony remarked.

Enos glanced at him. "That's exactly what it was. When I was with her, I felt tingles where I'd never felt tingles before. That gal could curl my toes with a look and a wink. It's the only time I think I've ever truly been in love. Although there have been six or seven other times I've come close."

"Do you make it a habit to visit boardin' houses?" Charley's parson back in Kentucky had regularly denounced harlots and those who visited them as lewd and sinful. Truth was though, he had thought about visiting a bawdy house himself but had never mustered the nerve. One time he got as far as the walk leading up to a fancy house in Denver when a vision of loveliness in a second-floor window whistled at him and waved a little pink handkerchief. It scared him so, he went and sat on a bench near the creek until his blood stopped boiling in his veins.

"Sure," Enos answered. "Doesn't everyone? We're human, ain't we? We've got needs. When we're hungry, we need to eat. When we're thirsty, we need to drink. When we're cravin' companionship, we need to—"

"That will be quite enough," Charley said.

Enos chuckled. "You're sure a caution. I like you, pup, but you've got a heap of learnin' to do. Life ain't no fairy tale with ladies in castles waitin' for their knights in shinin' armor to come sweep 'em off their dainty feet. Life is sweat and misery and more sweat and joy, and anything else is dribblin's from the pie."

Much to Charley's annoyance, Melissa was gazing at Howard as if he were a fount of worldly wisdom. "That's your opinion. Folks are entitled to opinions of their own, last I heard."

"No need to get all frothy on me. Sure, a man can have all the opinions he wants. But opinions are like buffalo chips. There are a million of 'em, and it doesn't do to say one is any better than the other. They're all made of the same manure."

Melissa and Tony burst out laughing, but not Charley. He would never share the buffalo hunter's sour outlook on things. There had to be more to life than Enos let on. There just *had* to. "Shouldn't you take a shot at those antelope before they wander clear to Texas?"

"Is that your way of tellin' me I'm afflicted with leaky mouth?" Enos grinned. "I reckon I am at that. But that's why God gave the rest of you ears."

Melissa raised a hand to shield her eyes. "That will be quite a shot."

"Hardly, Missy. Not when they're so close you can practically reach out and touch 'em. Any runner worth his salt could pick those critters off without half tryin'." Turning to his horse, Howard opened a saddlebag, took out a spyglass, and handed it to Charley. "Do the honors. Let me know exactly where the slug hits."

Charley extended the telescope to its full length and pressed it to his right eye. The eyepiece was adjustable, permitting him to focus on the prong-horns with perfect clarity. There were eight all told, each with the distinctive markings of their kind: reddish-brown on their upper bodies and along the outside of their legs, white across their lower sides, their chests, and their rumps. Something peculiar struck him. "I don't see any males."

Enos had taken a box of shells from a pocket in his buffalo coat and set it on the ground. "You won't. This time of year, bucks and does keep to themselves. In the fall, when the males are in rut, they'll get together again. Come wintertime, there are herds of a hundred or more." He squinted toward the ante-lope. "I'll pick a big doe. No sense in deprivin' a young one of the few years of life it might have left."

"How thoughtful of you, Enos," Melissa said.

"The young ones don't have much meat on 'em anyway." Howard opened the box and removed a linen cartridge. "Most runners don't mind buyin' a rifle off a store rack, but not me. Clarabelle here is custom-made. I got tired of shootin' buffs and not havin' 'em drop. The calibers most rifles are made in just don't have enough wallop. So I had Clarabelle made in .45-90."

Charley had used a .36 caliber rifle to hunt deer, so he had a fair inkling of how powerful Clarabelle must be and said so.

"She gets the job done, that's for sure. But if I had it to do over again, I'd have her made in .50-90 or more. There's been a few times when she's taken two shots to drop a buff, which is one too many." Enos worked the trigger guard, which doubled as a lever, lowering the breechblock. He inserted the long cartridge and moved the trigger guard back in place.

"Why does your rifle have two triggers?" Tony asked. "It only has one barrel."

Enos held out Clarabelle so they could all see. "After I thumb back the hammer, I squeeze the second trigger, which sets the first to what runners call a 'hair trigger.' The slightest squeeze and Clarabelle will go off. Makes it a lot easier to hit what I aim at."

"I'm not sure I understand," Melissa said. "How does that help you be more accurate?"

"Most triggers, Missy, have a lot of pull to 'em. You have to squeeze sort of hard. That tends to make a gun jerk, and that's the last thing you want in a huntin' rifle." Enos patted his Sharps. "With Clarabelle's, there's no jerkin' when I squeeze the hair trigger. The barrel stays nice and steady."

"Whenever you're ready," Charley said. He hadn't taken his eye off the antelope. Every twitch of an ear, every blink of an eye, was as plain as if he were standing next to them.

Enos tucked the Sharps to his shoulder and elevated the rear sights. "At this range I don't hardly need to bother," he bragged and sighted anyway. He stood rock-still. His breathing slowed. The hammer made a loud *click* when he pulled it back. He curled his forefinger around the rear trigger and squeezed, setting the first, then slid his finger to the first trigger but was careful not to touch it.

Charley was trying to watch Enos out of one eye and the pronghorns out of the other. "Which one are you fixin' to shoot?"

"The one on the far right."

It was a big doe. Charley could see her lips move when she dipped her head to nip grass. Raising it again, she stared in their direction. Standing side-on, she was as perfect a target as a man could ask for. He braced for the shot.

When it came, it was thunder unleashed. The loudest Charley had ever heard. At the boom, the pack animals whinnied, and one tried to rear, but Tony, thinking fast, gripped the lead rope with both hands and held on.

Charley had a problem of his own. His bay shied, and to maintain control he had to lower the telescope and tighten his hold on the reins. "There, there," he soothed. "Take it easy."

The blast rolled off across the prairie. Charley figured the rest of the pronghorns would be in full flight, but when he raised the spyglass, they were *all* right where they had been. Including the big doe, contentedly chewing grass. "I think you missed, Enos."

Howard was squinting at the antelope in disbelief. "It's been a spell. I must be more out of practice than I reckoned." He went through the motions of loading and setting the hair trigger.

This time only one of the pack animals acted up.

Charley never took the telescope off the big doe. She was staring at them all the while, as calm as could be. "I think you missed again."

Enos held Clarabelle at arm's length and looked at her like she had betrayed him. "This just can't be." He examined the sights, then muttered and marched to the pack horses. From one he took a metal tripod, which he unfolded and set up. On the top was a notch or groove into which he slid Clarabelle's barrel.

Melissa asked, "Does that help your aim much?"

"I've never missed when usin' it."

Charley glanced at Tony, who was as puzzled as he was, then out at the pronghorns. There had to be a logical explanation. For all his boasting, Enos's reputation as a marksman was well established. Thousands of buffalo had fallen to his Sharps, to say nothing of the target matches he had won before that fateful day he lost to Jesse Comstock.

"Shootin' is like anything else," Enos was saying while reloading. "If'n a man doesn't keep his hand in, he's apt to become a mite rusty." He squinted at the pronghorns. "Damned peculiar how they're just standin' there. But they'll do that sometimes."

Charley held his breath when Enos took aim, but he had to let it out again after a couple of minutes passed and no shot rang out. Enos was being absolutely certain. Under no conceivable circumstances could the next shot miss.

Yet it did.

Enos slowly lowered Clarabelle. He shut his eyes, took a step, and plunked down on his backside as if his legs had been knocked out from under him. "God, no. I thought it was all in my head, but it wasn't!"

Charley didn't like the sound of that. Dismounting, he hunkered beside the distraught frontiersman. "Thought what was all in your head?"

"The fuzziness." Enos placed Clarabelle in his lap. "For the last six months or so, things at a distance tend to get fuzzy on me. I first noticed it when I couldn't read the *Rocky Mountain News* sign from my shack like I always could."

"Your eyes are going out on you?" Charley could have slugged him. "Why didn't you mention it sooner?" Their whole manhunting scheme depended on Enos's ability to drop the Hoodoos from a safe distance.

Enos shrugged. "I figured it was all that city air gettin' to me. All that wood and coal smoke. Or maybe all the bug juice I was guzzlin'. Or both." He gazed at the clear sky. "Out here I thought it would be different. I thought I would be my old self again."

Tony climbed down but held on to the lead rope. "This changes everything," he told Charley. "You know that, don't you?"

"Let's not be hasty." This from Melissa, who joined them. "We've invested too much to turn back now."

"What will we do when we catch up to the Hoodoos? Beat them with sticks?" Tony brushed his hand across the revolver at his waist, a Massachusetts Arms Company .31 caliber patterned after a British version. "I haven't even shot this yet."

Charley looked down at his own holster. He had chosen a nickel-plated Allen & Wheelock Army .44 revolver. It was big and cumbersome, but it could knock a man down at fifty feet. "All we need is a little practice."

Melissa drew her pistol, a .31 caliber T. W. Cofer model. She had chosen it because it was "pretty"; it had walnut grips, and the barrel, cylinder, trigger, and hammer were nickel-plated, while the side plates, as well as the back strap and the top strap, were bronzed. "Now is as good a time as any to start. Charley, fetch some rocks."

Charley hopped to obey. He gathered up four about the size of his fist and deposited them in a row twenty paces out. "Who wants to go first?"

"I will," Melissa volunteered. Adopting a two-handed grip, she took aim, her left eye closed, the tip of her tongue sticking between her lips. Her trigger finger tightened, but the pistol didn't go off.

"Remember," Charley said. "It's single-action. You have to cock the hammer before you can shoot."

"I know that!" Her cheeks red, Melissa pulled the hammer back and set herself. When she fired, her arms jerked, and she turned her face away.

Five yards past the rocks, dirt spewed in a geyser.

"Permit me." Tony drew his pistol. He kept both eyes open when he shot, but he fared no better.

Charley looked at Enos, hoping the hunter would share some tips on how to shoot, but Howard was mired in self-pity. Unlimbering the .44, Charley tried to twirl it as he had seen some do. It slipped from his finger and fell on his foot. Snatching it up, he smiled sheepishly at Melissa and extended his right arm. Only then did he realize the pistol lacked sights. It had no front bead, no rear sight, nothing. He had chosen one of the few models that didn't have any. Looking down the barrel, he fired. His shot added another cloud of gunsmoke. It also left the rocks untouched.

"Not bad for our first try," Melissa encouraged them. "It will be weeks before we find the Hoodoos. All the time in the world to hone our skill."

"What skill?" Tony added some harsh words in Italian. "A ten-year-old with a slingshot could beat us."

Charley hated to admit it, but his friend was right. It would take a miracle for them to hit anything smaller than the broad side of a stagecoach. And miracles were in short supply.

Chapter Eleven

Painted Rock
Kansas

The settlement of Painted Rock owed its existence to two mistakes. The second was made by six families from Pennsylvania who believed they could travel from St. Joseph, Missouri, to Denver, Colorado, on their own. They refused to pay what they viewed as exorbitant fees charged by professional guides.

Their leader, Floyd Havershaw, a blacksmith, summed up their feelings best when he stood on a crate in St. Jo's public square and declared, "How hard can it be? Kansas is as flat as a flapjack, and eastern Colorado doesn't have a hill higher than I can spit over. I say we head due west and trust in Providence to watch over us."

Two wagon wheels broke in the first ten miles. A week later, half their horses ran off one night when the livestock was left untended, and it took four days to gather them up. Jack Taylor broke his foot when he accidently ran over it with his Conestoga. And Floyd Havershaw nearly lost a hand when the anvil in his wagon shifted and fell on it.

According to Floyd's map, they could shave a couple of hundred miles off their journey if they left the main trail and bore on a more southerly heading. Floyd had traced the map himself from an old book in the Scranton public library, so he had every confidence in it. They were supposed to strike the North Fork of the Solomon River after a few days but didn't. Floyd told everyone not to worry, that they were sure to strike the South Fork of the Solomon River in a few more days, and they would follow it west. Only the South Fork wasn't where the map said it should be either. That didn't stop them. They took their bearings by the sun and forged on.

The first mistake had been made by Sam Stowe years earlier. A Civil War veteran, he took the tales of gold nuggets in the Rockies waiting to be plucked off the ground seriously enough to ride a mule from Indiana to Colorado. Sam was so convinced he would strike it rich, he sold all his worldly goods for the provisions he needed. When he reached the mountains and discovered the gold wasn't waiting to jump into his arms, he became discouraged, turned right around, and headed for Indiana.

From another argonaut, Sam heard of a remarkable sight he hankered to see on his way home. As a small boy he had liked to collect unusual rocks. When he enlisted, he had two shelves crammed with everything from pieces of ruby quartz to marble to basalt. So when told about the mystery rock, he couldn't resist.

Not far from the Colorado border, a secondary trail looped through northwest Kansas, passing near a boulder as large as a log cabin. Remarkable for its size, it was unique in another respect. Every square inch was covered by strange paintings. Who had painted them was a mystery. The emigrants certainly didn't know. Nor did the Arapahos, the Kansa, or the Osage. The paintings had been there for as long as anyone in their tribes could remember.

Fittingly, the boulder became known as Painted Rock.

Sam found it without any problem, perched atop the north bank of a meandering stream. He spent the rest of that day and all of the next scrambling over it on his hands and knees, studying the figures and symbols. There were men with beaks and wings, animals with spear-shaped plates on their backs, enormous birds with buffalo in their talons. There were circles within circles and swirls within swirls. There were letters that did not resemble any letters known. Sam had never seen anything like it.

The following morning, Sam made his fateful mistake. He was preparing to depart and decided to clean his rifle. Only he forgot it was loaded. The slug tore off three toes and part of his foot. It wouldn't have been so bad except he was sitting with his boots touching Painted Rock, and the slug flattened when it hit the boulder and ricocheted out.

Sam needed two weeks to heal to where he could hobble with a crutch. By then he had thought it over and decided the accident was an omen. He had fallen in love with the prairie in general and that spot in particular. Always a loner by nature, it was right in keeping with his character to build a cabin and stay. He bought several cows and other essentials from emigrants on the main trail and was set.

The Indians didn't bother him. They watched from a distance as he spent every spare moment scampering over Painted Rock and decided that either his brain was in a whirl, which was their way of saying he was crazy, or he had been touched by the Great Mystery. In either case, it would be bad medicine to harm him.

Sam was content to live out his life a hermit, but it wasn't meant to be. Floyd Havershaw and the six wagons from Pennsylvania showed up. The pilgrims held a meeting and decided they had gone far enough. The ground was fertile, the stream ran year-round, and game was abundant. Overnight, Painted Rock became a settlement.

Sam wasn't pleased. He told them it was a free country, and they could do as they wanted, but they were to stay the hell away from his boulder or else.

Word of the new settlement spread. Most wagon trains stuck to the main trail, but now and again a small train or individual wagons rolled into Painted Rock to buy supplies. In addition to Sam's cabin, it now boasted six frame homes, Floyd Havershaw's combination blacksmith shop and stable, Jack Taylor's general store, and Tom Shadley's saloon, the Lucky Star.

The women of Painted Rock wanted the saloon shut down, but the men stood firm. When the women pointed out the settlement was too small to keep a saloon in business, the men assured them they were up to the task. When the women complained the men would stay out drinking to all hours, the men responded that the saloon was mainly for socializing, but to make the women happy they would close it every night at eleven.

All went well until Abigail Reece and Susie Kline arrived. They had been run out of Independence for lewd and lascivious acts the local newspaper would not dare print and were on their way to Denver to take up employment at a bawdy house. Painted Rock suited them better. Both ladies were long at the tooth, with Susie pushing fifty, but well preserved. Abigail looked fifteen years younger than she was and swore by Aunt Gertrude's Facial Cream and Life Extender.

The decent women in Painted Rock protested when the two doves took up residence above the saloon. Their husbands made mention of Christian charity and promised the doves would share no more than drinks and talk.

No one in Painted Rock paid much attention to five strangers who stayed overnight from time to time. They looked like ordinary cowboys. Their white-haired leader said they were cattle buyers. The youngest favored pearl-handled Colts and often entertained the settlement's children by setting up empty bottles on the bank of Painted Creek and putting on a show of speed and skill that dazzled his young audience.

The settlers had heard of the Hoodoos. Everyone had. But no one connected the five strangers who passed through every few months with the five notorious horse thieves until Abigail confided to Tom Shadley, the saloon owner, that the young one with the pearl-handled pistols was Kid Falon.

Shadley told Floyd Havershaw, and Havershaw called a town meeting. Every adult was obliged to attend, including Sam Stowe, who continued to resent the settlement and everyone in it and wished they would all come down with the plague and die.

"We have us a predicament," Floyd began and related what he had learned but not the name of the person who had discovered the Kid's identity or how she had discovered it. "The Hoodoos are wanted in four territories. They're thieves and killers, and we've been harboring them. What do we do about it?"

"Why should we do anything?" Jack Taylor said. "They've never bothered us. They come, they drink, they sleep, they ride off. That's it. I say let them go on doing as they please, and we'll all live longer."

Tom Shadley stood. "I, for one, wouldn't care to rile them. We've all heard the stories about how many men they've killed. So long as they're peaceable, why should we care who they are or what they do?"

"Bunch of yellow curs," Sam Stowe groused. "Is this why you called me away from my stove and my supper? If any of you had a lick of gumption, you would do what any law-abiding citizen should do and send word to the army. In case you haven't heard, your precious Hoodoos killed a couple of soldiers a while ago, and there's a seven thousand dollar bounty on their miserable heads." Sam rose and limped toward the door. "I might try to collect it my own self."

"Sam, wait!" Floyd called in vain.

"Someone had better set that grump straight, or he'll cause us no end of grief," Tom Shadley said.

"I'll try," Jack Taylor offered. "I'm the only one in town he'll talk to anyhow."

Over an hour was spent debating how best to deal with the Hoodoos. The only decision they reached was to put off making a decision for another week to give everyone time to mull it over.

"There's no rush," Floyd said. "It's only been three weeks since they were here last. Generally, they don't visit us but once every couple of months."

The very next day, the Hoodoos rode in.

It was early afternoon, and the five hard cases were caked with the dust of many miles. After putting up their horses at Floyd Havershaw's establishment and paying to have their mounts fed and tended to, they repaired to the Lucky Star.

"Drinks all around," Brock Alvord said as they lined up at the bar.

"Make mine a bottle," Big Ben Brody commanded.

Tom Shadley had been taking inventory when they came in. He took inventory once a day just to have something to do. "Sure thing, Mr. Alvord." Years ago Tom had learned the secret to keeping his customers happy was to always remember their favorite brands. It made them feel like they were important enough for him to go to the trouble. He selected two bottles and turned. "Here you go."

The Hoodoos were as straight as rails and as stern-faced as temperance pushers. "Is something the matter?" Tom asked.

"How did you find out who I am?" Brock Alvord demanded. "I never told you."

Kid Falon had his hands on his pearl-handled Colts. "I reckon if you know, everybody must know."

"And here we thought they were as dumb as stumps and would never figure it out." Curly Means laughed.

"Maybe we should clean out this two-bit town," Jack Noonon suggested.

Brock Alvord took the bottles, passed one to Big Ben Brody, and opened the other. "How about it, barkeep? Should we be mad at you folks for tryin' to trick us?"

"We only found out last night!" Shadley bleated. "And it doesn't make any difference to us who you boys are. You've never mistreated anyone here. Fact is, I like you fellas."

Curley Means grinned and nudged Noonan. "Did you hear that, Missouri? He likes us. Why don't you hop over the bar and give him a big kiss?"

"Why don't I cut off your carrot and shove it down your throat?"

Big Ben Brody roared, and the tension evaporated. The Hoodoos relaxed. Alvord poured drinks.

Tom Shadley mopped perspiration from his balding pate with his apron and thanked God for his deliverance.

Shoes clacked on the stairs. Down sashayed Abigail and Susie in their finest frillery. They had brushed their hair and splashed on so much perfume the entire saloon filled with the musky fragrance.

"Abby, darlin'!" Kid Falon hollered. Lifting her, he swung her completely around and planted a kiss on her full red lips. "Have you missed me? You're all I've thought about since I left."

"I'll vouch for that," Curly Means said.

Susie ambled over to Curly and contrived to rub her hip against his. "How about buying a girl a drink, handsome?"

Curly raised a finger to the brim of his hat. "Thanks for the offer, ma'am, but there are two things I never have any truck with. One is dogs. The other is anything and everything female."

"How about you?" Susie said to Noonan.

"How about me?" Big Ben said. Bottle in hand, he looped a huge arm around her slender waist. "It's about time the two of us were better acquainted."

Kid Falon steered Abigail toward a table. "You and me need to talk, beautiful. I've been doin' a lot of thinkin', and there's something important I want to say." He held out a chair for her, then dragged his close enough that the two chairs touched.

Abigail gave a toss of her long red hair. A sad look crept into her blue eyes, and she said softly, "I'd rather you didn't."

"Huh? You don't even know what I'm about to say." The Kid lifted his voice to bawl, "Fetch us a bottle of our own over here, Shadley, and be quick about it!"

As soon as Tom scurried off, Abigail leaned forward and placed a hand on the Kid's arm. "Do you have any idea how old I am?"

"What's that got to do with anything?" Falon kissed her on the cheek. "You're the prettiest filly this side of the Divide, and I have big plans for you and me."

"Kid, listen to me."

Falon took both her hands in his and squeezed. "I've never met a girl like you. That last time, when we spent all night in your room, was the best night of my life. I want more nights like that, Abby. I want them to never end. I've pondered it considerable, and I've decided I'd like to be your man permanent-like, if you'll have me."

"First off, I'm a woman, not a girl. Second, you don't know a damn thing about me. Third, you should drink at a lot more troughs before you decide to hitch your horse to just one. Fourth, one night isn't the same as true love. Fifth, and this is the most important, get it through your handsome head that I'm old enough to be your ma."

"My ma ain't that old," the Kid responded. "Besides, age don't hardly matter. Curly says it's the heart that counts, and my heart is fit to burst with how I feel about you." Hope lit his young face like a flame flaring on a candle. "What do you say? We'll rustle us up a parson and do this proper."

"You're loco."

Kid Falon slid his hands off hers and frowned. "Don't talk like that, Abby. I've never opened up to anyone like I'm openin' up to you, and I don't much like havin' my face slapped."

"Kid, Kid, Kid," Abigail said tenderly and shook her head. "What am I to do with you? How can I make you understand? I've seen this sort of puppy love more times than I can count. I'm one of the first women you ever had, aren't I? I made you feel good, real good, and you're mistaking that good feeling for love. But it's not. There's a fancy word for it a drummer told me once. Infatuation. That's what ails you. In-fat-u-a-tion."

The Kid's frown became a scowl. "I've had plenty of women. You hear me? Plenty! Don't flatter yourself you're the first. As for that infatted business, what the hell does a damn drummer know anyhow? All they do is jabber. Hell, if a drummer walked through that door right now, he'd be dead before he took two steps."

"This one sold encyclopedias. He knew a lot about darned-near everything. Why, he could recite all the Presidents' birthdays from memory."

"Bid deal. So he could read. I can read too. I got as far as the sixth grade, and my teacher always said I was one of the smartest in her class. Smart enough to know when I care for someone, and when I don't." Now the Kid was glowering. "You're lucky I don't get up from this table and never talk to you again."

Abigail reached for him, but he pulled away. "Please, Kid. Calm down. I didn't mean to upset you."

"Well, you damn sure did. I haven't been this mad since that time a cowboy stepped on my foot at a dance and then had the gall to say I stepped on his. It was his fault, him bouncin' around with his gal like they was tryin' to stomp snakes."

"You're getting yourself agitated," Abigail said.

"So what? I can agitate myself if I damn well want to." Kid Falon looked around the room and hitched at his gunbelt. "I have me half a notion to kill someone just for the killin'."

"Please, no." Abigail glanced at Brock Alvord, but he was absorbed in a discussion with Tom Shadley. "Everyone would blame me for settin' you off."

"There won't be anyone left to blame you for nothin'," the Kid declared.

In her anxiety, Abigail clutched his arm. "You would kill women and children? I know you like to throw lead, but that's despicable. How can you expect me to go on caring for a man who would do such a thing?"

"Then you do care!" The Kid clasped her to him and kissed her in a heated display of passion.

Abigail tried to pry loose, but the Kid swooped her onto his lap and nuzzled her ear. "What's that scent you always wear? I swear, I couldn't get it out of my nose the whole time I was away. Even when I was downwind of Big Ben after a meal of beans, all I'd smell was you."

"I'm flattered." Abigail stopped resisting, removed his wide-brimmed hat, and set it on the table. "But I still think you're loco. It will never work. Not with the life you lead and the life I lead. We won't get to see each other but for short spells."

"Who says I aim to steal horses the rest of my life?" Kid Falon playfully ran a hand along her thigh. "And who says you'll go on workin' in saloons? As soon as we're hitched, that's all over. We'll buy you a house, and you can cook and mend my clothes and do all the stuff other women do for their menfolk."

"Oh, Kid." Abigail chuckled. "I'm not the domestic type. Never have been, never will be." She ran a finger through his fine hair. "I've always had a restless streak. It's why I left home at fifteen and wound up workin' at a St. Louis whorehouse—"

Kid Falon suddenly gripped her by the shoulders and shook her fiercely. "Don't ever say that again. You ain't no whore."

"I'm not no preacher's wife neither. Hell, Kid. You're looking at me with blinders on. Don't make me out to be more than I am. I've been around the racetrack enough times to curl your toes."

The door opened, and in limped Sam Stowe. He was wearing his Union uniform and carrying a Spencer carbine. Two locals at a corner table saw him and blanched. "Hoodoos!" Sam cried and took another shuffling step. "Your days of thievin' and murderin' are over!"

Curly Means looked up from the game of solitaire he was playing and grinned. "Well, bless your Yankee soul! I could use some entertainment."

Big Ben Brody lowered his whiskey bottle. "What rock did that snail crawl out from under?"

"Painted Rock, most likely," Curly answered, and they laughed.

Not John Noonan. "If there's anything I hate worse than a scum-suckin' Yankee, I've yet to meet it."

"Hoodoos!" Sam cried again, limping farther into the room. "I'm placin' all of you under arrest!"

Tom Shadley looked fit to have a conniption. "Sam! What in God's name do you think you're doing? You don't have the authority to arrest anyone. Take that rifle and get out of here before you bring trouble down on all our heads."

Sam shook his. "I aim to lock these varmints in my root cellar and go for the army, and no one is stoppin' me. Someone in this town has to show they have some sand." He pointed the Spencer in the general direction of Big Ben Brody and John Noonan. "We'll start with you two. Unbuckle your gunbelts and step away from that table."

John Noonan swore. "This is plumb ridiculous. If you're not careful, I'll take that rifle from you and shove it up your ass."

"I'd pay to see that!" Curly Means whooped and fished in his pocket. "Here you are! Ten dollars! But only if you do it with his pants on."

Sam swiveled the Spencer toward the curly-mopped Hoodoo. "Quit your funnin'. None of you are takin' this serious enough. I fought in the war. I killed my share. I'm not a man to be trifled with."

"Oh, perish forbid," Curly said and laughed louder than ever.

Brock Alvord turned from the bar. Pushing his hat back, he raised a half-full glass. "Listen, mister. We don't want any trouble. Why don't you lean that rifle against the wall and come have a drink with me?"

"All I want from you is your gunbelt."

Tom Shadley came around the end of the counter. "Damn it, Sam. You're being unreasonable. We told you not to do this."

Sam Stowe trained the Spencer on him. "That's far enough. I don't trust you any more than I do these horse thieves. You're nothin' but a butt-peddler."

"I am not!"

"Fart in my ear, why don't you? How stupid do

you reckon I am? You've been tail-tradin' these two floozies to every man in Painted Rock except me. That's what I get for lettin' you folks settle here. There ain't one of you with the morals of Old Scratch hisself."

Kid Falon moved Abigail off his lap and stood. "I've listened to this coot long enough."

Sam leveled the Spencer at him. "You're the gunsman, ain't you? The one who thinks he's so slick. You with your silver-studded gunbelt and your hundred-dollar pistols and your whore on your—"

The Kid's right hand was at his side one instant, holding a Colt the next. The revolver spat lead and smoke.

Sam Stowe was smashed against the wall, a ragged hole in his left shoulder. His finger involuntarily tightened on the Spencer's trigger, and the rifle discharged.

Abigail Reece cried out, staggered, and gripped a chair to keep from falling. She stared at a scarlet smear spreading across her bosom and exclaimed, "I've been shot!"

"*Abby!*" Kid Falon swept her into his arms just as she collapsed. Her eyelids fluttered, and her full lips moved, but all that came out was a trickle of blood. "This can't be happenin'!"

Susie Kline, Brock Alvord, and Curly Means rushed over. Susie grasped her friend's hand and shook it. "Abby? Abby? Hang on! We'll find someone to help!"

"Kid," Abigail said, fixing her blue eyes on Falon. "For what it's worth, I'd have said yes." Then she gasped, stiffened, and died.

For a few moments, Kid Falon held her close. Then, his face as hard as granite, he gently laid her down.

He drew his Colts with slow deliberation. With equal deliberation he advanced on Sam Stowe, who had slumped to the floor but was conscious. "And you called us murderers?"

Sam weakly raised a blood-drenched hand. "Didn't mean—" he croaked.

"You son of a bitch." The Kid sent a slug into Sam Stowe's other shoulder. "You miserable rotten son of a bitch." He shot Sam in the right leg, then the left. He shot Sam in both arms. He shot Sam in both knees. By then he was standing over the bullet-riddled veteran, and with the same slow deliberation, he placed the muzzles of his Colts against Sam Stowe's eyes and squeezed both triggers.

The gunfire brought everyone in town. The men filed in, then stood back, aghast, as Kid Falon carried Abby to the bar and arranged her on her back with her hands cupped at her waist. "I should burn this whole place down!" he snarled. Instead, he drank himself into a stupor and the next morning had to be helped onto his horse by Brock Alvord.

Tom Shadley was at the hitch rail to see them off. "I hope you won't hold last night against us, Mr. Alvord. Sam always was a contrary cuss."

"See that the woman is buried. Have a headstone carved." Brock flipped a gold piece to him. "We'd stick around for the funeral, but we have somewhere to be in a few days." He gigged his horse, and all the Hoodoos but one trotted westward.

"The boss might be willin' to forgive and forget, but I ain't the type." Kid Falon jabbed a finger at Shadley. "You'll be seein' me again, barkeep. You and the rest of these sheep. Count on it."

Tom Shadley shivered.

Chapter Twelve

Southwest Nebraska Territory

Justice Department Agent William Shores and the Shoshone warrior Red Fox had been riding south for days with no sign of the outlaws Shores was after. Red Fox repeatedly reined up and climbed down to inspect the ground. When he was done, he always swung up, pointed, and declared, "Bad whites go that way, Brother John."

Shores was no tracker, but he had two good eyes, and he never saw tracks of any kind. He never saw the charred remains of a campfire or anything else that would prove they were really following the Hoodoos and not just aimlessly scouring the prairie. By the fifth day, he couldn't keep quiet any longer and turned to the old warrior in exasperation. "Are you sure we're still on their trail?"

"Yes, Brother John. They ten, twelve sleeps ahead. But we catch."

"I'd sure as hell better, or my boss will drown me in the Potomac." Shores scratched a bug bite on his neck. "That's assuming I live long enough to make it back to Washington. The mosquitoes last night about ate me alive." He scratched another bite. "I thought they are only found near water."

"We were near creek," Red Fox informed him.

"We were? Why didn't you say something? I could use a bath." Shores had not had one since Cheyenne, and he was a little on the rank side. Many Westerners, and, to be fair, many from the East, had an aversion to water. Regular bathing was believed to weaken the constitution and make one sickly. Shores disagreed. In Chicago he had grown fond of taking a hot bath daily. So much so, he now owned his very own porcelain tub.

"We be near other water soon, Brother John."

Shores was astounded by the Shoshone's remarkable knack for always knowing where water was. They hadn't gone thirsty once, for which he was grateful, given that daytime temperatures hovered near one hundred degrees. Today was no exception.

Removing his hat, Shores flicked a quick glance at the sun. "I don't see how you stand this heat." The old Indian never seemed to tire, never seemed to need water or to eat much food.

"Land hard, man hard," was Red Fox's reply.

"Where I'm from, a man doesn't need to be hard to survive. All it takes is money." And money was something Shores wouldn't mind having more of. The assistant director had promised that if he arrested or slew the Hoodoos, he would be entitled to the bounty. Seven thousand dollars was a sizeable amount.

"You whites and money. It be silly."

"You wouldn't think so if you were in my boots," Shores assured him. "Without it, a white man can't buy clothes to wear or food for the table."

"Make clothes, shoot food," was the warrior's solution.

"If only it were that simple." Every time Shores tried to get the white view across to the old man, he had the impression he was talking to a stone wall. Shoshone ways and white ways were worlds apart.

"Bear," Red Fox announced and extended an arm.

"What the hell do you mean, 'bear'?" Shores asked. But by then he had spotted it himself, a large, hairy form plodding ponderously toward them from the northeast. "Must be a black bear." The morning sun lent its coat a cinnamon hue, but he was well aware black bears were not always black.

"No. Grizzly."

"That can't be." The last Shores had heard, the only grizzlies left were in the mountains. Once quite numerous on the plains, they had been exterminated to the point where no one ever saw them there anymore.

"Grizzly," the Shoshone repeated. "Him see us, Brother John."

"Don't sit there and tell me you can see its face from here." Shores could barely tell it was a bear. He gauged the distance and wasn't worried. The grizzly had to be a quarter of a mile off, and their horses were fresh from a night of rest.

"Young bear," Red Fox told him. "Hungry bear."

"Can you hear its stomach growl?" Shores grinned. Sometimes the old Indian was too preposterous to be believed.

"No. It run now. Come eat us, Brother John."

Shores looked again, and damned if the grizzly wasn't loping toward them at a rapid if ungainly pace. "Damn stupid bear. It's too far off. It can never catch us."

"Stupid white man. Bear faster. Maybe catch horses." Red Fox slapped his heels against his paint and lit out of there like his life depended on it.

Perhaps it did. Shores was appalled to see the grizzly barreling toward them like a steam engine at full steam. He pricked the claybank with his spurs and galloped after the Shoshone. Every ten or fifteen seconds he looked over his shoulder and saw the grizzly had gained.

Soon the bear was close enough for Shores to distinguish its massive head and the bulging hump atop its broad front shoulders. *God, but the thing looks bigger than the claybank,* he thought. He had his Winchester in its scabbard, but he wasn't positive he could hit the bear while riding flat out. And hadn't he heard grizzly skulls were inches thick and deflected anything short of a cannon ball?

Red Fox was motioning for him to ride faster.

Shores knuckled down to do just that. He didn't glance at the grizzly again for a while, and when he did, he wished he hadn't. The bear was less than thirty feet behind him. Its maw gaped wide, exposing teeth as long as daggers.

Goosebumps prickled Shores's spine and up over his scalp. He imagined those teeth shearing into the claybank's rear legs and the horse taking a tumble. He imagined being spilled into the long grass. Imagined the grizzly reaching him before he could stand. He might get off a shot, maybe two, but it wouldn't be enough, and the bear would open him up like a husked ear of corn. "God help me," he breathed.

Red Fox had let go of his reins, twisted at the waist, and was notching an arrow to his bow. Pulling the string back to his cheek, he held the bow steady.

Shores was sure he could hear the *thud-thud-thud* of the grizzly's paws. He didn't want to look back again because he was afraid of what he would see, but, steeling himself, he did. And saw exactly what he had feared.

Mere yards separated the claybank's flying hooves from the grizzly's teeth and claws. The bear was huffing and puffing but showed no signs of slowing. If anything, the nearness of its prey had lent it speed.

Shores reached down for his rifle, but in so doing he shifted his weight in the saddle and the claybank slowed. Not much, only a trifle, yet it was sufficient incentive for the grizzly to take a prodigious bound and swipe at the claybank's hindquarters. The claybank squealed, and Shores felt its rear legs start to sweep out from under it. He tensed to try and leap clear. But somehow the claybank stayed up, and another few seconds took it out of the bear's reach.

The grizzly, though, wasn't about to quit. Uttering a roar that blistered Shores's ears, it surged forward.

Shores had momentarily forgotten about Red Fox. Now he saw the Shoshone let fly with the arrow. He glanced back, thinking the warrior had gone for the neck or the throat. The shaft, however, embedded itself in the ground in *front* of the bear. Shores couldn't believe Red Fox had missed. The old man nocked a second arrow and sent it after the first, and once again the arrow bit into the earth in front of the bear instead of into the bear's flesh.

So much for the stories about Indian prowess with a bow, Shores thought. Red Fox had to be the worst archer in the history of the world. Red Fox let loose a third shaft, and this too struck the ground in front of the bear. That was when Shores noticed something he hadn't noticed before. Each time an arrow hit, the grizzly slowed. And each time the bear slowed, the claybank and the paint increased their lead.

Another arrow flew. The grizzly swerved to avoid it and lurched to a stop. Its sides heaving, it watched them race off, voicing a snarl of frustration at being thwarted.

They hadn't gone two hundred yards when Red Fox reined up. Against his better judgment, Shores did the same, wheeling the claybank so he could keep an anxious eye on the bear. "Why did you stop so soon?"

"Need arrows, Brother John. Wait bear go. Then get them." The old Shoshone had the patient air of a parent enlightening a small child.

"But we're too close." Shores shucked his Winchester out. "If that monster comes after us again, we might not get away in time."

"Bear tired, Brother John. Bear go rest. See?"

The grizzly had turned and was shambling north, its head hung low in fatigue. It looked back at them once and grunted.

Shores had something else to gripe about. "Why in hell didn't you shoot that damn thing instead of into the ground? I'd rather it was dead so it won't ever go after anyone else."

"Take many arrows kill grizzly. By then grizzly eat you." Red Fox kneed the paint. "Get arrows now. Much work to make. Not lose them."

"I'll wait here." Shores was tired of the Shoshone treating him like an idiot who couldn't pull on his own boots without help. Maybe he wasn't a savvy frontiersman, but he was a grown man and could get by just fine on his own.

Dismounting, Shores squatted and angrily plucked at the buffalo grass. He would still rather be on his own. But without Red Fox it would take a lot longer to find the Hoodoos, and Shores dearly wanted to complete his assignment and return to Washington, D. C. and his comfortable life there. He had a nice apartment and nice clothes, he ate at nice restaurants. The wilderness held no appeal for him at all. Quite the opposite. Given his choice between a stroll down a tree-lined avenue and spending an entire day in the saddle sweating to death, constantly bothered by dust and insects, he would choose the city every time.

Shores supposed some would consider it sacrilege for a Texan to feel that way. But not all Texans lived in the country, and not all Texans thought a horse was God's gift to creation.

Red Fox, Shores saw, was taking his sweet time collecting the arrows. He picked at his teeth with a blade of grass and thought about what he would do with all the money he would get for the Hoodoos. Seven thousand dollars was enough for a nice house. For new clothes. For a gold watch. Or maybe he would just hold on to it. Eventually he hoped to meet the right young woman and settle down. But he was in no rush. Three Washington lovelies were dating him at the moment, and he liked the variety.

Shores straightened and stretched. He was feeling restless, which he attributed to his narrow escape from the bear. It had set his blood to racing, and it would be a while before he was his old self.

The claybank nuzzled him, and Shores patted its neck. It wasn't a bad horse, but he would be damned if he would let himself grow attached to it. Once his job was done, he would take it back to the livery in Cheyenne, and that would be that.

After a while, Red Fox rejoined him. "Better hurry, Brother John. Rain come later. Much rain, much thunder."

Shores tilted his head. There wasn't a cloud in the sky. "What makes you think we're in for a thunderstorm?"

The Shoshone sniffed. "Smell in air."

Shores sniffed a few times, but all he smelled was horse sweat and dust. "Do you read palms too?"

"Sorry, Brother John?"

"Never mind." Shores forked leather and clucked to the claybank. "Come on, old man. Let's pretend one of us knows what he's doing. I'd like to find the Hoodoos before next year."

"We find before half moon," Red Fox predicted. "Many die, Brother John. Maybe me. Maybe you."

Shores hoped the old man was wrong.

Denver
Colorado Territory

The building was in a crowded section of the city decent people avoided after dark. Ubel Gunther climbed to the third floor, avoiding litter and stains of questionable origin. The stink caused him to breathe through his mouth instead of his nose . . . when he breathed at all.

"These people live like swine," Hans remarked.

"Swine have their uses," Ubel observed. "Perhaps this one will be the right one."

"Mr. Radtke isn't happy it's taking us so long. He says we should have left days ago."

"Are you saying I'm not performing my duties efficiently? That you could do it better?"

Hans's beefy face mirrored sudden fear. "I would never say a thing like that, Mr. Gunther. I know my place. Mr. Radtke trusts you. That's enough for me."

"He trusts me enough to know these things can

take time," Ubel said, mollified. "It's not my fault most of these so-called scouts and trackers are drunks or braggarts or worse."

"The next one comes highly recommended."

"They all came highly recommended," Ubel reminded him. "And they have all proven worthless." He went from door to door until he came to Room 34. He rapped with his cane.

"Go away!" someone demanded. A female someone.

"Is this Mr. Trask's apartment? Mr. Blue Raven Trask?" Ubel put an ear to the door and heard rustling.

"Who are you? What do you want?"

"My name is Ubel Gunther. I would like to tender a business proposition. May I speak with him?"

The door opened a crack, and a brown eye peeked out. "That's all you want my husband for?"

"Why else would I seek him out?" Ubel was growing impatient with her timidity. "Please, madam. I am in need of a tracker, and I have been informed he is one of the best."

"There's none better," the woman confirmed. "But he told me not to tell anyone where he went."

"What harm can it do?"

"He's got enemies, mister. Maybe you didn't hear, but he's the one who tracked down those stage robbers a while back. Their friends have sworn to get even with him. Just the other night, one tried to knife him in the back."

This was news to Ubel. "What happened?"

"Blue cut him from ear to ear." The woman opened the door wider. She had a pleasant face and fine brown hair and was a half-blood. "I'm his missus, Nora."

Ubel doffed his bowler. "My name is Gunther. I'm extremely pleased to make your acquaintance. Would you prefer I leave an address where I can be reached, and you can have him contact me at his convenience?"

"You sure do spout a lot of fancy words." Nora gnawed on her lip. "No, you won't need to go to that much trouble. He's at the billiard hall at the end of the block. He'll be the one wearin' the headband. Tell him I sent you. And if I'm wrong about you, and you try to kill him, I'm sorry."

"Sorry you sent us?"

"Sorry for you, mister. He don't kill easy. He'll do the both of you before you can blink." Nora smiled and shut the door.

The billiard hall catered to some of Denver's rougher element. Hans stayed by the door as Ubel walked past two billiard tables to one at the rear. The glances cast his way were rife with distrust and more than a little envy. Leaning on his cane, he addressed a short, wiry man in buckskins and a rawhide headband. "Blue Raven Trask? Your wife said I would find you here. We've been told you are an excellent tracker, and my employer would like to hire your services."

Trask bent over the table to take a shot. Since it was against the law to wear a sidearm within the city limits, he did not appear to be wearing a revolver, although the right side of his shirt bulged suspiciously. On his other hip, wedged under his belt, was a tomahawk.

When there was no reply, Ubel said, "I would be grateful for a few moments so you can hear me out. I've already interviewed eight men who failed to impress me. I hope I'm not wasting my time again."

Trask stroked his stick, and the cue ball struck the seven with a sharp *crack*. The seven disappeared down a side pocket.

"You are the man, are you not, who rescued the farmer's wife abducted by Yellow Badger's renegades last year?"

"That was me." Trask changed position to take another shot.

"Where did you learn to track, if you don't mind my asking?"

"In case you can't tell, mister, I'm a breed. My father was Arapaho. He started teachin' me to read sign almost as soon as I could walk. There aren't but a handful of men better than me in the whole country."

"Then you are exactly the person I need." Ubel offered his hand. "Name your price and give me a list of what we will need, and we can be on our way."

Again Trask stroked the stick, and again a ball shot down a hole. "First things first. I don't take just any work. If it's not legal, find someone else."

"You have scruples?"

"Why wouldn't I? Because I'm half-and-half?" Trask unfurled and placed his hand on the tomahawk. "I should have known you would be one of *those*."

Ubel was unfazed by the slur. "I am not a bigot, Mr. Trask. The truth be known, the circumstances of your birth could not matter less to me. I simply meant that most of the men I have talked to so far have not shown your aversion to lawbreaking. They do not care what the job is."

"I'm not them. What are the particulars?"

"A young man whose name would be of no interest to you stole a considerable sum of money from my employer. This young man and several friends left Denver three days ago, traveling east. Naturally, my employer would like to have him tracked down. That is all there is to it. Are you interested?"

Trask wasn't one to bandy words. "It'll cost you two hundred dollars. In advance. I'll find them for you, you can bank on that. But once I do, my work is over, and I go my own way. Agreed?"

"Your terms are more than agreeable." Ubel offered his hand, and Blue Raven Trask shook.

"A few more things," the tracker said. "I don't take to being bossed around. You don't tell me what to do, ever. You ride when I say to ride, you stop when I say to stop. If we run into Injuns, you let me handle the palaverin'."

"When can we depart?"

"That depends on how many are going and how soon you can get your hands on what we'll need."

Walking side by side, they moved toward the street. Ubel saw Hans gesture at a cluster of men near the front. A broomstick in a vest and high boots had a knife in his hand, low down against his leg. The man was staring hard at Trask, but Trask did not appear to have noticed. "There will be four in my party, including myself." Ubel changed his grip on his cane so he could swing it like a club, then leaned to the side to whisper, "Mr. Trask, I think I should warn you—"

"No need," Trask said. He looked at the pool tables, at the window, at the portly proprietor, at everyone and everything except the men in the corner and the man holding the knife. "When he makes his move, get out of my way. This isn't your fight."

"Does it have something to do with the stage robbers your wife mentioned?"

Trask nodded. "Some folks just never learn." He was almost to the door, only a few yards from the men in the corner. Inexplicably, he turned his back to them, but as he did, his right hand drifted to his tomahawk.

The man in the vest didn't shout a threat or swear at Trask or give any other sign of his intentions. He simply raised his knife and sprang.

To Ubel, Trask's death seemed certain. The tracker had been a fool to turn his back like that. But then Trask spun with incredible swiftness, and the tomahawk met the descending stroke of his attacker's blade. Other patrons scrambled to make room as the man in the vest crouched and circled.

Trask stood as still as a statue. It was impossible to tell what he was thinking but not to tell that here was a man possessed of no fear whatsoever. He was as calm and as self-assured as a mountain lion.

"You were warned not to go after my cousins." The man in the vest broke his silence. "They'll spend eleven years in prison, thanks to you."

"I hope they remember to send flowers for your grave, Roarch," Trask said. Me, I plan to piss on it."

"You damned breed." Roarch attacked anew, weaving his knife in a savage series of arcs and slashes. He was skilled, very skilled, but every swing was countered by the tomahawk.

It wasn't often Ubel Gunther was impressed, but he was impressed now. The half-breed was unbelievably quick and undeniably deadly. It occurred to him that here was a potential valuable ally. Trask had said he would go his separate way once their quarry was located, but Ubel wondered if more money might induce him to change his mind. Not that Fabrizio or Pickett or the girl posed much of a threat. Ubel was thinking of the buffalo hunter. Enos Howard was known to be a marksman, able to drop an animal or a man from a great distance. Getting close enough to dispose of them might be difficult, and Ubel was a firm believer in eliminating difficulties before they became a problem.

Roarch was swearing up a storm. With good reason. Trask was slowly but inexorably forcing him toward one of the pool tables. Soon he would have his back to it and be hemmed in. "You stinkin' breed!" he screamed and redoubled his efforts to kill Trask. He was no slouch with a knife, but he just wasn't good enough, and it wasn't long before he realized it and worry replaced the fury contorting his face.

The end came with stunning rapidity.

Trask feinted to the left, and when Roarch parried, he sidestepped, shifted, and buried the tomahawk in Roarch's temple. Roarch died on his feet, his mouth opening and closing like that of a goldfish out of water. He melted beside the table. No one else moved. No one else spoke.

Trask wasn't even breathing heavily. "This will delay us," he said to Ubel. "The police will want to question me."

"Leave them to me," Ubel said. "My employer has considerable influence." More than considerable. Radtke often invited the mayor and the chief of police to his best boarding house at no cost to them. Ubel smiled and put a hand on Trask's shoulder. "While we are waiting, I have another proposition for you."

Chapter Thirteen

Northeastern Colorado

Charley Pickett wouldn't care if it took forever to find the Hoodoos. Over two weeks in Melissa Patterson's company had increased his feelings for her to the point where he never wanted the search to end. During the day, he rode by her side as much as possible. At night, they stayed up late, staring at the stars and talking.

Tony left them pretty much to themselves. He had grown unusually quiet. When Charley asked why, Tony blamed it on the heat and the flies. Charley had a hunch there was more involved, but he did not badger Tony about it.

Charley was more concerned about Enos Howard. The buffalo hunter had fallen into a sulk. He wouldn't speak unless spoken to, and he guzzled whiskey from the moment he woke up until the moment he passed out at night.

"What the dickens is the matter with you?" Charley had asked the evening before. "Why are you actin' like you sat on a corncob?"

"You have eyes, pup, but you don't see. You have

ears, but they're stuffed with wax." Enos wet his throat, lowered the bottle, and sighed. "My big plan has unraveled. I'm not the man I used to be."

"So you can't shoot the moon's eyes out. Your life isn't over."

"It might as well be," Enos said forlornly. "My eyes should have cleared up by now, but they haven't. I'm good out to about a hundred yards, but any farther than that and I couldn't hit the ass end of a buff if my life depended on it." He swilled more rotgut. "If it ain't chickens, it's feathers."

"We change our plan," Charley proposed. "Instead of you pickin' the Hoodoos off from a mile away, we'll sneak in close."

Enos arched an eyebrow. "Get in close to Kid Falon? To hombres like Brock Alvord and Curly Means? Land o' Goshen, boy, they'd splatter your brains without half tryin'."

"Not if we take them by surprise. And that's where you come in. You can see well enough to track. Once we find them, we wait until they least expect any trouble. With a little luck, we can take them without havin' to fire a shot."

"Did your ma drop you on your noggin when she was liftin' you out of your crib? No one has ever taken the Hoodoos by surprise, and no one ever will. They ain't like ordinary men. They sleep with one eye open. The smallest noise will bring 'em out from under their blankets with their six-guns blazin'."

"Are you sayin' it's impossible?"

"I'm sayin' if a toad had wings, it wouldn't bump its butt when it hopped. I'm sayin' if we had a lick of sense, we'd turn these nags around and light a shuck for Denver while we still can." Enos held out the bottle, but Charley shook his head. "I don't much mind committin' suicide. With my eyes gone, I'm a waste of hide. But what about Missy? She's young. She's pretty. She has her whole blamed life ahead of her. It ain't right to lead her into the valley of the shadow."

"She made the same choice we did," Charley said defensively.

"Choice, hell. She's blinded by the money. The three of you think it's the answer to your prayers, but all it will buy you is maggots eatin' your innards. I'm sorry I ever agreed to this egg hunt. Now I'll have your deaths on my conscience as well as my own."

"We're not going to die."

"Mighty big words for someone who ain't ever kilt a person. It's not the same as squashin' a bug. It sticks in your craw and festers and sores until some nights you wake up screamin'. One of those Blackfeet I shot wasn't much older than you, and once a month, like clockwork, I see his shocked face and how he reached out to an older Injun who must have been his pa."

"I thought you hated Indians."

"What on earth for? The only ones I'm not fond of are the ones who try to lift my hair." Enos gazed into the distance, but he wasn't seeing the prairie. "I had me a Crow wife once, but she couldn't stand my bellyachin' and went back to her people. I'd take her for my wife again in a split-second if she'd have me, but by now she's probably got a Crow husband and a passel of younguns more than half-growed." He shook himself and glanced at Charley. "We're tiltin' at windmills, boy. Take my advice. Turn around before it's too late."

"Why don't we put it to a vote?"

"The four of us are a democracy now, is that it?" the buffalo runner had said. "Hell, if that's the case, let's squat on this land and claim it as our own country."

Charley grinned at the recollection and drifted back to ride alongside Melissa. It was her turn to lead the pack horses. "How are you holdin' up?" At least once a day he asked her that to show how considerate he was.

"This is the happiest I've been since the deaths of my parents, and I owe it all to you."

"Shucks. I haven't done anything special." Charley tried not to blush, but it was hopeless.

"This hunt was your idea, so you deserve the credit." Melissa's smile was honey and wine mixed. "You're quite a man, Charley Pickett, and I hope you don't mind my saying so."

Charley swore he was going to float right up out of his saddle, he felt so light-headed. She had never complimented him so straightforwardly before, and he couldn't think of anything better to say than "Thanks."

Melissa wasn't done. "One day you'll make some woman awful happy. Call me a hussy, but I'll wish it were me."

Charley's brain about shut down from shock. She couldn't be hinting what he thought she was hinting. They hadn't as much as kissed yet. Several times he had been tempted to plant one on her cheek, but his courage always deserted him. She was looking at him, her eyes wide, as if waiting, but his tongue had turned to lead. He was almost glad when Enos hollered back to them.

"We'll rein up and rest in those cottonwoods yonder!"

Where there were cottonwoods there was often water, although in this instance they found none. Enos explained it was below ground, and if they dug far enough, they would strike it. But since their waterskins were nearly full, they forewent the effort.

Leaving Enos to nurse a bottle, Charley led Melissa and Tony off about fifty yards. He had collected a few dead limbs, and, breaking them into six-inch lengths, he jammed the pieces into the ground as targets.

"That should do us." Backing off twenty paces, Charley drew his revolver, aimed carefully, and fired. The stick he had selected burst in half.

"Well done!" Melissa exclaimed, clapping. "You're getting better and better every day."

Pride gushed through Charley like hot water from a geyser. "I want to be able to do my part when the time comes."

Tony was shaking his head and frowning. "Who are we trying to kid, *mi amico*? Kid Falon could put six bullets into you in the time it took you to shoot once. And I am worse than you." To demonstrate, he leveled his revolver and fired. The shot kicked up dirt half a foot from the sticks. "See? I am horrible at this. I much prefer my stiletto."

"My turn," Melissa said. Her pistol gleamed in the sunlight like a jewel. Spreading her legs wide, she extended both arms and took aim. As always when she was intensely concentrating, the tip of her tongue poked from between her lips. She fired twice. At each blast, a stick dissolved.

Charley whooped and leaped into the air. "Did you see her, Tony? She could be a sharpshooter, this girl!"

"She did well," Tony conceded. "Just not well

enough. Not when our lives are at stake if we lose against the Hoodoos." He looked at them. "And we *will* lose."

Melissa asked, "Why must you always look at the bleak side of things?"

Tony corrected her. "I look at things as they are. Not as I or you or anyone else might wish them to be. In Naples, the city where I was born and raised, there are men much like these Hoodoos. They are called the *Camorra*. They rob and kill as they please and there is little the *polizia* or anyone else can do. No one opposes them because to do so is to ask for your last rites."

"You can't hardly compare them to the Hoodoos," Charley commented.

"On the contrary, I can. Oh, the *Camorra* do not ride horses, and they use shotguns and stilettos instead of rifles and revolvers, but they are just as deadly. Everyone rightly fears them. They go where they please, do what they please. They have no conscience; they show no mercy. A list of those they have killed would be longer than my leg."

"You carry a stiletto," Melissa said.

Charley didn't get what that had to do with anything. His friend wasn't a cold-hearted killer. "I'm wearing a pistol, but that doesn't make me an outlaw."

Tony was staring at Melissa. "You think you know everything. But you are only partly right. Those who join the *Camorra* must swear a blood oath. An oath that binds them to the *Camorra* from that day on. They must never betray it, or they forfeit their lives. Nor are they permitted to leave the *Camorra* if they grow tired of the bloodshed. To protect itself, to keep its secrets, the *Camorra* assassinates anyone who tries."

"Why would anyone want to join an outfit like that?" Charley wondered.

"It is a blood bond passed from father to son. A bond that must never be broken, or it brings shame on the heads of the entire family."

Melissa was giving Tony a strange look. "So it's impossible to quit once you're in?"

"Those who want to leave have one choice. To flee the country. To travel as far and as fast as they can and pray the *Camorra* never learns where they are." Tony gazed at the surrounding plain. "Even this is not far enough."

Charley aimed at a stick. "Let's keep practicing. We need to be ready when we find the Hoodoos."

Tony muttered something, then said louder, "Has anything I have said sunk in? We can practice for a century and still not be ready. As Americans are so fond of saying, we are digging our own grave."

Melissa tilted her head. "If you feel that way, why have you stayed with us this far?"

Tony nodded at Charley. "He is my friend."

"That's all?"

"What more is needed? In Italy, loyalty to one's friends is almost as sacred as loyalty to one's family. Charley stuck with me when my life was in danger. I can do no less for him."

"Commendable," Melissa said. "There is more to you than you've let on."

"There is more to everyone," Tony said. "And never enough space on a headstone for all of it."

Nebraska Territory

Things had been going so well.

William Shores was confident it would not be long before he had the Hoodoos in his gun sights. The old Shoshone was holding to a pace that would wear out most people and came close to wearing out Shores. They were in the saddle from first light until the last glimmer of twilight. Breakfast consisted of jerky for Shores and a few dried roots for Red Fox. They never stopped at midday. Supper was usually rabbit stew, the rabbit courtesy of Red Fox.

The old warrior had a sense of urgency about him. He was eager to catch those who had slain his brother.

Shores didn't mind. He was equally eager to finish up and go back to his old life. He missed it even more when along about the fourteenth day he made the mistake of spreading his blankets over a hole in the ground that was home to a legion of resentful ants. He woke up the next morning covered with them and with so many bites it looked like he had the measles. The bites itched fiercely. He couldn't stop scratching until Red Fox prepared an ointment from a packet of herbs the warrior carried in a small leather pouch.

That very night a thunderstorm lashed the prairie for hours. The rain came down in sheets, and it wasn't long before Shores was soaked to the skin. The next morning Red Fox broke the bad news.

"Rain wash away sign, Brother John."

"We can't just give up," Shores snapped. He had tried to start a fire, but everything was too wet, and now he was huddled under a dripping blanket, his body cold as ice, his temper red hot. "Search around while I change into my other clothes."

Grunting, Red Fox climbed on the paint and rode off. He did not seem the least bit fazed by the wet and the chill.

Stuffed into Shores's saddlebags was the suit he had worn when he arrived in Cheyenne. As soon as Red Fox was out of sight, Shores pulled out the shirt, jacket, and pants, and his extra socks, and slipped into them. They were wonderfully dry, but he was still ice-cold, so he stood and paced, swinging his arms to increase the circulation.

It did no good. Shores's teeth started chattering, and he couldn't make them stop. The feeling of being cold alternated with hot flashes where it felt as if his skin were coated with burning kerosene. He was coming down with something, but he would not let a little sickness stop him.

Red Fox was gone over an hour. His expression was eloquent testimony to the success of his search. "I sorry, Brother John. No can follow bad whites."

"We'll keep heading southwest," Shores proposed. "Sooner or later we'll strike their trail again." He was glad to get under way. He thought it would warm him, but by the middle of the morning he was no better. Quite the contrary. The hot spells were more frequent and lasted longer, and he constantly perspired.

By noon, Shores could barely sit in the saddle. He was as weak as a newborn kitten, and his mouth felt filled with cotton. His chin kept drooping, and he could not keep his eyes open.

Shores was suddenly conscious that the claybank had halted. He looked up, his vision swimming. The paint was beside the claybank. Red Fox placed a palm on his forehead.

"Brother John sick. Need rest. I make tea."

"Forget it. We'll stop when we usually do. The tea can wait." Shores flicked his reins. The sea of grass around them rose and fell like the waves on the surface of an ocean. It had a nauseating effect. Bile rose in his throat, but he swallowed it down and moved on, holding his head high to show the Shoshone he was tougher than the old Indian thought. The prairie stopped heaving, and the dizziness lessened, and for a few minutes all went well.

Then Shores bent his neck to squint up at the sun. Something about the simple movement caused his head to spike with throbbing pain and his body to blaze as hot as the fiery orb he was looking at. The ground and the sky switched places.

Shores did not realize he had passed out until he opened his eyes. He was on his back, covered by one of his blankets, and his head rested on his saddle. "What—?" he murmured, his tongue as thick as a railroad tie. He was caked with sweat and could not stop shivering.

A shadow fell across him. Red Fox squatted. "Tea ready soon. Brother John rest. We stay until better."

"Like hell. We're wasting time." Shores tried to rise, but he couldn't make it onto his elbows, let alone stand. Groaning, he sank back and cursed. But even that took too much out of him, so he subsided and grumbled, "What is wrong with me anyhow?"

"Maybe ant bites. Maybe rain. Maybe both." Red Fox turned to a small fire. On a flat rock beside it was Shores's coffeepot. He lifted the lid, peered inside, and stirred whatever he was concocting with one of Shores's wooden spoons.

"Been helping yourself, I see?" Shores was grateful for the old man's help, but he resented the Indian being so free with his belongings. It occurred to him how ridiculously easy it would be for the Shoshone to stab him between the ribs and make off with the claybank and everything else. He slid his right hand up under his left arm to his Smith & Wesson. No matter how sick he became, he mustn't relax his guard.

Shores closed his eyes, and when he opened them again the sky had darkened. He thought another thunderstorm was on top of them, but when he twisted his head to the west he saw that the sun had vanished from the sky. He had been out for hours. He also discovered they were in a hollow or basin of some kind.

Red Fox was squatting on his haunches by the fire, his thin arms folded across his spindly knees. The coffeepot had been slid back from the fire but was near enough to keep the contents warm. "Brother John, bear in winter, sleep same," he said and smiled.

Shores didn't find it at all humorous. They were squandering hours better spent in pursuit of the Hoo-doos. Worse, it was his own body that had betrayed him. Him! Who had never been ill a day in his life!

The Shoshone was filling Shores's tin coffee cup. He sniffed a few times, nodded in satisfaction, and slowly tilted the cup to Shores's mouth. "Sip slow," he cautioned.

Shores was unprepared for the harshly bitter taste. He coughed, and most of his mouthful dribbled down his chin.

"Again," Red Fox said. "Sip slow but swallow quick."

Once Shores got some down, the rest wasn't so

bad. He noticed no difference in his condition. Indeed, as the evening waned, he grew progressively worse. His fever climbed, his head throbbed, and every muscle in his body ached. The simple act of taking a breath became painful.

Shores drifted in and out of consciousness. Every time he glanced up, Red Fox was by the fire, watching him. *Waiting for me to die,* Shores suspected. But if that were the case, why was the old Indian going to so much trouble to help him. *Or was he?* Shores had a terrifying thought: *What if the tea was poison instead of medicine?*

Shores told himself he was being childish. There was no reason for Red Fox to kill him. But how much did he really know about the old man? Other than that Red Fox was Shoshone and the Hoodoos had murdered his brother? *Supposedly* murdered him, since it was entirely possible Red Fox had made the whole thing up. Maybe, just maybe, Red Fox was in league with the Hoodoos. Maybe, just maybe, the Hoodoos had learned he was after them and had sent Red Fox to do him in.

Beads of sweat trickled into Shores's eyes, making them sting. He blinked to clear them, but that only made it worse. A hand brushed his forehead, and he nearly jumped out of his skin.

"Brother John burn up," Red Fox said.

"Stop touching me," Shores croaked. He tried to draw the Smith & Wesson, but he was too weak even for that. Helplessness ate at him like an acid. Regret ate at him too. Regret he had given up his comfortable job with the Pinkertons to take the position at the Department of Justice. *Why couldn't I be content with what I had?* Ambition and restlessness were to blame for his plight.

Dimly, through his feverish haze, part of Shores realized he wasn't thinking lucidly. It was normal for a person to want to better themselves. He shouldn't fault himself for desiring to make something of himself. But the thought of dying here in the middle of the godforsaken wilderness was as bitter to swallow as the Indian's tea. His parents, his friends, would never know his fate. He would lie in a shallow unmarked grave, provided the Shoshone bothered to bury him, or become a feast for scavengers. It wasn't right. It wasn't fair.

"More tea, Brother John." Red Fox had refilled the tin cup. "Drink all. Then sleep more."

"I'm tired of sleeping," Shores griped, but that was exactly what he did. When next he woke up, it was the middle of the night, and he was worse than ever. His teeth were chattering again, so fiercely his jaw muscles hurt. His clothes were drenched, and it still felt as if he were being burned alive. The crackling of the fire drew his gaze to its dancing flames and to the hunkered form beside it. "Don't you ever sleep?"

"You bad sick, Brother John. Must watch." Red Fox filled the cup again. With water this time, not tea.

Shores's throat was parched. He gulped it down and asked for a second and then a third cup. He wanted more, but the warrior advised against it.

"Too much and belly hurt."

"It's my belly," Shores said but let it go. The old man had a point. He attempted to roll onto his side, but his body refused. The blood in his veins was molasses. He barely had the energy to pull the blanket up to his chin. He shut his eyes, and the very next heartbeat he was out to the world.

A hazy series of vague impressions filtered through Shores's consciousness: of drinking more tea, of having his brow mopped by Red Fox, of drinking water, of the sun and the stars taking repeated turns above him. Whenever he opened his eyes, he had the impression an age has passed since the last time.

The sun was blazing when Shores struggled up from the bottomless depths of a black well into the bright light of a new afternoon. His mouth was as dry as a desert, but the fever was gone, and he wasn't sweating as much. "Water," he rasped, but nothing happened. He looked toward the fire, which had gone out, and saw no trace of his companion. "Red Fox?"

There was no answer. Alarmed, Shores raised his head high enough to scan the basin. The only horse in sight was his claybank. "Oh God." Shores fought down panic and found the strength to prop himself on his elbows. The Shoshone was gone. The old man had deserted him!

Shores looked around. His Winchester was missing from its saddle scabbard. His rope was missing too. Red Fox had left the coffeepot, but his canteen was conspicuously absent.

Easing onto his side, Shores crawled to the coffeepot. One shake was enough to show it was empty. "Damn that scrawny red devil to hell!" Mad enough to chew nails, he threw the coffeepot down and wished he hadn't when waves of vertigo resulted. He collapsed, his stomach in upheaval. In his current condition, he wouldn't last long. He needed water, and he needed food . . . and a lot of both.

Hooves clomped to the north. Fearing he had been found by hostiles, Shores fumbled at his Smith & Wesson. He wrapped his fingers around the grips just as a rider appeared. Astonishment transfixed him like a lance. "Red Fox! You came back!"

The old Shoshone was holding the Winchester. Slung over his left shoulder was the canteen. Behind him, tied to the paint with Shores's rope, was a white-tailed buck. "Brother John need meat."

Shores removed his hand from his revolver and slowly sat up with his back against his saddle. He felt like a complete jackass. "I was worried there for a bit," he admitted.

"I be fine," Red Fox misconstrued. Hopping down, he untied the buck and let it plop to the ground. He drew his tomahawk, bent over, and set to work.

Shores absently scratched his chin. The amount of stubble puzzled him, and he asked, "How long was I out?" He figured two days, three at the most.

Red Fox let go of the tomahawk to hold up all his fingers and thumbs.

"My God." Shores was flabbergasted. At the rate they were going, it would take a year to find the Hoodoos.

Chapter Fourteen

Montana Territory

No one could ever figure out how the Hoodoos
were able to be in Colorado Territory one day and
Kansas Territory a few days later. Yet it was an indis-
putable fact that they somehow covered hundreds of
miles far more swiftly than everyone else. Time and
time again they were seen in one territory by reliable
witnesses and a short while later spotted in another
territory by others.

Rumors sprang up. Some claimed the Hoodoos
knew of Indian trails no one else did. Others said
their horses were bred especially for speed and en-
durance that far outstripped ordinary mounts. A few
believed the Hoodoos dabbled in dark and fearsome
magic, which explained not only their extraordinarily
swift animals but the inability of the army and the
law to end their vicious spree.

The true answer was much more down to earth.

Brock Alvord had traveled widely. He had been as
far west as California, as far north as Montana. He
had fought Blackfeet. He had fought Sioux. He had
survived encounters with Apaches and with Coman-

ches. And it was from the Comanches, those dreaded scourges of Texas, that he had learned the trick to covering ground faster than most thought humanly possible.

The Comanches were infamous for their lightning raids deep into settled regions, after which they melted into the wilds with impunity. No one could catch them, and a lot of lives had been lost before their secret was discovered: relays. Warriors with strings of fresh mounts waited at designated points along the line of escape.

Brock Alvord was quick to see the potential. He had been called a lot of things, many less than flattering, but "dumb" wasn't one of them. He rightly reasoned that the Comanche system would work well for someone in his chosen line of work. So, early on, Alvord had taken to keeping the best of the stolen horses for himself and his men, and to setting up relay sites.

The sites posed a challenge. They had to be near water. There had to be ample forage. There had to be shelter from the elements. But most importantly, the sites had to be where no one would find them.

Alvord searched and searched and found plenty of sites with water and grass but few that met all his requirements. Particularly the last. There was hardly a spring or water hole the Indians didn't know about, and they would no more hesitate to steal horses from him than he would from them.

The solution was staring Brock Alvord in the face for months before it came to him one night when he was half-drunk and playing poker with Curly Means and John Noonan, the first two to join his horse-stealing ring. The subject of hostiles came up, and Noonan mentioned how an uncle of his had been tortured and mutilated by Comanches some years back. It reminded Brock of his relay scheme and how it had fallen through because he couldn't find safe sites.

Shortly thereafter, their conversation had turned to the fur-trapping days of decades past. Curly Means mentioned how a friend of his had once found a cache in a river bank filled with old plews. "They were piled in a dugout with a buffalo hide and a foot of dirt over them. But heavy rains collapsed the dirt."

Just like that, a gem of a notion hit Brock Alvord like a thunderclap. He slapped down his cards and whooped like a drunken cowboy, and the next morning he lit a shuck for northwest Kansas with his new recruits in tow. They asked what the shovels and picks were for, but he saved his surprise until they came to one of the sites he had come across months before but chalked off as too risky.

Curly and Noonan about had fits when Brock informed them they were to dig away half a hill.

"What the hell for?" the tall Missourian demanded. Shoveling dirt did not suit him one bit.

"I want the world's biggest dugout," Brock elaborated. "Big enough for six horses and a two-month supply of hay and feed."

Curly caught on right away and worked with zeal, laughing at the joke they would play on the law and everyone else.

Covering the dugouts proved the hardest task. Brock tried buffalo hides. He tried canvas. Finally, he used a latticework of branches reinforced with rope, over which blankets were draped. Then grass and weeds were strewn over everything. From a distance it looked like the rest of the prairie.

Eleven more dugouts were constructed, scattered

throughout four territories. Some were in the sides of hills. Two were carved out of the walls of remote canyons. One, in the Tetons, was a cave the Hoodoos enlarged.

Another problem confronted Brock. What was he to do about the tracks the stolen horses would make? In the mountains there was plenty of rocky ground to throw pursuers off the scent, but not out on the prairie. He pondered long and hard and came up with the solution: burlap bags. Twenty or more large bags at each dugout were always kept filled with grass and leaves and whatever else grew in the general area. When a new herd was brought in, the Hoodoos took the bags and covered the last quarter mile or so of trail. It wouldn't fool a skilled tracker, but it would delay pursuers long enough for whoever was on lookout to warn the rest.

All that effort, and it was never put to the test. Brock's relays worked too well. That, and as he learned early on, the Indians he stole from rarely chased his gang past the boundaries of whichever reservations they lived on. The tribes who didn't live on a reservation, the wild ones Brock had expected the most trouble from, were reluctant to stir up trouble with the white man and bring the army down on their heads, so they, too, rarely chased the Hoodoos far.

A few tribes, though, didn't give a damn who stole their stock. They wouldn't give up short of the grave. Which was why Brock avoided stealing from the Blackfeet, whose fondness for white scalps was well known. Sioux territory was also taboo. Of late the Sioux had been slaying every white they caught and had been brazen enough to attack well-garrisoned forts.

The Crows were another matter. They had a long history of being generally friendly to whites. They also owned some fine horses. The band that Looks With His Ears belonged to was camped along Arrow Creek within hailing distance of the Crow Indian Agency.

Three hidden relays were between Painted Rock and the agency. The Hoodoos stopped at each to change mounts. It was close to midnight of the sixth day when they arrived.

Thanks to Sunset's detailed directions, Brock led his men right to a rise overlooking a circle of Crow tepees. It lay dark and quiet under the stars. At that time of night even the camp dogs were asleep.

The best horses were picketed in the center of the circle. More had been turned out to graze close by, but Brock was only interested in the horses in the circle.

"Do we ride on down and take 'em?" Curly Means asked. "Or do you want me to raise a ruckus by going after the outlyin' herds and draw off the bucks?"

"We stick together," Brock responded. "Big Ben and I will see to the horses. The Kid, Noonan, and you are to make damn sure we don't take an arrow in the back."

Kid Falon drew a pearl-handled Colt. "My pleasure. There's nothin' I like better than shootin' Injuns. I'll cover the tepees to the north."

Noonan shucked a Winchester and levered a round into the chamber. "I'll take the ones on the west."

"I reckon that leaves the rest for me." Curly chuckled. "The more lodges to watch, the more fun it will be." He palmed his revolver.

Brock Alvord loosened his rope. "Ready?" he said to Big Ben.

The giant already had his rope in hand. "Are we drivin' the horses out the same way we came in?"

"No. I want to fight shy of the agency cabins. We'll swing east for a couple of miles, then turn south. Kid, you and Curly bring up the rear. Noonan, once we're out of the village, you ride on ahead and take point. Don't get careless on me. Just because these are Crows doesn't mean their arrows can't turn you into pincushions."

"You're doin' wonders for my confidence." Curly Means grinned.

Brock motioned and spurred his horse down the slope. No sentries had been posted; the Crows felt safe with the agency headquarters so close. He saw a four-legged shape appear out of the inky shadow at the base of a tepee and cursed. He had hoped the camp dogs wouldn't give the alarm until his men were closer. Even so, they were almost to the bottom when the first dog barked, and in seconds they were in the circle.

John Noonan and Big Ben Brody let out with Rebel yells. Kid Falon whooped and hollered. Curly Means did what Curly always did and laughed for joy. More than any of the others, Curly thrived on the thrill, on the excitement.

Brock's gaze swept the picketed horses. They were indeed fine animals, just as Sunset had asserted. He counted nearly three dozen.

The racket was enough to raise the dead. It was only a few seconds before a lodge flap parted and a Crow warrior stuck his head out. A shot from the Kid snapped him around, and he scrambled back in.

Falon, Noonan, and Curly were all firing now. Brock reined up and vaulted to the ground to cut a picket rope. He worked swiftly. They had to be out of there before the Crows could get organized.

A warrior armed with a rifle burst from a lodge to the west and was promptly gunned down in his tracks by Noonan.

To the north two warriors charged from the same lodge, only to run full into the blazing Colts of Kid Falon.

Curly was having a grand old time. Cackling and firing, he kept the occupants of the tepees to the east and south pinned inside.

"Hurry!" Brock called to Big Ben, who had just dismounted to cut a rope. Ben had brawn to spare, but he wasn't particularly quick. His nickname in the Confederate unit he'd belonged to had been "Turtle," and it fit him like a shell.

Brock slashed another rope, and a third. The horses were nickering and milling. It wouldn't take much to spook them.

Shouts and screams came from the tepees. Some of the warriors were yelling back and forth. Working out what to do, Brock suspected, a hunch proven right when warriors charged from different tepees at the same time. The Kid and Noonan wounded two and drove the rest back.

Brock didn't go in for wholesale slaughter. It wasn't that he was an Indian lover. Far from it. Needless killing would incite the Indians into more determined pursuit. So, long ago, much to the Kid's displeasure, he had given a running order to the effect that his men were to kill only as a last resort. By and large they abided by his decision. The notable exception was the Kid, who had more last resorts than all the others combined.

Big Ben was severing the last of the ropes. Brock swung onto his mount and began to drive the Crow horses east. It didn't take much to set them in motion: a few swings of his rope and a few shouts, and taut nerves did the rest.

A warrior with a bow came from behind a tepee. Either he had been off in the woods the whole time, or he had cut a hole in the back of his lodge and forced his body through the opening. Now he raised his bow, an arrow nocked to fly.

Kid Falon fired two shots so rapidly they boomed a fraction of a second apart. Punched by the slugs, the Crow fell against the tepee and slid to the ground.

"Yeehaw!" Big Ben Brody had heaved his bulk into his saddle and was on the other side of the herd, goading stragglers.

Brock was pleased. So far it had gone smoothly. But he mustn't be cocky. They wouldn't be safe until they put a couple of hundred miles behind them.

The Crow horses filed between tepees. A dog came bounding out to yap at them and was promptly shot by Curly Means. As was inevitably the case, several other dogs had preceded it in death on Curly's side of the circle.

As the last of the horses thundered into the night, Brock looked back and howled like a wolf. It was the signal for the Kid, Noonan, and Curly to leave off harrying the Crows and catch up.

Brock concentrated on keeping the horses together. Across the way, Big Ben was swinging his rope and yipping like a seasoned cowhand. Only Curly Means, though, had ever actually been a puncher, and then only for a short while. As he once told Brock, "Spendin' the rest of my life smellin' the hind end of cows didn't appeal to me, so I took to ridin' the high lines."

No explanation was needed. In Brock's opinion, cowboys had to have the dustiest, dirtiest, most thankless job around. For a measly thirty dollars a month they worked themselves to the bone. That wasn't for Brock. He never liked hard work. Back in Illinois, he had spent more time at his favorite fishing hole and in frolicking with friends than doing the chores his parents wanted him to. One thing led to another, and on his sixteenth birthday his father gave him an ultimatum: Either start pulling his weight or get the hell out. Brock hadn't been back since.

The others had varied backgrounds. Noonan and Big Ben had served in the army of the Confederacy. When the war ended, they did what thousands of men their age were doing and drifted west. The Kid had never done much of anything except gamble and shoot anyone who looked at him crosswise.

Brock knew how the path he had chosen might well end. But he could never go back to leading a law-abiding life. All those years he watched his father work at a job he hated had taught him an invaluable lesson. The straight and narrow was more than a path: It was a cage. It hemmed people in as surely as if they were ringed by iron bars. They weren't free to do what they wanted, when they wanted. From cradle to grave they were slaves to laws and conduct that governed everything they did. That wasn't for him.

Pistols were cracking. Brock saw a handful of Crows running across the circle, but the Colts of the Kid and Curly dispersed them.

The country was fairly open. It wasn't long before Brock Alvord spotted the agency cabins. Earlier the cabins had been dark, but now lights had come on and people were standing outside in their nightshirts and robes, trying to divine what all the commotion was about.

From out of a corral near the largest cabin came a rider. He wore a nightshirt and pants and had a rifle in his left hand. And he was undeniably white.

An agency employee. Brock frowned. The last thing he wanted was a gunfight with a white man. The Hoodoos had gone unchecked as long as they had in large part because they never stole from whites and never killed whites when on a raid. It was Brock's cardinal rule.

When they weren't on raids, it was another matter. What his men did on their own time was none of Brock's affair. There had been shooting scrapes; most involved disputes over cards or women. Most but not all. The Kid had shot a few people for the hell of it. He always claimed self-defense afterward, but he wasn't fooling anyone. The Kid loved to kill. It was that simple.

That business with the cavalry troopers was typical. The Kid and Noonan had sat in on a card game with three soldiers. Poor losers, the boys in uniform had accused the Kid and Noonan of cheating. One hot word had led to another, and hot lead was slung. The result: three dead soldiers and a boost in the bounty on the Hoodoos.

The agency man Brock had spotted was angling to intercept the herd. "Stop!" he bawled. "Stop in the name of the United States government!"

Idiots were born every second. Placing his coiled rope over his saddle horn and sliding his leg against it to hold it in place, Brock yanked out his Winchester. He had to act before any of the others did. Particularly the Kid.

"Stop!" the man repeated and raised his rifle.

Firing a Winchester accurately from the back of a horse at full gallop took some doing. Fortunately, Brock had some experience. His shot brought the agency man's mount crashing to the ground and tumbled the rider into a wash.

In a cloud of dust, the stolen horses swept on by the cabins. Brock breathed a sigh of relief. He replaced his Winchester, reclaimed his rope, and spent the next several hours guiding the herd south. The horses were tired and flagging when he brought them to a halt, and his own mount was lathered with sweat.

Big Ben Brody came trotting around. "We did it! Those Crows are as easy to steal from as a passel of babies."

"We were lucky," Brock said.

"Hell, the Kid and me could wipe out that whole village by our lonesome."

Brock doubted it. The Crows were formidable warriors who for years had held their own against the Blackfeet and the Sioux.

Curly Means trotted up. "There's no sign of anybody on our trail. The Kid and me flipped to see who rides drag, and he lost."

"I want both of you back there until we reach the first relay," Brock instructed him.

"How about after?"

"Flip another coin. Just so we get these horses to the Bar K without losing any." Brock had a potential buyer in mind. The last time he delivered rustled horses to Will Seever, the owner of the Bar K in Colorado Territory, Seever had expressed an interest in acquiring more.

Curly shook his head. "No, I meant after we deliver them."

"I haven't thought that far ahead. What does it matter?" Brock would do as he always did and hide most of his money in a secret hole at one of their relays. He had thousands squirreled away and planned to have thousands more before he called it quits. If he lived that long.

"The Kid has been makin' noise about Painted Rock," Curly said.

Brock had been expecting something like this. "Talk to him. Use that charm of yours. Persuade him to let it be. Abby's death was an accident. That should be that."

Curly lifted his reins. "I'll try, *amigo*. But you know how the Kid is when he's made up his mind. If you hear a shot, come a runnin'. He might blow my head off for stickin' my nose in."

Brock tried to dismiss it as of no consequence, but for the rest of the night and well into the next morning he mulled over how to make his case. By then he was convinced no one was chasing them. They stayed a whole day at the next relay to rest the herd. Brock used the opportunity to sound the Kid out.

Kid Falon was seated on an upended barrel, cleaning one of his Colts by candlelight. "I'm thinkin' of buyin' me a derringer to keep in my boot like Curly does," he said as Brock walked up. "Any you can recommend?"

"I've never used a hideout gun myself," Brock responded. "And it's not guns I want to talk about. It's Painted Rock."

The Kid looked at him. "We tote our own skillets

when we're not stealin' cayuses for you. That's always been how it was. Unless you aim to change things."

"No, not at all." Brock was under no delusions. The Kid and the others permitted him to lead them because it was in their best interests. But they wouldn't hesitate to strike off on their own if he ever presumed to step over the invisible line he had no right to cross.

"Then why the hound-dog face?"

Brock sat on another barrel. "Those soldier boys were bad enough. We don't need to make it worse."

"Some pills can't be swallowed. It's not as if I'm on the peck. If ever a man had cause, it's me."

"How many, then?"

The Kid twirled the Colt and gave it a final wipe. "Every mother's son. And then I'm burnin' the place down."

"Some might say that's a little extreme." Brock was choosing his words with care.

"Killin' Abby was extreme. That gal never hurt a soul in her life. Sure, it was that loco cripple who set the tumbleweed rollin'. But the rest of those no-accounts are as guilty as he is. Remember what the barkeep said to the crip? 'We told you not to do this.' His exact words. Those people knew, Brock. They should have warned us he was lookin' for trouble."

"It could push the bounty on us up to ten thousand. Maybe higher."

Kid Falon grinned. "That's as much as they're offerin' for Jesse James. Why, we'd be plumb famous."

"The James boys have every manhunter and Pinkerton in the country after them," Brock noted. "I don't know about you, but I'd get a crick in my neck from lookin' over my shoulder all the time."

"I dare a damned Pinkerton or any other gunny to try and buck me out in gore," the Kid blustered. "My lead-chuckers will put sawdust in their beards soon enough."

Brock could see there was no reasoning with him, but he tried once more anyway. "One of my conditions for lettin' you join was that you try to avoid makin' wolf meat of white men."

"You can't blame those soldiers on me. I was sittin' there behavin' myself until they accused Noonan of dealin' from the bottom of the deck and took to callin' us names. They jerked their hardware first. We jerked our final."

"I was there, if you'll recollect." Brock had to admit the troopers had asked for trouble. Too much bug juice and poor poker skills had planted many a gent on boot hill. "All I'm askin' is that you think it over."

The Kid didn't reply, and that was where it stood until they arrived, over a week and a half later, at the Bar K, located in southeast Colorado Territory. Will Seever was all too happy to take the horses off their hands and invited them to stay overnight in his bunkhouse.

Brock Alvord thanked him but declined. Kid Falon and Noonan were about as fond of punchers as Curly was of dogs, and it wouldn't do to put temptation in front of them. He touched his hat brim and rode off.

A mile from the ranch, Brock reined up and swung his mount to face the rest. "All of you know what the Kid has in mind. Anyone who wants to ride with him can. But you should know I'm dead set against it. Whoever wants can go with me to Denver. We'll meet up there at Darnell's saloon in a month."

The others glanced at one another.

"Well?" Brock prompted and looked at Big Ben Brody. "Let's hear it. Are you goin' with the Kid or me?"

Big Ben shifted in his saddle. "There isn't an hombre I admire more than you, boss. You know that. But what those folks did was just plain wrong. I'm with the Kid on this. Sorry."

"Noonan?" Brock said.

"A man should always stick by his pards. If the Kid is dead set on a killin' spree, I say roll the dice and let 'em fall."

"Curly?" Brock had a sinking sensation deep in his gut.

Curly grinned. "Last time we were there, I saw three or four dogs waltzin' around as healthy as you please. We can't have that, can we?"

So there it was. Brock Alvord hid his disappointment. "All right. If that's how you want it, count me in."

The Kid leaned on his saddle horn. "You're throwin' in with us after all the jabberin' you did about how we should get shed of the idea?"

"We've ridden together this long," Brock said and shrugged.

"All right, then." The Kid's smile was downright vicious. "The good people of Painted Rock better start countin' the days. Their time on this earth is over."

Chapter Fifteen

Northeast Colorado Territory

Charley Pickett was so happy to be spending so much time with Melissa Patterson that weeks went by before he realized they were wandering back and forth across the prairie without accomplishing anything. That evening around the campfire, he brought it up.

"Why are you lookin' at me, pup?" Enos Howard demanded and upended a bottle. After a few swallows, he said, "I can't pull sign out of thin air. Until we strike their trail, all we can do is twiddle our thumbs."

"But that's like looking for a sewing needle in a haystack," Melissa mentioned. "It could take forever. At this rate, our supplies will run out long before we find it."

Tony was roasting the rabbit they were having for supper. Melissa had shot it with her rifle from fifty yards off when Enos couldn't be bothered to try. "How will we know it even *is* their trail? It could be anyone's."

"There are five of them," Enos said. "Any more, any less, it's not the Hoodoos."

"It could be five cowboys for all we know," Tony said.

"Maybe we should pay Fort Sedgewick a visit," Charley suggested before they could argue. "The army might have a clue to their whereabouts."

"I'll take you there, but I won't go into the fort," Enos said. "I know a couple of the scouts assigned there. They'll laugh me to scorn if they see me with greeners like you."

"Or is it you don't want them to see you drunk?" Tony rotated the trimmed branch they were using for a spit.

Enos lowered the bottle in midswallow. "Watch that mouth of yours, kid. You're startin' to get me riled."

"I am not a 'kid,' *signor*. I am a grown man, and you will treat me with the respect a grown man deserves."

"You're a peckerwood, is what you are," Enos retorted. "All you've done this whole hunt is grouse about how we're in over our heads."

"We are," Tony said. "And if your brain was not soaked in whiskey, you would realize it."

Enos started to rise, but Charley sprang between them. "Enough! Enos, you don't have to go into the fort with us if you don't want to. Tony, quit insultin' him all the time. I thought by now the two of you would get along better."

"He brings it on himself." Tony straightened. "I have never met a man more *arrogante*. It is a wonder no one has buried him long before now."

Charley felt sure Howard would take offense, but

the buffalo hunter was gazing to the northeast. "Did you hear somethin'?"

"I had an inspiration." Enos chuckled. "Why in blue blazes didn't I think of this sooner? If anyone can help us, he'd be the coon."

Melissa asked, "Who are you talking about?"

"Eli Brandenberg. He has a soddy a couple of days' ride from here. Sells drinks and dry goods and ammunition. Buffalo runners stop there all the time. So do a lot of folks usin' the main trail. They gab up a storm. If anyone has heard what part of the country the Hoodoos are in, it would be Eli."

"Rumors are not very dependable," Tony remarked.

"It's better than having nothin' to go on at all," Charley said. "We'll head for Brandenberg's at first light." Although he would just as soon spend the rest of his life wandering the prairie with Melissa.

"I'll drink to that." Enos resumed guzzling. He was a lot more subdued than he used to be and was still conspicuous by his absence at their daily target shoots.

Soon the rabbit was roasted. Charley tore off a leg and ate ravenously. He glanced at Melissa every now and then, admiring the dainty way she held a piece of meat and how she took tiny bites instead of wolfing the food like he did. She was as delicate as fine china and twice as pretty.

Tony didn't have much of an appetite. He nibbled at a piece, then rose and walked off into the darkness.

Excusing himself, Charley followed. In his estimation it was high time he got to the bottom of whatever was bothering his friend.

There was no moon. Charley barely made Tony

out, standing in the middle of some mesquite, his hands shoved in his pockets. "Are you as tired of rabbit as I am?" he joked.

"I want to be alone."

"Nothin' doin'. You've been keepin' to yourself ever since we left Denver, and I'd like to know why. Is it something I've done? Is it Melissa?"

"It is both," Tony said.

The blunt answer threw Charley off his mental stride. He groped for the right thing to say. "I'm sorry if I've upset you. You're about the best friend I've ever had, and I'd rather eat dirt than have you down at the shanks on my account."

"It is not you. It is your love for the girl."

Now Charley was doubly confused and more than a little put out. "I never said I was in love with her."

"Oh, please. Anyone with eyes can see the longing in yours when you look at her. Like Enos with Clarabelle, you have been struck by the thunderbolt." Tony paused. "I should know. I have been struck too."

"You've got a gal stashed away somewhere?" Charley grinned and clapped him on the back. "Why didn't you say so?"

Tony sighed. "Why talk about that which can never be mine? Her name is Maria, and she lives in Naples. We have been in love since we were twelve." Tony brightened and took his hands from his pockets. "Oh, if only you could meet her, *mio amico*! Her beauty is like a rose you are afraid to touch for fear you will crush it. When she moves, her body flows like water. Her hair always has the scent of strawberries, and her skin is as creamy as milk."

Charley had never heard Tony talk like this. "Sounds to me like that thunderbolt seared you clear down to your toes. If you feel that way, why didn't you bring her to America with you?"

Tony's joyful mood disappeared. "Because the *Camorra* would kill her as well as me, and that I could not bear."

"The *Camorra*? That outfit in Italy you told us about?" Charley was slow, but eventually he caught on. "You're the one who tried to quit them! And you had to leave Italy or they would have killed you!"

"*Si*. I never lived in New York, I never stabbed anyone there. I am sorry I lied. I thought it best to keep my past secret." Tony placed a hand on Charley's shoulder. "Can you forgive me?"

"There's nothin' to forgive."

"My *madre* and *padre* are in Naples. My *padre* wants nothing to do with me because I disgraced our family. It would make him greatly happy if I were to put a *pistola* to my head and pull the trigger."

"But you did right quittin' a bunch of killers."

"*Mio padre* would not agree. He has belonged to the *Camorra* all his life. As did his father and his father before him. I broke the chain and brought down everlasting shame on the Fabrizios."

Charley couldn't understand a father turning against his own son. "How did Maria feel?"

"It was for her I did it. She wanted no part of the *Camorra* way of life, no part of the violence. So we went to my father. I thought he would sympathize. I thought he would help us. Instead, he informed the *Camorra*, and men were sent to murder me. Had it not been for my mother, who warned me and slipped me enough money for passage to America, I would not be here right now."

"Why didn't Maria come with you?"

"My mother did not have enough for the both of

us. I promised to send for Maria as soon as I can. It has been over a year and I have yet to raise the money." Tony sighed. "Now you know the real reason I joined this insane hunt of yours. It is not for money for San Francisco. It is for money to bring the woman who has claimed my heart to me."

Charley wasn't angry that Tony had lied to him. He couldn't begin to imagine the torment his friend must be suffering.

"Whenever I see you with Melissa, it reminds me of the happiness I shared with Maria and how much I want to hold her in my arms again. The sadness is almost more than I can bear. That is why I have been so quiet." Tony paused. "You should tell her, you know."

"Tell who what?"

"Melissa. How much you care for her. You do neither of you any favors by keeping it inside. Women like to hear those things, Charley. They need to be sure of your devotion. Then they will freely and gladly give theirs."

Charley would have explained it wasn't that simple, but a slender figure came walking toward them.

"Here you two are. I was getting worried." Melissa smiled. "What's the big attraction out here?"

"Men talk," Tony said and smiled at Charley. "I was just leaving. My appetite has returned. I better grab some rabbit before Howard eats it all."

Suddenly Charley was alone with the woman he adored. She was so close, their shoulders touched. His body prickled as with a heat rash, and his mouth went dry. "Nice night," he said.

"Did you ever see so many stars?" Melissa was gazing upward, her throat pale and smooth in the starlight. "There's something about the air out here. You can see a lot more than back East."

"I always liked lookin' at the night sky when I was little," Charley confided. "I'd try to find the constellations." He pointed. "There's the Big Dipper." His finger moved. "And that one there is the Little Dipper."

"We should try and count them all sometime," Melissa said. "I bet there are thousands."

A lump formed in Charley's throat when her hand found his and gently squeezed. He repaid the courtesy, his mind racing like a thoroughbred. She had never done that before; what did it mean? Was she expecting him to kiss her? Or would she slap his face and stomp off in a huff? Better to play it safe, he decided, and replied, "It would take an entire night. I don't count fast."

"You're too hard on yourself, Charley. You have more worthy qualities than you think."

The compliment made his ears burn. "If I do, they're pretty well hidden." Charley grinned, trying to be poised and calm, but his insides were swirling like butter in a butter churn. "A man has to know his limits."

"But not carp on them. And it's a man's strengths that count most." Melissa turned and looked at him as she had never looked at him before.

Charley sensed an important moment had arrived. He yearned to kiss her, but he was afraid to. Yet he was also positive that if he stood there like a tree stump, it would upset her. So he compromised. He tried flattery. And since he wasn't all that good with words, he borrowed some. "Have I ever told you your beauty is like a rose?"

Melissa gave a tiny gasp. "No, you haven't. I would remember a thing like that." She leaned closer. "You really think so?"

Charley nodded. Emboldened, he went on. "When you move, your body is all pretty and sparkly like water in a mountain stream."

"No one has ever said anything like that to me before."

Charley's face was an inch from hers. He breathed deep and said, "You always smell like fresh straw."

Melissa leaned against him. Her warm breath fanned his cheek.

"Your skin is like a bowl of milk. I sometimes wish I were a cat so I could lap it up."

"Lap all you want," Melissa said softly, her arms rising around his neck.

The next fifteen minutes were paradise. Her kisses were molten honey, and the sensations she sparked in him were as delicious as hot apple pie. He never wanted to stop, but at length she eased back a trifle and rested her head on his shoulder.

"This is the happiest day of my life."

The next words came out of Charley's mouth in a rush. He had no conscious awareness of wanting to say them at that exact moment, although he had been thinking about saying them ever since he met her. "Will you marry me?"

Her gasp this time was a lot louder.

Charley waited. And waited some more. And when he couldn't take the suspense any longer, he said, "Well?"

"A man should never ask a question like that lightly."

Of all the things she could say, that was one Charley hadn't foreseen. He pondered it, trying to unravel its true meaning. Women were unusual that way. They said one thing but meant something else. In this instance, the best he could reply was, "I've never been more serious about anything in my life. You're all I think about. But I would understand if you don't feel the same. I'm not the best catch in the pond."

"Oh, Charley."

"If I've stepped too far past the rail, just say so, and I'll never bring it up again."

"Men are so silly."

Charley took that as confirmation she wasn't interested in tying the knot. The celestial spectacle above them seemed to break apart and come crashing down to earth.

"I don't mean to be. It's just how I am."

"Yes, Charley," Melissa said and kissed his neck. Something damp trickled down it.

Was that a tear? Charley wondered. She had him so confused, it was pitiful. "Yes, what? Yes, I'm silly? Yes, I went too far and should never bring the subject up again?"

"Yes, I will marry you."

Charley never had every part of his body freeze up on him before. His tongue, his mouth, his heart, everything stopped, and soon his chest started to hurt because he wasn't breathing. He sucked in a long breath and let it out again to get his lungs to work. "You mean that? Cross your heart?"

"Kiss me, Charley."

He did. Again and again and again. Joy filled him until he was fit to explode, and when she leaned her cheek on his shoulder again, he was panting and tingling clear down to his toes. "I'll be a suck-egg mule."

"You'll be my husband, Charley Pickett. We might

never be rich, but we'll have each other. We'll live on a small farm and raise as many children as you want, and when we're old and grey, we'll sit on rocking chairs on our porch and look back at all the happy times, and we'll be content. When we go to our graves, we'll go knowing we did the best we could with what we had, and no one can ask more."

"Yes!" Charley said, seeing it all so plain, as if they had already lived it. "That's exactly how it will be." He hugged her, and tears filled his eyes. It didn't make sense to be crying at the most joyous moment of his life, and he tried to blink them away.

"When did you have in mind, Charley? I'm not fussy. If you want a justice of the peace instead of a minister, that's fine by me. All I ask is that I get to wear a new dress, and I want some flowers I can press in a book and save to always remind me of the occasion."

Charley hadn't thought that far ahead and admitted it.

"That's all right. First we'll settle this Hoodoo business. Then you can take me anywhere in the world you want us to go. Anywhere at all. I'm not one of those women who will always be making demands, Charley. A house, a farm, children: that's all I want."

To Charley that seemed an awful lot, but all that was down the road. Right now the important thing was that she had said yes. He felt her hand caress the back of his neck, and he had a terrible thought. "Oh Lordy! What have I done?"

Melissa pulled back. "Having second thoughts?"

"Never in a million years." Charley grasped her small hands in his big ones. "I just realized. When a man proposes, he's supposed to give his girl a ring."

His voice broke, and his eyes misted over worse than ever. "I don't have one."

"Is that all?" Melissa touched his damp cheek. "You sweet, adorable infant, you. The ring isn't important right now. It's the love that counts." She paused. "You do love me, don't you?"

Charley was shocked on two accounts. First, he didn't much like being called an "infant." It implied he wasn't mature enough to know what he was doing. Second, he wouldn't have asked her to marry him if he didn't love her. "I love you more than any man has ever loved any woman ever."

"Then why don't you say it."

Charley thought he just had, but he humored her. "I love you." He was rewarded with another fifteen minutes of passion the likes of which about scorched him alive. His wedding night promised to be a night most men would die for.

Melissa put her forehead on his chest and gripped his arms tight. "You do things to me." She trembled, then looked up, as radiant as the sun. "We should get back. Do we tell the others or keep it our little secret?"

"Whichever you want." Were it up to Charley, he would shout it to the world at the top of his lungs.

"I'd rather keep it to ourselves. It's more special that way."

Arm in arm, they headed toward the fire. Charley's feet weren't touching the ground. He was floating along like a leaf blown on the wind.

Enos was flat on his back, his arms wrapped around an empty bottle. His snores were loud enough to be heard in Arkansas.

"Back so soon?" Tony was eating some rabbit. He

grinned at Charley, who was sure his face must be beet red.

Melissa detached herself, walked over to Tony, and thrust out her hand. "I'm declaring a truce between us. From this moment on, what you did in Denver is forgotten."

"I had already forgotten it. You are the one who will not."

Charley had to find out. "I don't suppose either of you would see fit to finally tell me what has been going on?"

"He touched me," Melissa said.

"Touched you how?" Charley asked, and even as he said it, he knew, or thought he did, and blazing fury coursed through his veins, fury as surprising as it was intense, because this was Tony they were talking about, and Tony was his best friend.

Tony muttered something in Italian. "How many times must I say I am sorry for the same offense? Accidents happen. Believe it or not, not everyone is as anxious to put their hands on you as Charley is."

"You shouldn't say things like that," Charley said, barely able to keep himself under control. He glanced at Melissa. "Tell me," he commanded and received another surprise when, without any hesitation, she did.

"Tony used to stop by every day and buy a potato, just like you. He would always say how much I reminded him of a girl he knew in the Old Country. The kind of things men always say when they want a woman to be interested in them."

Charley thought of Maria, and his fury melted like mountain snow under a midday sun. Melissa had jumped to the wrong conclusion.

"Anyway, one day I turned to get some potatoes

out of my sack, and it was closer than I thought, and I tripped over it. Next thing I knew, Tony had his hands around me, and was touching my—'' Melissa looked down at her chest. ''He says he caught me so I wouldn't hurt myself, but I know how men are.''

To Charley's horror, a snort burst from his lips, followed by a loud cackle. Right away he clamped a hand over his mouth, but the harm had been done. The gleam in his fiancée's eyes had nothing to do with love.

''Find that funny, do you?'' Melissa's tone was as brittle as eggshells. ''The woman you're going to marry groped by another man?''

Tony rose. ''Did I hear right?'' He beamed at Charley. ''You have proposed, and she accepted?'' Laughing heartily, Tony embraced him. ''I congratulate you, my friend! I wish the two of you all the happiness in the world.''

''I'd like you to be there as my best man.''

''I would be honored.'' Tony spread his arms wide to hug Melissa, but she held out a palm, stopping him.

''Explain yourself, Charley Pickett.''

Charley took her hand and sat her down and told her about Maria, Tony's true love, and all Tony had been through. He concluded with, ''If you love me, you have to trust me. And if you trust me, you have to trust my choice in friends.''

''I trust you with all my heart,'' Melissa said, and rising, she gave Tony a hug.

After that they sat around the fire talking until the wee hours of the morning. Charley couldn't stop glancing at her and touching her arm to prove it was real and not a dream.

Melissa was curious about Maria. Tony answered

her many questions openly and honestly, and presently she said, "We'll help you do whatever needs to be done to bring her over. Maybe we could make it a double wedding."

"I would like nothing better. But there are complications. Her father does not want her to have anything to do with me. He fears the *Camorra*, and rightly so. He might keep her in Naples against her will."

They were quiet awhile after that, until Melissa said, "I'm curious. Where did you learn English so well?"

"It is taught in the schools. Many of my countrymen practice it as a second language."

Enos Howard chose that moment to smack his lips and roll onto his side.

"I guess we should turn in," Melissa said. "Our curmudgeon of a buffalo hunter wants to ride out at dawn. Says it will take us about two days to reach Eli's. Then, if we're lucky, it's on to the Hoodoos."

The rosy inner glow that had sheathed Charley like a bubble burst. He crawled under his blankets, but he couldn't sleep. His emotions were in turmoil. Now that Melissa had declared her love, it changed everything.

Charley realized Mr. Leeds had been right. He had no business bringing Melissa along. There was no excuse for placing her life in jeopardy. It was pure selfishness. If she came to harm, it would be his fault and his alone. And when dealing with cutthroats like the Hoodoos, that was a very real possibility.

What in God's name had he done?

Chapter Sixteen

Nebraska Territory

The swaying motion lulled Federal Agent William Shores into dozing off, as it had so many times. The sun was an hour higher in the sky when a slight jolt awakened him. He raised his head and beheld grass, grass, and more grass for as far as the eye could see. Shores was sick to death of it. Just as he was sick to death of being treated like an invalid. His fever was long gone, and he had regained much of his strength, but Red Fox insisted he was not yet recovered enough to ride. "What do you call this thing again?"

"Travois, Brother John. Many tribes use."

Shores had to admit it was a great idea. The old Shoshone had chopped down a few saplings and fashioned them into a crude but serviceable platform. He had then lashed the two long poles on either side of the paint, climbed back on, and off they went. The claybank plodded along behind them, linked by a rope to the travois.

They had been traveling steadily south for days, making for the nearest settlement. Once there, Shores hoped to learn the latest news about the Hoodoos.

"How much longer before we get to this place you mentioned?"

"Five, six sleeps, maybe more," Red Fox answered. "Prairie big, Brother John. Your patience small."

Shores was impatient all right. He was impatient to get back on his feet. He was impatient to find the Hoodoos and wrap his assignment up. He was impatient to part company with the old man. Most of all, he was impatient with the West and everything in it: the grass, the dust, the bugs, the sun, the sweaty smell of the horses, the worse smell when they used their hind ends for what hind ends were made for.

With nothing better to do, Shores twisted to his left. His saddlebags were on the travois beside him. Opening one, he rummaged inside for the drawings he had made of the symbols Mat-ta-vish had drawn in the dirt. He had not looked at them since he showed them to O. T. Quarrel, and he had no idea why he had an urge to look at them now.

There were two. They did not contain much detail, but there was no doubt what they were. One was a buffalo. Its horns and hump and overall shape were unmistakable. The other reminded Shores of a jellyfish, but that couldn't be. Mat-ta-vish had never been anywhere near an ocean. Mat-ta-vish's sister believed it was a star. So the two drawings translated into "Buffalo Star." Shores had asked her if the name held special significance, but she was as puzzled as he was.

Shores eased partway onto his side so he could face Red Fox. "Did your brother's wife mention the drawings he spent the last few moments of his life making?"

"Drawings?" The old Shoshone glanced down.

"These." Shores handed the paper up to him. "I think they're a clue of some kind. An important clue. Is there a place your people call Buffalo Star? Or could it be the name of someone?"

"Not name," the old warrior said, the lines in his seamed countenance doubling. "Not Buffalo Star."

"What do they mean then?"

"One be white buffalo."

"What's the difference? Buffalo, white buffalo—it's all the same, isn't it?"

Red Fox spoke slowly. "White buffalo special. White buffalo rare. To Indian, much good medicine."

"What about the star? What does that mean?"

"Star mean star."

"So you're saying it's Good Medicine Star?" Which made even less sense to Shores than the other. Maybe he was wrong, and the drawings had nothing to do with the Hoodoos. Maybe they were symbols with special meaning for Mat-ta-vish and no one else. He mentioned as much.

"No. Drawings be about bad whites. So must think like whites." Red Fox pursed his lips in contemplation. "To your people, white buffalo be good luck. Like rabbitfoot soldier at fort have."

"Carrying a rabbit's foot for luck is a silly superstition," Shores said. "So is thinking an albino buffalo is special."

The old warrior leaned down and handed the paper to him. "Much whites not know."

"You're smarter than us, is that it? Look at you. Running around half naked. Using a bow and arrow. And you live in a dwelling made of hides. What do you know about the world that we don't? Have you read the Bible? Or Plato? Have you ever been to Europe? Africa? Asia? Hell, your people know next to nothing about life. And the sad thing is, they know so little, they don't realize how little it really is."

If Red Fox was offended, he didn't show it. "Indians know all need to know. How to hunt. How to skin animals. How to make clothes. Before whites come, Indian happy. Go where we want, do what we want. Now must live on reservation. Must wear white clothes. Must send children to white school. Cannot count coup, cannot raid enemies. Indian unhappy."

"Don't blame me. I wasn't a party to the treaties." Shores stared at the drawings. "Good Luck Star?" he said aloud, as baffled as ever. He shoved the paper into his saddlebags and lay with one hand under his head. He couldn't wait to reach the settlement. If they had a telegraph, he would send an update to the assistant director and request the latest information on his quarry. It was probably too much to hope for. Just as it was probably too much to expect them to have a decent hotel where he could treat himself to a hot bath and a night's sleep in a soft bed.

What was the settlement called again? Shores had to think a bit before he recalled the name the Shoshone had told him.

Painted Rock.

Colorado-Nebraska Border

Eli Brandenberg was plucking a chicken out by the henhouse when four riders appeared to the southwest. His dog barked to warn him. Placing it in the storeroom, he took his rifle and a telescope and went back out. He looked through the telescope and saw a big buffalo hunter doing the same. The other man lowered his and grinned. "I'll be damned," Eli said.

Eli had a jug on the counter waiting when Enos Howard barreled into the soddy like he owned it and clapped Eli on the shoulder near hard enough to knock him down.

"Eli, you scoundrel! It does this coon good to see your ugly self again." Enos introduced his companions and told them to take a seat. "How about grub all around? And a pot of that coffee of yours that can float a horseshoe." Eno's eyes narrowed and he lightly touched the muzzle of his Sharps to one of Eli's many bruises. "What the hell happened to you? Did an ornery horse try to stomp you to death?"

"I'd rather not talk about it."

"It's your face," Enos said with a shrug. He uncorked the jug, crooked his arm, and gulped. "Lawsy! You still make some of the best corn liquor this side of Beulah land."

"I try," Eli said, somewhat appeased. "Where have you been keepin' yourself? It's been a year, almost a year and a half, since I saw you last." He gave the three young ones at the table a once-over. "And since when do you take up with tadpoles? Have you given up the buffs to tend babies?"

"Be nice. They're green, but they have gumption. We've partnered up on a special hunt."

"I haven't seen any buffalo in a month of Sundays. Time was, I'd see four or five big herds a year, but you buffalo hunters are killin' 'em off faster than the cows can drop calves."

"It's buffalo *runners*, Eli. You should know that. And my buff days are over. I've got me a whole new line of work."

"But you just said you were on a hunt."

"Not the kind of hunt you think."

Charley Pickett called out, "These tadpoles would

like to have some food and drink, if you don't mind. The lady here is hungry."

Enos grinned at Eli. "You have to excuse the pup. He's in love." He ambled to their table, swung a chair around, and straddled it. "Overheard us, did you?"

"Every word," Charley said. "It's hard not to when you're always bellowing like a bull."

"Folks have been sayin' I talk too loud since I was knee-high to a prairie dog. But I'm not one of those who talks as quiet as they live."

Melissa had taken a brush from her bag and was running it through her hair. "I'm not sure I follow you."

"Life was meant to be lived, Missy. Not like a mouse in a cage. But like a griz, the lord of all creation. Bears are hardly ever quiet. They're always gruntin' and snortin' and growlin' and rumblin' and livin' life the fullest they know how. They don't do anything in half-measures. It's full to the brim for them, and that's exactly how I like to live. Full to the brim."

Tony removed his cap. "The strange thing is, I understand what you are saying. Even stranger, I agree."

"You? You could have fooled me. Until a few days ago, you were as quiet as a lump of coal and just about as lively."

"I have had a lot on my mind. More than you can possibly suspect."

"That's the trouble with younguns nowadays. You think too damn much. It bogs your brain down in thoughts when you should be usin' it to live."

Tony said, "No one would ever accuse you of bogging down your brain."

"Exactly. I leave the piddlin' stuff for those who like to fret. Me, I take each day as it comes. I grab it by the horns and wrestle it to the ground, and then I put my foot on its neck and whoop like a Crow."

"I haven't noticed you doing much whoopin' except when you're drunk," Charley commented.

"Hell, boy, you've yet to see me when I really hit the liquor. All I've been doin' is what you might call sociable drinkin'."

"In that case," Tony was grinning, "you are surely the most sociable person I have ever met."

Enos laughed and declared, "Will wonders never cease! You do have a sense of humor! Keep this up, and pretty soon you might even learn how to have some fun."

Eli arrived. He had put his grimy apron on and was carrying a scuffed wooden tray with four glasses and a pitcher of water. "What would you folks like?" He rattled off the list of the foods and drinks he had available.

"Oh, I would die for some eggs!" Melissa declared. "I saw your chickens when we rode up, and I was hoping you would have some. With a little of that pork sausage you mentioned."

"I'll have to double-check the sausage to be sure," Eli told her. "It's been hangin' in the cellar a spell. It was salted proper, but sometimes the meat turns. I'll nibble a piece to see if it's spoiled."

"Thank you. That's most considerate."

Eli nervously shifted his weight from one foot to the other. Women always made him uncomfortable. The way they moved, the way they thought things out, they were so different in everything they did. It was spooky. He never knew what to say around them or quite what to do. Once he had tried courting a girl, but it hadn't worked out. They would sit for hours without saying a word. Just sit there on her father's porch, staring off into space. Finally he stopped going over to visit and hadn't felt the need for female companionship since.

"I'd like a slab of venison," Charley began. "Three or four baked potatoes, a mountain of pork and beans, half a loaf of bread with butter, and a pot of coffee to wash it down."

"Is that all?"

"Eggs sounds nice to me too," Tony said. "With the yolks intact, if you please. And toast and jam."

"Just bring me a jug," Enos directed.

Melissa stopped brushing her hair and wagged the brush at him. "You should eat too. Treat yourself. Who knows how long it will be before we find the Hoodoos."

Eli, in the act of turning, stopped. "What do you have to do with those miserable snakes, girl?"

Enos grinned. "That's who we're after. You're lookin' at four genuine manhunters. We've been scourin' all over creation for those buzzards and were hopin' maybe you had word of which territory they've been seen in lately."

Eli stared at each of them and made a sound reminiscent of one of his chickens being strangled. "Are you addlepated? Why, Big Ben Brody alone could take the four of you with one hand and both legs hogtied, and he's the least dangerous of the whole bunch."

"You let us worry about that," Charley said.

Shaking his head at the buffalo hunter, Eli commented, "I'd expect such foolishness from these three. They're so wet behind the ears, they're drippin' sap. But you should know better, Enos. You've been bloodied, and you've blooded more than your share. You'll only get these tadpoles killed."

"This was their brainstorm, not mine. When they first told me, I laughed till my sides were fit to split. And I still think they're loco. But I gave 'em my word, and I'm with 'em until the end."

"It's the bounty, isn't it? All that money has you droolin'? Of all the simpleminded silliness, this takes the cake."

Charley's jaw twitched. "When we want your opinion, mister, we'll ask for it. And don't insult the lady again, or you'll answer to me."

Enos gestured. "Now, now. Let's not snip. I'm sure Eli didn't mean anything personal. He's only being considerate. Right, Eli?"

Eli was thinking. He still ached from the beating he had taken, and two of his front teeth were so loose they might fall out any day now. He had never hated anyone as much as he hated the Hoodoos. Hate so potent that sometimes, when he thought about what they had done, his head swam and his temples pounded, and he couldn't hardly see for the red haze in front of his eyes. He spent hours daydreaming about paying them back. About staking them out over ant hills or sneaking up in the dead of night and slitting their throats. He wanted them dead, stone dead, Brock Alvord most of all. Brock was the one he had always liked and respected. And look at what the man had done.

"Got a bee in your ear?" Enos prompted.

Eli slid a chair from another table over to theirs and sat. "What if I could tell you how you can go about settin' a trap for the Hoodoos? A trap they would never suspect? It could mean the difference between your livin' and dyin'."

The four manhunters looked at one another, then leaned toward him. Charley Pickett said, "We're all ears, mister."

"Not so fast, boy. There's a condition. If I help, you take me with you. I want to be there when you tangle with them. And I want to be the one who blows out Brock Alvord's wick."

Enos tugged on his beard. "What's gotten into you, Eli? As I recollect, you never were much for spillin' blood."

"I have my reasons."

"I suppose you also want a share of the bounty?" Enos said. "Seems to me, you callin' us simpleminded is like the pot callin' the kettle black."

"The reward is all yours."

Again the four manhunters looked at one another. Tony Fabrizio remarked, "I have never met a man who has no interest in money. Why else would you want to go along?"

"Ask me no questions, and I'll tell you no lies."

Enos was frowning. "You worry me, Eli. It's too much to ask you to explain, is it?"

Eli couldn't if he wanted. The words would choke off in his throat. His humiliation ran bone deep. So did his craving for revenge. "Do you want to hear about me or the Hoodoos?" He did not wait for an answer. "I happen to know Kid Falon has taken a shine to a certain saloon gal and pays her a visit every chance he gets. I know where the saloon is. I know the name of the saloon. And wherever you find him, the rest of those bastards are bound to be."

Enos was quick to see the possibilities. "We could lie in wait for 'em and pick 'em off like buffs from a blind."

Eli nodded. "Five of us and five of them. We each

choose one and blast away. All I ask is that Brock Alvord is mine. Do we have a deal?"

"And there is nothing you want in exchange?" Tony asked. "Nothing at all?"

Eli remembered a trading post he had stopped at on his trek west. The owner kept the pickled hand of a hostile who once tried to scalp him in a jar and displayed it for all to see. "I'd like Brock Alvord's ears."

"What in the world for?" asked Melissa.

Enos dismissed her question with a wave. "Who cares so long as he helps us find the Hoodoos?" He extended his hand. "We have a deal, Brandenberg. And you know me. I'm as good as my word." He leaned toward Eli. "So tell me. Where is this saloon at?"

"Painted Rock."

Northeast Colorado Territory

Ubel Gunther was not one to complain, but he had reached the point where if he never rode another horse for as long as he lived, it would be too soon to suit him. His lower back ached constantly, and his right foot was sore from where one of the pack animals had stepped on it when he was stripping the packs off.

Ubel's associates were in worse shape than he was. Hans, Oscar, Rutger, and Arne were not used to riding for weeks on end. All four were as stiff-legged as brooms at the end of each day and could not sit down without wincing. Oscar was the worst. He needed to place a folded blanket between his buttocks and his saddle or he could not ride at all, and at night he had to lie on his side because sitting up straight was torment.

Most frontiersmen would have been amused at their expense, but Trask merely offered to make an Indian potion that would soothe their sore muscles. Ubel politely declined. To him, using the potion would be a sign of weakness, evidence he and the others were not tough enough to endure petty discomforts. Then, too, he did not trust anything "Indian." That included the tracker.

Trask was not a typical breed. The ones Ubel had encountered at Radtke's boarding houses and gambling dens were temperamental, explosive men who turned violent at the drop of an insult. Men who looked down their noses at everyone because everyone looked down their noses at them.

Not Trask. He was always as calm as the prairie when no wind was blowing. His self-control was superb. It was impossible to gauge his feelings by his expression. The man would make a great poker player, but by his own admission he never gambled. He also hardly ever imbibed strong spirits, another atypical trait.

Ubel prided himself on his ability to read people with the same ease he read a newspaper, but Trask baffled him. The times he tried to engage Trask in conversation, the tracker was as laconic as a Spartan.

Now, under yet another burning midday sun, Ubel brought his mount up next to the half-blood's piebald. "How far behind them would you say we are?"

Trask answered without taking his eyes off the plain ahead. "The same as the last time you asked. About two days, a little less."

"Can't we push on and overtake them sooner?"

"Sure. And tire out our horses. So if they catch

wind of us, they'll leave us eatin' their dust. If you're not happy with how I do my job, say so."

"Have I complained once this whole time? Your skill is everything we were told it was." Ubel was mystified by Trask's uncanny ability to read sign where there did not appear to be any. Their fifth day out, an afternoon thunderstorm disgorged a torrent of heavy rain, erasing the hoofprints they had been following. Or so it seemed to Ubel's untrained eye. But Trask pressed on, and the next morning they came on the charred embers of a campfire made by Fabrizio's party. Ubel never doubted the breed's ability after that.

"They've been headin' northeast for several days now. Makin' for Eli's, unless I miss my guess."

"Where?"

"Not a 'where'—a 'who.' Eli Brandenberg sells liquor and trade goods. He has the only waterin' hole for hundreds of miles."

"Is he a friend of yours?" Ubel entertained hopes of sleeping in a bed for a change. He would pay good money for the privilege.

"Hardly. He can't stand Indians or breeds. I never buy supplies from him." Trask rested his Spencer across his pommel. He always rode with the rifle in one hand, his reins in the other. "But he might know where Fabrizio is bound if you ask him real polite."

"Leave that to me." Ubel let a minute go by before he brought up what else was on his mind. "Have you given my offer more thought?"

"No need. My answer is still the same. I'm a tracker, not an assassin. I won't take part in killin'. Told you that before we left Denver." Trask looked at him. "I've been open and honest with you from the beginnin', which is more than I can say about you. You fed me the notion we're after a pack of city dwellers. But I know better. One is a buffalo runner."

"A what?"

"A white who hunts buffalo. His buffalo coat leaves its imprint when he sleeps. So does the stock of his Sharps when he leans on it. All those empty bottles we found were his. He's the one you must worry about."

"I've met him," Ubel revealed. "Enos Howard is his name. He's a loudmouth drunk, nothing more. I did not think it was important enough to tell you, or I would have."

"The name has a rep attached. That drunk can put a bullet through our skulls from a thousand yards away. Another reason we should be careful about how close we get."

"All I care about, all my employer cares about, are Tony Fabrizio and his friend, Pickett. If the others don't interfere, they can go their way in peace. If not, if this buffalo hunter tries to stop us, we will dispose of him. Sharps or no Sharps."

"I admire a man with confidence," Trask said. "You'll need every ounce you have."

Two days later they spied a sod structure in the distance. Ubel wanted to spread his men out and converge on foot, but Trask insisted on circling wide to search for sign. "Never go into a painter's den without first seein' if it's inside," was how he put it.

The tracker found hoofprints leading to the southeast. "It's them. With someone else along. They lit out yesterday mornin'." He was on one knee, running his fingers over the ground.

"If only we knew where they were heading," Ubel mentioned.

Trask uncurled and stared off across the expanse of shimmering grass. "If they keep on as they are, there's only one place they could be goin'. It's a small settlement in the middle of nowhere called Painted Rock."

Chapter Seventeen

Painted Rock
Kansas

Tom Shadley was sweeping the floor of the Lucky Star when he heard riders ride up to the hitch rail outside. He thought little of it. Spurs jangled, and the door was shoved wide. Shadley glanced up with a smile on his face. It froze there, just as he froze with his broom in midsweep. "Kid! We weren't expecting you back so soon!"

"I bet you weren't," Kid Falon said. He grinned at Susie Kline, drew his right Colt, and shot Tom Shadley through the head.

It was so quick, so unexpected, the dove never screamed. One second Shadley was alive and well and humming to himself, the next he was a lifeless husk with a bullet hole smack between his wide-open eyes.

The Kid stalked to the bar. Two locals hastily backed toward the wall, each as pale as paper. Twirling the Colt into its holster, Kid Falon helped himself to the bottle they had been sharing.

Into the saloon filed the rest of the Hoodoos. Curly

Means went to Shadley's body, said, "I'd like some redeye, barkeep," and laughed. Brock Alvord walked past it, frowning. Noonan didn't waste a glance. Big Ben, though, hunkered and went through Shadley's pockets. The money he found, along with a folding knife engraved with a scantily clad woman, he stuck into his own.

Kid Falon jabbed a finger at the locals. "Round up everyone who lives here. Every man, woman, and child. Any who give you sass, we'll fetch ourselves. And tell them we won't be nearly as nice about it."

"And have everyone bring their dogs," Curly Means added. "On a leash."

The oldest man nodded vigorously. "Yes, sir. Right away, sir." The pair bolted like jackrabbits fleeing ravening wolves.

"Look at 'em go!" The Kid chortled and moved around the bar. "Belly up, gents. The drinks are on me." To Susie he said, "Get upstairs and stay there." Then his gaze alighted on Brock Alvord. "What's eatin' you? You look as if someone shoved a rifle up your ass and was fixin' to squeeze the trigger."

"We've crossed a line we can never cross back over. From here on, everything has changed." Brock indicated a bottle of whiskey, and the Kid gave it to him. "Stealin' horses is one thing, treein' a town is another. No one will want to do business with us after this."

"Get that from your crystal ball, did you? Hell, Brock. You're gettin' to be as squeamish as an old woman. When folks hear about that coot with the rifle who shot Abby, they'll understand."

Curly reached across the bar to grab a bottle for himself. "It's not as if we're goin' to kill the females and the brats."

"Who says we're not?" Kid Falon asked.

Brock bent his head so the Kid couldn't see his face and went over to a table to join Noonan and Big Ben. Noonan was honing the bone-handled knife. Big Ben was amusing himself by biting into a gold coin he had found on Shadley. "I need to know where you boys stand."

"I stand behind whoever is top dog," Noonan said.

Big Ben quit chomping for a moment. "You're about the smartest man I've ever met, Brock, and I'd follow you anywhere. But this town did the Kid and the rest of us wrong. They've got what's comin' to them."

The first to arrive was Jack Taylor, the owner of the general store. He took one look at Shadley and recoiled in stark terror. "Poor Tom!" Wringing his hands, he looked at Brock Alvord. "Why would you allow such a thing? We've always done right by the Hoodoos, haven't we?"

Kid Falon pounded the bar and snapped, "Talk to me, not him! I'm the one who lost the gal he loved."

Beads of sweat broke out on Taylor. "But we buried her decent, just like you wanted. Over by the creek where it's shady. And Floyd carved the nicest headstone you'd ever want to see."

"Did he carve one for the varmint who shot her?"

"Sure. But nowhere near as fine." Jack Taylor smiled. And died. A slug from the Kid's Colt cored his left eye and burst through the rear of his cranium. Taylor tottered like he was adrift on a wave-tossed raft, then collapsed in a heap.

Brock Alvord downed a third of his bottle in twice as many swallows. He looked at Noonan and Big Ben, but neither met his gaze. "All my effort, all my plannin', all for nothin'."

Again the door swung open, framing the muscular bulk of Floyd Havershaw, Painted Rock's founding father. His shirt was off, and his hairy chest was slick with sweat. Clutched in his ham-sized right hand was his blacksmith hammer. "What's all the shooting about?" He stopped as if he had run into a wall, and his arms slumped to his sides. "Lord Almighty, no!"

The Kid hopped up onto the bar and swung his legs over the front. "Been workin' hard, have you, blacksmith?" He still held the smoking Colt. "Poundin' your anvil so loud you didn't hear us ride up?"

"You murdered them! My two best friends!"

"I'd give you the same, but I hear Abby would be proud of her headstone." Kid Falon flipped his Colt into the air, caught it with a deft flick of his arm, spun the pistol forward, spun the pistol backward, border-shifted, border-shifted a second time, cocked the hammer, and shot Havershaw in the left knee.

Floyd cried out as he fell, his heavy hammer thumping beside him. A thin red geyser misted the floor until he clamped a hand over the hole.

Kid Falon slid off the bar and methodically commenced reloading. "You'll limp the rest of your life, but it's more than Abby can do, so count your blessin's."

"Bastard!" Floyd was red in the face, his veins bulging, his big arms twitching in a paroxysm of rage. "Put those guns down, you scalawag, and fight me man to man! I'll break you in half!"

"Some folks don't have enough brains to grease a skillet." Kid Falon shot him in the other knee.

A howl was torn from Floyd Havershaw's throat. Doubling over, he sputtered and shook, the lower half of each pant leg stained crimson.

Voices arose outside, among them that of the old

man who had gone to do the Kid's bidding. "We're all here, mister! Is it safe for us to come in?"

"It's a hell of a lot safer than if you don't!" Kid Falon rejoined. "Hurry it up! I'm about to lose my patience."

In they came, fear on every face, their movements stiff and awkward, mothers clasping children, sisters and brothers clinging to one another, the men with their heads bowed and their hands up. Three of the women broke into tears. So did many of the children. A little girl ran to Havershaw and threw her arms around his shoulders, crying, "Pa! Oh Pa!"

"Ain't this touchin' as hell?" The Kid drew his other Colt.

Curly Means was in motion. "Hold on there, pard." He walked in among the townspeople, taking leashes from those who had brought their dogs. A mongrel with a leather collar growled and refused to budge until Curly kicked it in the ribs. Yelping, it allowed him to drag it out with the others.

"What is he going to do with Fluffy?" a boy asked.

"Hush!" his mother scolded him.

Kid Falon strutted across the room, and they drew back in fright. "My pard is fixin' to do what I should do to all of you, only I'm too kindhearted." He scanned their pale faces and focused on the old man. "Go over to the general store and bring me all the rope you can find."

"Rope?"

"I didn't say daises." The Kid fired into the floor near the old man's feet, and the man was out the door in a flash.

Mrs. Havershaw looked up from her stricken husband. "You're a despicable human being, young man! Someone should have hung you long ago."

"Any volunteers for the job?" Kid Falon asked, and when no one replied, he had them take hold of the blacksmith and marched them outside and across the dusty street to the cabin that had once belonged to Sam Stowe. "This should do us."

Brock Alvord, Noonan, and Big Ben came out to see what the Kid was up to. Big Ben became more interested in Curly, who had tied three of the dogs to the hitch rail and was fashioning a noose from his rope for the fourth. "You aimin' to do one right after the other?"

"And end my hemp social too soon?" Curly's grin was sadistic. "One an hour should be about right." He bent to slip the noose over the black dog's neck but it whined and pulled away. A stern "Stay!" rooted it in place, and the deed was done. Taking the other end, he climbed onto his horse, looped the rope around his saddle horn, and laughed. "It's moments like this that make life worthwhile."

"You are one loco hombre," Noonan said.

"And damn proud of it." Yipping lustily, Curly applied his spurs and galloped down the street. In the blink of an eye, the rope went taut and the dog was brutally jerked off its feet and dragged. It yelped and tried to stand, but the horse was moving too fast.

From over by the cabin came a high-pitched scream. The boy who owned the dog had his hands to his cheeks, his eyes wide in horror. "No! Let Fluffy go!" He started to run to the dog, but his mother grabbed hold of him and wouldn't let him go no matter how hard he struggled.

Kid Falon ordered the citizens of Painted Rock to form a ring around the cabin and stand with their backs to it. He made a slow circuit, his Colts covering them, his grin as sadistic as Curly's had been.

"What in blazes is he up to?" Big Ben wondered.

"Whatever it is," Noonan said, "I sure wouldn't want to be one of those settlers."

Brock Alvord didn't comment, but his expression showed exactly how he felt.

A howl pierced the air. Curly had reached the end of the street and wheeled his mount. The rope whipped like a snake, snapping the black dog like a bobber at the end of a fishing line.

Big Ben chortled. "That Curly sure is comical."

Out of the general store trudged the old man, laden with coils of rope. Hastening to the cabin, he deposited them at the Kid's feet. "Here you go, Mr. Falon, sir."

"What are you givin' them to me for, you old coot?" The Kid motioned. "I want you to tie all the ropes together to make one long one."

Curly galloped past the saloon, swinging his hat and hollering like a drunken cowboy. The dog still had some life left; its legs moved weakly.

The boy who owned it was bawling.

"Shut that brat up," Kid Falon growled at the mother, "or I'll give him something to really cry about."

Big Ben leaned against a post. "My pa used to say that to me all the time. He took a switch to me once too often, and I had to break his back."

"You killed your own pa?" Brock Alvord had not liked his own father much, but he had never stooped to that.

"What do you take me for? I left him a cripple so his switchin' days were over. Then I lit out and haven't been home since." Big Ben sighed. "I paid a fella once to write my ma a letter. But either he didn't know his letters like he claimed, or she never got it, because she never wrote me back.''

Curly, cackling merrily, was galloping toward the huge painted boulder. Fluffy had gone limp and was flopping and bouncing like a wind-tossed tumbleweed.

Noonan casually observed, ''We should be glad it wasn't a hog that bit him. He'd sure wear out a lot of horses.''

Over at the cabin, the old man was going from one person to the next, looping rope around their necks, wrists, and ankles.

Big Ben Brody scratched his temple. ''What in hell is the Kid makin' that old geezer do? I never saw the like in all my born days.''

''It's an old Injun trick,'' Noonan said. ''Tyin' folks out under the hot sun and bakin' them alive.''

Brock Alvord pulled his hat brim low and strode toward the cabin. ''Kid, I want a word with you.'' He nodded at the terrified inhabitants. ''This ain't right. Shootin' unarmed men was bad enough. Makin' the women and children suffer is takin' it too far.''

''Abby was a woman, wasn't she?'' Kid Falon retorted. ''But she wasn't good enough for the uppity females here. She told me how they looked down their noses at her and wouldn't even give her the time of day.''

''And the children?'' Brock stared at a weeping girl. ''What's your excuse for hog-tyin' them?''

''Since when do any of us need excuses? I can't help it if you're softhearted. Go drown your conscience in drink and leave me be.''

Brock looked the Kid in the eyes. ''I can't let you do this.''

"The hell you say!" Kid Falon declared and shot him.

Justice Department Agent William Shores was dozing in the saddle when the old Shoshone made a comment that penetrated his lethargy.

"There be Painted Rock, Brother John."

Shores willed his head to rise and blinked in the glare of the afternoon sun. He was fit enough to ride, but he still did not feel like his old self. The sickness had sapped too much vitality. He hoped that after a few days of rest, of sleeping in a bed and eating three nourishing meals daily, he would fully recover. "I hope to God I can find a room to rent."

Red Fox rose a few inches off the paint. "Something strange, Brother John."

"What?" To Shores, everything looked perfectly ordinary. The settlement had a single dusty street, a few houses, a store, a saloon, and a stable. And over near a huge boulder stood a cabin. A cabin with a lot of people ringing it, women and children and a few men, their backs to the four walls. "What the hell?"

"Bodies," the Shoshone said, pointing with a gnarled finger.

Now it was Shores who rose in the stirrups. He saw a man on his back not far from the cabin. In the middle of the street lay a black dog, its head twisted at an unnatural angle. At a hitch rail in front of the saloon five horses were tied. So were three dogs.

Red Fox reined in. "This bad medicine."

"Spare me your superstitious drivel." Shores clucked to the claybank. "Follow me." The situation merited immediate investigation. Some of the people at the cabin had seen him, but none acknowledged the hand he raised in greeting. He went to call out, then saw that someone had trussed them up like lambs for the slaughter. Bringing the claybank to a halt, he drew his Smith & Wesson.

"You were right. Something is very wrong here," Shores said for the old warrior's benefit and swung down.

One of the women tried to move her arms as if to warn him to get out of there. Another was shaking her head at him. A boy with a tear-streaked face was gazing at the dead dog.

Shores walked to the dead man. The victim had been shot twice high in the chest, and when he fell, his hat had come off. His features betrayed great surprise. Shores stared at the man's close-cropped snow white hair and trimmed white beard and was reminded of the description he had been given of Brock Alvord. *What a coincidence,* he thought. The man even had blue eyes like Alvord.

Gruff voices from the saloon alerted Shores the killer must still be in Painted Rock. Crouching, he crept to the near corner, then along the wall to a window. It was raised halfway, and the dingy brown curtains had been tied back. Raising his right eye to the sill, he spotted a big bearded man at a table glumly regarding two others over by the bar. One had curly hair that spilled over his ears. The other was barely old enough to shave and wore pearl-handled Colts.

"—no call to do that, damn it!" the curly-mopped man was saying. "He was the boss of this outfit, in case you've forgotten."

"I ain't forgettin' nothing. But *you* seem to be forgettin' that didn't give him the right to butt in like he done." The younger man leaned his elbows on the counter. Besides, who says we need him anymore? We know all his contacts. We know where the relays are. Why can't we carry on without him?"

"And who's going to lead us? You?"

"Watch your tone with me, Curly Means."

Shores stepped back. "Curly Means?" he whispered and happened to glance at the name of the saloon: *The Lucky Star.* A keg of black powder went off in his skull. At last he understood the significance of Mat-ta-vish's drawings. He also realized he was alone. Red Fox had disappeared. *Good riddance,* he told himself. He didn't need the old warrior's help anyway. Darting to the corner, he cat-stepped toward the rear. There had to be a back door. He would get the drop on them. Better yet, he would shoot them while their backs were turned. He wasn't taking chances with a gun-shark like Kid Falon.

One of his spurs jingled, and Shores stopped, appalled by his carelessness. He swiftly removed both and set them in the grass.

Shores didn't give the outhouse a second glance. Cocking the Smith & Wesson, he gingerly tried the latch of the back door. Metal scraped on metal, but not loud enough to be heard from up front. Cracking the door open, he peered down a narrow hall. It was deserted. He stayed close to the wall, where there was less likelihood of a floorboard creaking, and he slunk past a small kitchen to the doorway to the saloon.

Big Ben Brody was still at the table. Curly Means had found a jar of pickled eggs and was filling his belly. Kid Falon had his back to Shores and was saying, "Why do we even need a leader? We should each have an equal say. And each get an equal share.

I never did think it was right of Brock to take an extra ten percent for himself."

Tingling with suppressed excitement, Shores took precise aim at the center of the Kid's back. He curled his forefinger around the Smith & Wesson's trigger and was heartbeats from ending the Kid's blood-drenched career when a hard object gouged him behind his left ear and a voice laced with a Southern accent warned, "I wouldn't do that, mister. Not unless you're partial to havin' your head blown off."

A hand came from behind and relieved Shores of his revolver.

Shores remembered the outhouse and wanted to beat his head against the jamb. Instead, he elevated his arms. "John Noonan, I presume?"

"None other." Noonan shoved him into the saloon. "Lookee what I found, boys. This polecat was fixin' to backshoot the Kid."

Kid Falon spun and glowered. "Another pack rat comes out of its hidey-hole. I know just what to do with him."

"Wait." Curly Means was about to pop an entire egg in his mouth, but he dropped it back in the jar. Looking Shores up and down, he said, "This swivel dude ain't no local. He's store-bought from bottom to top."

"That he is," the Kid thoughtfully agreed and filled his left hand with a Colt. "Who the hell are you, four-flusher? And why would you want me toes down? I never set eyes on you before."

Shores desperately tried to think of a lie they would believe, but his mind had gone as blank as a newly cleaned blackboard.

"Catamount got your tongue?" Noonan holstered

his pistol and poked his hands into each of Shores's pockets. "What does this say?" he asked, handing Shores's identification to Curly.

Big Ben Brody rose and lumbered over. "Want me to break a few of his bones to loosen his tongue?"

"No need." Curly grinned like a bobcat that had caught a chipmunk to play with. "What we have here is Mr. William E. Shores from the United States Department of Justice."

"Never heard of him or it," Kid Falon said.

"He's some sort of federal John Law," Curly explained. "Hails all the way from Washington, D.C. Looks like Brock was right. Gunnin' down those soldiers made people sit up and take notice."

"To hell with Brock, and to hell with this federal." The Kid gripped Shores by the front of the shirt and hauled him toward the front door. "Mighty stupid, if you ask me, to come all this way to dig your own grave."

Shores was tempted to grab for the Kid's Colt, but he knew he would be dead before he touched it. The other Hoodoos were tagging along, and to them he said, "You owe it to yourselves to hear me out."

"Did I say you could talk, four-flusher?" Kid Falon demanded and swung his left arm out and down.

Shores ducked, but he was much too slow. Excruciating pain nearly blacked him out. His knees buckled, but Big Ben Brody's huge arms encircled him, and he was hefted like a sack of potatoes out into the street and dumped onto his hands and knees.

John Noonan said, "Any last words?"

Blood dripping down his face, Shores felt the muzzle of the Kid's Colt pressed to his forehead. He braced for the blast and the black veil of oblivion but was granted a momentary reprieve.

"Hold on, Kid," Curly Means urged. "I've got me a better idea."

The people at the cabin were watching aghast, as if they knew what was to come. Shores searched for some sign of Red Fox but couldn't find him. For all the old Indian's talk about how he wanted revenge for his brother, when push came to shove, Red Fox had turned tail. Shores didn't blame him though. The Shoshone had shown more common sense than he had.

Hooves drummed. Curly Means rode up, uncurling a rope as he came. "I've always wanted to do this with a human being."

Shores wondered what the Hoodoo was up to, then noticed the black dog a few feet away. Its eyes bulged, and its tongue lolled limp in the dirt. The cause of death was self-evident: the middle of its neck bore the inch-deep imprint of a rope. "No!" Shores glanced at Curly Means just as a noose settled over his head. He reached up to tear it off, but Curly had already applied his spurs.

The ground rushed up to meet Shores's face, and he was dragged down the center of the street. Dust swirled into his mouth, his nose, his eyes. Frantic, he clawed at the rope. Waves of pain washed through him. He couldn't breathe. He could hardly see. Somehow he got his knees under him, but he was wrenched flat again. His lungs ached abominably, to the point where he thought they would explode.

Dimly, Shores realized Curly Means had turned and was galloping back the way they had come. He thought his neck would snap when his body suddenly whipped around.

The other Hoodoos were hollering encouragement. Shores was ebbing fast. He had not had much energy to begin with, and the lack of breath was more than his body could endure. Again he heard Curly change direction. This time his neck would break; there was no escaping it. Thankfully, his consciousness faded, and his last thought before he pitched into the abyss was that this was a damn stupid way to die.

Chapter Eighteen

Ubel Gunther did not know what to think. He and his men were approaching Painted Rock from the northwest. Their view of the saloon and the street in front of it was blocked by the enormous boulder that gave the settlement its name, so they were quite close when they observed some men in wide-brimmed hats and slickers whooping and laughing while another was dragging someone dressed in a suit at the end of a rope. The rider reached the north end of the street and reined sharply around. As he did, an old Indian raced from concealment at the side of a house and slashed the cowboy's rope with a tomahawk. The man in the suit rolled up against a picket fence. Before the rider realized the rope had been cut, the Indian had the man in the suit draped over a slim shoulder and was loping toward a stand of trees.

"What is that all about?" Hans wondered. He had his rifle out.

"Drunken cowboys," Ubel guessed. "They won't bother us if we don't bother them." He scanned the hamlet. "I don't see Fabrizio or his party. We have beaten them here. *Gut.*"

The idea had come to Gunther two nights earlier.

He had been warming himself by the fire when Trask mentioned they should reach Painted Rock in a few days. "Exactly how many, I can't rightly say. But we're close. The people you're after won't get there much ahead of you."

"I wish we could arrive before they do and arrange a suitable reception," Ubel said. Then it hit him: Why couldn't they? He posed the question to Trask.

"They're not more than ten to twelve miles ahead. Swing wide to the north, ride all night, and by morning you'll be in front of them. All you have to do after that is head due southeast."

"I should have thought of this sooner." Ubel had shot to his feet. "We leave this minute." At a snap of his fingers, Hans and the rest began gathering up their saddle blankets and saddles. Trask, though, continued sipping coffee. "You will join us, will you not?"

"I will not."

"But we need you to guide us to the settlement. And don't forget. My offer of an additional five hundred dollars still stands."

"You just don't hear so good, do you? I'm a tracker. Not an assassin. I also told you the day we met that as soon as my job was done, we'd go our own ways. That time has come. At first light, I'm lightin' a shuck for Denver and my wife."

"I have never met anyone who would pass up five hundred dollars," Ubel commented.

"Blame my Arapaho half. I'm not as fond of money as most whites are. To me, it's a means to an end, not an end in itself."

On that philosophical note, they had parted company.

Ubel had done as Trask advised, and now here

they were at Painted Rock with plenty of time to set a trap. Fabrizio and his friends would ride right into their blazing rifles.

Oscar was staring at the only log cabin in Painted Rock. "Why are those people tied to that building?"

Intent on the commotion, Ubel hadn't noticed them. Nor the bodies of a man and a dog in the street. Neither were acceptable. Fabrizio would see the bodies and be on his guard when he rode in. It was all due to the rowdy cowhands, Ubel reasoned. Reaching under his jacket, he loosened his revolver in its holster.

The four drunks were fanning out and moving toward the trees. They stopped at the sight of Ubel and his men, and a big ox with a bushy beard declared, "I swear! This place is gettin' more crowded by the minute!"

"Greetings, gentlemen," Ubel said cordially, touching his cane to his hat. "Is it me, or are you doing your utmost to turn this quaint bastion of civilization into a model of anarchy?"

A cowboy with curly hair whistled in mock admiration. "Lord Almighty, but don't he talk pretty? His tongue must be solid silver."

"Maybe we should invite 'em for a drink," suggested a swarthy cowboy with a bone-handled knife on his hip.

The youngest cowboy, who wore matching pearl-handled Colts, spat in the dust. "I wouldn't be caught dead with a bunch of yacks wearin' chamber pots on their heads. Especially when these yacks must be more John Laws."

"I beg your pardon?" Ubel said. "You suspect we're law officers?" The idea amused him. "Nothing could be further from the truth."

"So you say," the young one responded. "Then who the hell are you, mister? And what are you doing here?"

Hans leveled his rifle. "You will not talk to Mr. Gunther in that tone of voice, cowboy."

"Is that a fact?" The young one's Colts blossomed in his hands as if from out of thin air.

"No—!" Ubel exclaimed. He hoped to avoid a needless confrontation. But his hope was dashed when the young hothead shot Hans in the chest. Quick as thought, the young one swiveled toward Arne. The other cowboys were unlimbering their hardware, and the next instant the settlement rocked to artificial thunder. Hot lead flew every which way.

Bending low, Ubel spurred his mount toward a gap between the general store and the saloon. "Follow me!" he shouted. He drew his revolver and twisted just as a slug whipped his bowler from his head. Another nicked his left arm. He saw Hans on the ground but still alive, feverishly working his Winchester. Oscar and Rutger were close behind him, but Arne must not have heard his command and was racing toward the cabin.

The cowboy with the bone-handled knife fanned his pistol twice. Rutger's horse whinnied and tumbled, throwing Rutger clear. He hit hard but rolled and sprang erect, all in the same motion. Sprinting for the gap, he sent shot after shot at the dispersing cowboys.

Ubel galloped to the rear of the buildings. Swinging down from his saddle, he holstered his revolver and pulled the Winchester out. Moments later, Oscar joined him. Ubel led him on foot toward the front, where Rutger was reloading. The gunfire had stopped.

"I hit one," Rutger reported. "The big one. I saw him stumble, but he made it to cover."

All the cowboys had. Ubel didn't see them anywhere. Hans was dead. Over near the cabin lay Arne's horse. Arne was alive but wounded and had crawled behind it. He waved to them.

"Damn stupid cowboys!" Oscar fumed.

Ubel was thinking about the young one with the pearl-handled Colts. Not many could afford such pistols. A matched set cost a hundred dollars, three months' wages for a cowhand. "Pearl-handled pistol," Ubel said to himself and recalled something Leeds had told them before they killed him. "Damn me for not remembering sooner! Those are not cowboys! They are the Hoodoos!"

"Who?" Rutger asked.

"A pack of horse thieves and killers. The stableman told us Fabrizio and his friends were going after them for the bounty money." Ubel had read the newspaper accounts. "The young one is Kid Falon. I do not remember the rest of their names. But they are not to be taken lightly."

Oscar peeked out, then had to jerk back when a slug struck the wall inches from his head. "They are good shots."

Ubel was incensed. This was the last thing he needed. Fabrizio's party might arrive at any moment. "We must kill these Hoodoos, and quickly. Rutger, stay here and keep them pinned down. Oscar, come with me."

It was common knowledge that all things being equal, a man with a rifle had an advantage over someone armed with a pistol. Rifles shot a lot farther and were more accurate. To capitalize, Ubel led

Oscar to the rear of the buildings, past their horses, and out onto the prairie. They stayed low, using weeds and grass to screen them, and went over a hundred yards, well beyond the effective range of a revolver, then looped to the north to come up on the Hoodoos from the rear. Only there was no sign of them.

"Where did they get to?" Oscar whispered.

From the vicinity of where Arne lay sheltered behind his horse came gunfire. There was the heavy boom of a rifle followed by the lighter crack of pistols. Rutger's rifle entered the fray, and after a long flurry of shots, silence fell.

Oscar glanced expectantly at Ubel, who would just as soon circle around the settlement and pick the Hoodoos off from the safety of the plain. But Arne and Rutger might need their help.

"Keep down." Ubel jogged toward the northernmost house, a small frame structure. He ran along the north side, under an open window, to a yard bordering the street. He saw Arne sprawled across the horse, as dead as his animal. He did not see Rutger at the corner of the general store. "This is not good."

"What will we do?"

A ladder propped against the front of the store gave Ubel an inspiration. "We will climb onto a roof and slay these Hoodoos when they show themselves." He turned, took two steps, and froze.

"Howdy." Kid Falon was leaning out the window, a Colt in each hand. "I'm plumb pleased you've made this so easy."

"Listen to me," Ubel said. His rifle was pointed at the ground. So was Oscar's. "This is senseless. Our fight isn't with you. In fact, I will pay you to help us kill the people we are after."

The Kid grinned. "I don't work for chamber pots."

The last sight Ubel Gunther saw were the twin muzzles of the Kid's pearl-handled Colts spewing smoke and lead.

Charley Pickett was riding alongside Melissa Patterson, as he always did since that night they had declared their mutual love, and she was telling him about an eccentric aunt of hers who once owned over fifty cats, when Enos Howard, who was in the lead, reined up and raised an arm for them to do the same.

"Did you hear that?"

"Hear what?" Charley asked.

"Shots," the buffalo hunter said. "I thought I heard some a while ago and now I'm sure of it."

"I heard them too," Eli Brandenberg confirmed. Cradled in his left arm was a scattergun he never set down, even when he slept.

Tony Fabrizio was in charge of the pack animals, and as he came up, he asked, "Why have we stopped?"

"Could be trouble," Enos said. From his saddlebags he slid his spyglass, and as he had done countless times, he searched the prairie beyond. "Nothin' except some trees to the southeast. We'll head for them. Everyone keep your eyes skinned and your hardware handy."

Eli affectionately patted his scattergun. "Buckshot means buryin', and I've got two barrels ready."

"Be mighty careful where you point that cannon when you shoot," Charley cautioned. When he was younger, he had used his pa's shotgun on occasion, including the time he shot a raccoon that had been sneaking into the henhouse. The coon came bolting out a hole it had made in the fence, and he cut loose with 12-gauge buckshot. It blew the raccoon apart.

On they rode. Soon the trees were visible with the unaided eye. So were a cluster of buildings.

"That's got to be Painted Rock," Enos announced. "One of us should go on ahead to see if the Hoodoos are there."

"No." Charley vetoed the notion. "We stick together." He would rather Melissa stayed out on the plain where she would be safe, but he knew better than to say anything. She would only refuse.

Enos was resorting to his spyglass again. "My eyes must be worse than I reckoned. I'd swear I see a bunch of folks tied to a cabin." Slowing, he handed the telescope to Charley. "Have a look-see."

The people were there, Charley confirmed, looking as miserable as could be. So were a lot of dead men and dead horses. And, strangely enough, a dead dog. When he mentioned the latter, Enos snorted.

"That would be Curly Means's handiwork. Folks say he hates dogs as much as Southerners hate carpetbaggers. And if he's there, so are the rest of the Hoodoos." Howard reined in. "It might be smart to sneak in on foot from here. Someone has to stay with the critters, though, so they don't stray off on us."

"That will be Melissa's job," Charley said, swinging down. As he had predicted, she didn't like it.

"Why me? Why don't we draw straws to see who stays?"

"Because I want you to." Charley looked right at her when he said it, expecting her to object, but much to his surprise she gave in.

"If you think it's for the best, I'll do it. But if you run into trouble, give a yell, and I'll come as quick as I can."

Charley would do no such thing. He refused to place her life in more danger than he already had. But he smiled and nodded, then followed Enos, Eli, and Tony, who were hiking east instead of toward Painted Rock. "Why are we going this way?"

Enos pointed at a belt of cottonwoods bordering a creek. "We'll come in from that direction so the trees hide us."

They had to constantly remind Eli to keep low. A bundle of nervous excitement, he kept rising up onto the tips of his toes to scan the settlement and mutter, "Where *are* they? Where *are* they?"

The gentle gurgle of the creek was the only sound Charley heard until they had crossed it and crouched behind trees. Then he heard the soft sobbing of several women and the moans of a barrel-chested man who had been shot a couple of times either before or after he was tied to the cabin.

"I'll be damned!" Enos whispered, his telescope trained on a pair of bodies at the side of the nearest house. He glanced at Tony. "It's that fancy-pants from Denver, the one who has it in for you."

"Ubel Gunther?" Tony took the telescope to see for himself. His bewilderment mirrored Charley's. *"Madrina di Dio.* It is him. The other one is another of Radtke's men. But what are they doing here?"

"Looking for us, I suspect," was the best Charley could come up with.

"Who cares about them?" Eli Brandenberg was bobbing up and down to see over a patch of weeds. "I want to know where the Hoodoos are. Brock Alvord most of all."

Enos reclaimed his telescope and after a minute swore lustily. "Looks like someone beat you to it, hoss. Alvord is one of those lyin' in the street."

"That can't be." Eli stood and stepped from hiding.

"Get down!" Charley whispered, but he was wasting his breath. Eli tramped toward the bodies, oblivious to all else. Charley started to go after him, but Tony grabbed his wrist.

"Would you make the same mistake he is?"

Gunshots shattered the deceptive quiet. They came from the saloon, or near it, and on their heels rose muffled shouts and the slam of a door.

"Some of fancy-pant's boys must be alive and swappin' lead with the Hoodoos," Enos speculated. "It can work in our favor." He beckoned them, then ran toward the frame house.

Charley preferred to hunker in the vegetation, but when Tony hurried after the buffalo hunter, he followed. Ubel Gunther and the other man had been shot through the head, their rifles left where they fell. Shoving the heavy Allen & Wheelock Army .44 into its holster, Charley snatched up Gunther's rifle and tossed the other rifle to Tony.

"Here's the plan, pups," Enos said. "One of us stays and watches the street while the other two hunt for the Hoodoos."

"We should stick together," Charley reiterated. For their mutual protection, if nothing else. He heard a voice and looked out. Eli was standing over a white-haired body, talking to it as if it were alive. "Do you see what I see?"

"He's gone loco!" Enos exclaimed.

Charley was inclined to believe it when Eli stepped back, cocked the scattergun, pointed it at Brock Alvord, and let the corpse have both barrels full in the

face. There wasn't much of it left. Giggling, Eli broke
the scattergun open to reload. "That's what you get
for what you did to me!"

Suddenly another man was there next to Brandenberg. A mammoth, bearded brute who roared like
a beast, threw both arms wide, and enfolded Eli in
them.

Charley thumbed back the Winchester's hammer
and stroked the trigger, but the hammer fell on an
empty chamber. He jacked the lever, feeding a cartridge from the magazine, but before he could fire,
the big man lifted Eli off the ground and shook him
as a bear might shake a badger.

"That's Big Ben Brody!" Enos cried, whipping
Clarabelle to his shoulder. He aimed, fired, and
missed.

"Let go of Eli!" Charley hollered. He tried to fix a
bead, but Brody was swinging Eli back and forth,
and he couldn't get a clear shot. They all heard the
sharp *crack* of Eli's spine and saw blood gush from
Eli's mouth. Big Ben Brody shook Eli a few more
times, then cast him to the dirt.

Clarabelle boomed a second time. Brody was jolted
sideways as if kicked by a mule. His legs, as big
around as oak trees, buckled from under him, and
he toppled, raising puffs of dust.

"I'll be a nanny goat! I hit him!" Enos crowed and
kissed Clarabelle. "I'm not as useless as I thought!"

Tony plucked at their sleeves. "We must hide. The
other Hoodoos will be after us."

"Let 'em come!" Enos bellowed. "By God, I've
never been afeared of any mother's son, and I'm not
afeared now! I'm hell with the bark on! Part alligator
and part snapper! Show me a coon out for my hide,
and I'll show you a hide fit for a rug!"

He would have ranted on and on, but Charley pulled him to the rear of the house, saying, "Hush up! One lucky shot, and you think you're Daniel Boone!" He went to clamp a hand over Enos's mouth to stifle another outburst, but it wasn't necessary. The buffalo hunter was staring at another body a few buildings down.

"That's not one of Gunther's dandies. He's wearin' a slicker."

"What are those sticks pokin' out of his chest?" Charley wondered.

Rifles level, they crept closer.

"God Almighty!" Enos breathed. "That there is John Noonan, the Missouri Terror! Someone put four arrows into him and lifted his hair to boot."

Not all the scalp was gone. About half. A knife had been inserted at the hairline, then the skin peeled back like the peel on an apple. Queasiness overcame Charley, and he averted his eyes. "Who would do such a thing?"

"A Shoshone." Enos was examining the arrows. He tapped an empty sheath attached to the killer's belt. "And he used Noonan's knife to do the scalpin'."

Tony's brow knit. "What is a Shoshone doing in Painted Rock?"

"You're askin' me?" Enos snickered. "My brain would explode if I tried to make sense of this mess."

A metallic *click* warned them they were not alone. A curly-headed man with the barbed tip of an arrow sticking from his shirt had a Colt fixed on them. He fit the description of Curly Means. Incredibly, he was grinning. "Where the hell did you three come from?"

"We're just passin' through," Enos replied, holding his Sharps behind his back. "We couldn't help bu notice everybody is killin' everybody else, so we ducked back here until all the shootin' stops."

Curly looked at Noonan. "So this is where he got to." His Colt dipped, and he tottered against the wall, scarlet oozing down over his lower lip and chin. "Don't this beat all? Done in by a damned redskin old enough to be Methuselah."

"Who?" Charley asked, but it fell on ears that couldn't hear. The Hoodoo's eyes were glazing, and his Colt had fallen from fingers gone limp.

"I am so confused," Tony said.

Enos moved ahead. "Stay behind me. There's only one of these cutthroats left, but he's the worst of the bunch."

Charley knew who he was referring to: Kid Falon. They found another of Gunther's men between the general store and the saloon. Inside the saloon were two more bodies. Townsmen, from the looks of them.

"This is a regular massacre," Enos remarked. "Someone has a heap of buryin' to do, and it won't be me."

"It won't be me either," declared someone behind them.

Charley turned.

Kid Falon stood in the doorway, his Colts trained on them. He took a step, his eyes as flinty as quartz. "Drop the artillery, or I'll drop you." When their rifles had thunked to the floor, he studied them, then said, "I heard a buffalo gun go off earlier. And now one of my pards is lyin' out in the street with a hole in him as big as a pumpkin." He gestured at the Sharps. "Guess which one of you I'm killin' first?"

Enos licked his lips. "I don't suppose you'd give me a sportin' chance?"

The Kid's laugh was more like a growl. "If life was fair, money would grow on trees."

Others might have cowed in fear, but Enos jutted his chin defiantly and thrust out his chest. "I figured you for yellow. Do your worst, you polecat."

Charley couldn't stand there and let Enos be murdered. He was standing sideways, and he lowered his right hand to his .44, hoping Falon wouldn't notice. But the Kid did and barked, "Don't even think it!" The very next second, the Kid snapped his head toward the street as if he had heard something, and Charley clawed out the .44.

Kid Falon spun and fired.

Charley was in motion, diving for the nearest table. Enos and Tony were also seeking cover, Tony with his revolver out. Charley and Tony squeezed off shots at the same instant, but they both must have missed, because the Kid was gliding to the right, his pistols cracking one after the other. Charley's hat went flying. He landed on his shoulder as holes sprouted in the table. Wood chips stung his face. He fired at the Kid, but his slug hit the wall. Tony was also shooting and having no more success.

Falon aimed both Colts right at Charley. He would not miss this time.

There was the crack of a shot. Charley flinched and waited for the dark to claim him but nothing happened. It was Kid Falon who pitched onto his Colts, briefly convulsed, and died.

In the doorway was Melissa, tendrils of gunsmoke curling from the barrel of her revolver. She rushed inside. "Is anyone hurt?"

Charley slowly stood and looked down at himself. He shook his right leg. He shook his left. He wriggled both arms and grinned. "I'll be damned."

Tony had taken a slug through the fleshy part of his left arm. It had gone clean through and was hardly bleeding at all.

"Good shootin', Missy," Enos complimented her. Chuckling, he rolled Kid Falon over. "This man-huntin' sure was easier than I thought it would be. Maybe we should do it for a livin'. After we turn these buzzards in for the reward, how about if we go after the James gang?"

Some pieces of the jigsaw forever remained a mystery.

After freeing the settlers, Charley and his friends made a thorough search of the settlement but never came across the Shoshone. They did find a half-dead man with severe rope burns on his neck lying in a flower patch. Mrs. Shadley offered to nurse him back to health so they put him in her parlor. Months later, Charley heard the man worked for the government, and that when he was fit enough to return to Washington, D.C., Mrs. Shadley had gone along as his new wife.

Out of gratitude, the people of Painted Rock let them have whatever they wanted, including extra pack horses, canvas to wrap the bodies in, and a buckboard to transport them. By the second week of the trip back to Denver, the smell was so rank, they flipped a coin each morning; the loser had to drive the buckboard.

The *Rocky Mountain News* carried their story on the front page, and for a while they were the toast of the city. Walter Radtke didn't dare touch them.

Enos soaked up enough liquor to kill twenty men, dallied with any woman who looked at him twice, then had to leave Denver in a hurry after the mayor's older sister went to His Honor and accused Enos of trifling with her affections. Later, Charley was told Enos had drifted into Arizona, went off into the Superstition Mountains in search of gold, and vanished.

Tony Fabrizio wasted no time leaving for New York. He planned to send Maria the money for her passage. Then they would find somewhere they could live without fear of retribution. "If there is such a place," Tony said the last night before he left. He shook Charley's hand. "You have made my fondest dream possible. For that I can never thank you enough."

"I am proud to call you my friend," Charley said.

Tony gave them an address in New York City where he could be reached. Charley wrote to him twice but never received an answer. Charley liked to think things worked out, and Tony and Maria lived long and happy lives together.

As for Charley and Melissa, they were married two days after they reached Denver. Eventually they moved to Kentucky and bought a farm next to Charley's parents. Five children and fifty years later, they often sat in their rocking chairs in the cool of the evening and reminisced about their days as manhunters.

One such night, with stars twinkling above and cows lolling in the meadow by their barn, Melissa looked thoughtfully at Charley. "Tell me true. If you had it to do all over again, would you do it the same?"

Charley smiled and clasped her hand.

"What do you think?"

SIGNET BOOKS   (0451)

JUDSON GRAY

RANSOM RIDERS   20418-2

When Penn and McCutcheon are ambushed on their way to rescue a millionaire's kidnapped niece, they start to fear that the kidnapping was an inside job.

CAYWOOD VALLEY FEUD   20656-8

Penn and McCutcheon are back! This novel of the American frontier takes readers to the Ozarks, where a mysterious gunman has been terrorizing an Ozark family called Caywood—picking them off one by one. The gunman's description matches McCutcheon's good friend Jake Penn. And now, he must find Penn and prove him innocent before more blood is spilled.

S308

Penguin Group (USA) Inc.
Online

Your Internet gateway to a virtual environment with
hundreds of entertaining and enlightening books
from Penguin Group (USA) Inc.

*While you're there, get the latest buzz on
the best authors and books around—*

Tom Clancy, Patricia Cornwell, W.E.B. Griffin,
Nora Roberts, William Gibson, Robin Cook,
Brian Jacques, Catherine Coulter, Stephen King,
Ken Follett, Terry McMillan, and many more!

**Penguin Group (USA) Inc. Online is located at
http://www.penguin.com**

PENGUIN GROUP (USA)INC. NEWS

Every month you'll get an inside look at our upcom-
ing books and new features on our site. This is an
ongoing effort to provide you with the most
up-to-date information about
our books and authors.

Subscribe to Penguin Group (USA) Inc. News at
http://www.penguin.com/newsletters